Bad husband

Thank you for purchasing *Bad Husband.* To be notified of new releases join my mailing list on my website at: www.sheystahl.com

Printed in the United States of America

Copy Editing: Becky Johnson, Hot Tree Editing
Proofreading: Janet Johnson & Ashley Schow
BETA Reading: Lauren Zimmerman
Cover Image: Copyright © Sara Eirew
Cover Designer: © Sara Eirew
Interior Formatting: Shey Stahl

My husband and I have never considered divorce.
Murder sometimes, but never divorce.

~ Joyce Brothers

For anyone who has ever been married and
knows how hard it can be.

Bad husband

RIDLEY COOPER IS ON A MISSION.
AND IF THERE'S ONE THING HE'S GOOD AT,

it's getting what he wants.

WHAT'S HE NOT SO GOOD AT?

Being a husband.

AT LEAST THAT'S WHAT HIS WIFE WOULD SAY.

1

A TRUE "WHAT THE FUCK" MOMENT

I think with any story, there's a beginning, a middle, and the end.

And just so we're clear, we're at the end. Right now. Or at least, in many ways, it feels that way with the way my heart wants to jump out of my chest and into my brain, a place it's never been. Believe me, the two are seldom on speaking terms. One leads, the other follows at will like a lost puppy trying to find his way.

You see that guy standing there, staring at a stack of papers in his hand? The confused one.

No, not Brantley. He's reading instructions to the framing nail gun our trainee jammed earlier today and then managed to shoot himself in the foot with. How is beyond me, unless he was doing it purposely. If you've ever met Trey, you'd totally understand how *that's* possible.

I'm confusing you, aren't I?

Welcome to my current situation.

Take a look around the framed house to the kitchen. Look at the guy *next* to Brantley, to the left leaned up against a counter. The one wearing a look of mystification as he scans over the words Petition for Dissolution of Marriage.

I'll say it again, because it certainly doesn't feel real to me either. Petition for Dissolution of Marriage.

Divorce? That means divorce, right?

I've been married to Madison for eight years… hell, remember just an hour ago when I fucked her against the shower wall? Did any warning bells go off in your head when she was screaming my name I'd be served with this today?

Oh wait, you weren't there yet. Sorry. Let's rewind a moment here and then you can give me your take.

Three hours ago, I'm in the shower, but there's my wife, Madison, standing at the sink brushing her teeth with nothing on. Look at her for a second. Long dark hair she keeps curled most of the time, beautiful wide blue eyes and that heart-shaped face.

Go lower, and you'll see hips most men only dream of touching and long legs… well, you get the point by now. Hot wife.

I actually started dating Madison back in college for her body. Don't sound so surprised. It's a fact of being a warm-blooded male. Ninety percent of the time we go based off looks at the first glance.

I *married* her for her heart, but still, she has an amazing body so naturally, I see her naked, I look. Or more importantly, I grab, or whatever else she'll let me get away with. Today she lets me get away with more.

Fast forward a little bit here, and I manage to get her in the shower with me.

See those two people, she's bent over the bench seat in the shower, hands splayed out over the tile, steam rolling between their bodies, eyes closed, hands grabbing at any angle they can to keep from one, falling, and two, never wanting to part.

That's Madison and me. We have an amazing sex life. Or so I thought.

We actually started with sex. Met at a Halloween party off campus, found out we actually had three classes together at ASU and then fucked the rest of the night. Honestly, it was one of the best nights of my life.

Me, I was in love that first night. It took Mad another month or so… maybe like six. I can be a bit… hmmm… what's the right word here? Intense? Nah, that's not right. I'll think of one and get back to you.

For now, let's just focus on the facts. We had sex this morning, and it was good, right? It seemed that way to me.

And now this? Shit just doesn't add up, does it? How did we go from, "Fuck me harder!" to a petition to…. I glance down and read the title once more. A petition to dissolve marriage.

What the shit?

"Why do you look like you saw a ghost?" Brantley stands in front of me, his wide burly shoulders blocking my view of the sunlight streaming between the two by fours in what will soon be the dining room.

I look up at him then back at the papers. I don't know if I can form words. It's like the time Madison told me she was pregnant. I sat there for ten minutes trying to formulate a reply, but I couldn't. I don't even know why I couldn't reply to her then.

Maybe because she was giving me a blow job at the time and I thought to myself, who tells you they're pregnant in the middle of a blow job?

Madison does. She has impeccable timing like that.

Blinking rapidly, I hand the papers to Brantley, still rendered speechless. I mean, what the fuck?

Brantley snorts, reading through it. That's more than I did. I just scanned the title and freaked the fuck out.

Swallowing back the lump rising in my throat, my heart continues to pound. I'm sure I'm having a heart attack. Rapid heartbeat, sweating… I think I feel some left arm pain too.

No, wait, that was Brantley. He punched me.

"Dude, what the fuck is this? Mad filed for divorce?"

Scrubbing my hands down my face, I stare at him. "I don't know."

He waves at my phone in my pocket. "Well… call her."

Digging my phone out, I swipe the screen and select her name. Guess what?

Yep. Straight to voice mail.

"Voice mail," I tell Brantley holding up the phone, and his brow pulls together. Brantley's been my best friend for twenty years. He knows Madison as well I do. Hell, he's our son's godparent.

Oh right, did I mention we have kids together?

Yeah, two. Callan and Noah. Callan's almost seven and Noah's three. Makes this even more bizarre.

I'm a good dad. Okay, I work a lot but I provide a comfortable life for them, one where Madison only works because she wants to.

So why?

"Okay, let's think here," Brantley begins, pacing the floor, his boots making a scuffing noise from the thick layer of dust. "Have you guys been fighting?"

I try to think about it. We've been married for a while. Of course we fight, but never once has either of us mentioned divorce. That I know of. I know we say some shit in the heat of the moment, and I sometimes lose interest when she's bitching about random crap, but divorce… what the actual fuck? I think I'd remember the warning signs.

Frustration takes over, and I rip the papers off the counter and stare at them once more. I'm a man of action. I see a problem and I fix it.

"Got any suggestions, guys?" Trey's staring at his foot just as I'm beginning to take action. The one with the nail through the top of it. He's bleeding all over the fucking place.

"Yeah, go to the hospital," Brantley tells him, shaking his head in disbelief at the trail of blood Trey left from the back sliding doors to the kitchen. "Shit, man, it looks like a crime scene in here. How are we gonna get that off the subfloor?"

I don't know why Brantley's surprised by this. This is like the third time in two weeks Trey's hurt himself on a jobsite. He's the reason we have to carry such high industrial insurance and have the city up our ass over his last mix up when he fell off a roof and broke his ass.

Where was I?

Right. The "what the fuck" moment. I'm having it again.

Action. I need to take action.

"The city will be here at 12:30 for the electrical inspection." I hand Brantley the inspector's business card and roll the papers in my hand. "Stay here. I'm going to find out what the hell this is about."

He nods but doesn't say anything else.

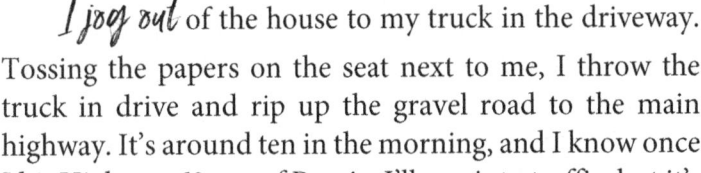

I jog out of the house to my truck in the driveway. Tossing the papers on the seat next to me, I throw the truck in drive and rip up the gravel road to the main highway. It's around ten in the morning, and I know once I hit Highway 60 out of Peoria, I'll run into traffic, but it's not like I could have stayed at the jobsite and wondered what the hell this meant.

My mind races through memories trying to pinpoint one where she might have hinted to this.

Have you ever seen one of those old fashion phone books? You know the ones I'm talking about with the letters on the front of the metal clipboard looking thing. My dad used to have one. You'd take the plastic slider to the letter the person's name started with and then flip it open and there'd be these cards in it with phone numbers.

That's me right now. Sliding through memories trying to pinpoint the right one. There had to be a reason. Was this something like that movie *Mr. and Mrs. Smith* where she's not at all who she said she was when we married? Had she been hired to kill me and her only way out was divorce? That'd I'd understand. I mean, good for her for taking the noble way out here. I'd take divorce over being shot in the back any day. I'll miss the sex, but I'll get over it eventually. No one wants a hit man for a wife. Think about it.

It takes me a half an hour to reach West Bay Salon where Madison is a massage therapist during the day.

That's right, I said massage therapist. Believe me when I say I've voiced my opinion about said job before.

Why you ask?

Well, let me tell you *who* her clients are.

Professional baseball players. Lots of them.

I don't like it one bit.

Is that why she served me with divorce papers? Is she leaving me for Derek Jeter?

If she is, I want season tickets in the settlement so I can heckle his wife-stealing ass.

Once I'm in the parking lot, I park my work truck next to a Mercedes and a Lexus. I weave through the cars like a man on a mission, papers in hand. Fuck yeah, I'm on a mission.

I yank the large glass door open, my calloused hardworking hands probably the only ones to pull open these doors.

Maybe not the greatest entrance, but forgive me here because the moment I'm through the door and standing in the marble entryway that greets these pretentious bitches who come here, I slam the papers on the counter. "Where the fuck is Madison Cooper?"

Too harsh?

Maybe so.

The young girl behind the counter jumps at the sound of my voice. "She's with a client, *sir*."

Sir? Who calls people sir these days? Right. She's like fourteen. Everyone over the age of eighteen is probably a sir in her world.

I lean into the counter and make eye contact with her. I can be intimating when I need to be, which is 85 percent of the time. I do run my own construction company and have four employees. I need to be intimating from time to time.

"You tell Madison, her *husband* is looking for her and she'd better call him the minute she's done or else I will be back here, waiting for her."

The cheerleader behind the counter gasps at me, unsure if I'm serious, or just mentally unstable. A little of both today. "I uh…." Her cheeks heat crimson, eyes darting from my mouth to my eyes and the little bit of dark scruff on my jaw. She's checking me out?

I'm attractive. I know I am. I lift weights, I run, I take care of myself. That's not me being conceited. That's me being confident. There's a difference between confident and conceited.

How you ask? That's like saying you've got a big dick when you've actually got something your fist can't even handle. Then you compensate by driving a lifted Chevy with balls hanging from your tailgate.

What's confident?

Snagging a chick like Madison when in reality, she's so far out of your league you'd need binoculars to see the playing field. Confidence is the key here.

"I'll tell her you stopped by," the girl finally says after clearing her throat.

Knocking my knuckles against the granite counter, I wait for her eyes to meet mine again. "You do that, *honey*. And *if* she doesn't call me, like she's supposed to, I'm coming back here and asking for you…" My eyes drift to her name tag. "Penelope."

Was that too much? The look on her face says it might be. It's something similar to the look girls give their fathers when they know they're in trouble. And I'm giving her one that's similar to the one a father might use when said daughter tells him she'll be out past her curfew and dating a guy named Tool who drives a black van with blacked-out windows.

We break eye contact as I slide the papers back off the counter and I turn to walk out.

Once I'm in the truck, I have no idea what to do next aside from call my lawyer and see if this is a joke. Maybe it's not real?

Glancing to my right, I look at the date wondering if it's an April Fool's bullshit.

February 24th.

Nope. Not a joke.

Did I forget Valentine's Day?

Pulling at my hair, I rack my brain for what we did on Valentine's Day… oh right, we went out to dinner at that steak house she loves.

See, we celebrated it. Okay, so we had to go out three days later because I was stuck in Denver on a job. Maybe knock me down a point for that one. She was pretty pissed.

And her birthday… it's a week before Valentine's Day. I worked my ass off and bought her those diamond earrings she wanted.

See? No selfless prick here. I treat her good. I may not have a lot of time, but still, I do what I can in between working fourteen hour days.

Running your own business isn't easy, and when you don't want to partner with a bigger company, you do what you can. I want the quality of Cooper Custom Homes to remain custom and not this commercialized bullshit you run into with these mass housing markets.

Back to my point. This Petition for Dissolution of Marriage.

Oh God, I can't think about it anymore. It's making me nauseous.

Dialing up Frank's number, he answers on about the third ring. "Hey, bro, what's up?"

He's not formal with me. Clearly. Mostly because we're friends outside of his lawyering duties. "What's a petition for dissolution of marriage?"

He thinks about it. I can almost picture him running his hand over his jaw or tapping his black pen obsessively against his rosewood Gran Palais desk. "It's a petition for divorce. Why?"

"Madison filed for divorce. I was served this morning."

He must be shocked because he's really fucking quiet like he's trying to decide the final play call at the Superbowl. Either that or he knows, and he's hiding it.

My temper flares as a rush of emotions hit me. "Did you know about this?" I shout, my words blistering through the cab of my truck. "You knew, didn't you?"

"No!" he shouts over my accusing tone. "I didn't know, Ridley. I swear." There may or may not be a few events that have occurred in the past where he's weary of my temper. Okay, I'll just come out and say it. He's terrified of me. I guess when you threaten to nail another man's dick to the wall over a poker game, he tends to be a little scared of you when you get angry. It was a long time ago. At least two months ago. Before you go thinking I have anger issues, I wasn't serious. It's not like I had the nail gun with me at the time. "Were you guys having problems? I wasn't aware you were."

"We weren't… that I knew of. Well, maybe a little, but she's never mentioned divorce to me." The heart attack feeling returns and I can barely breathe. Or maybe it's like an anxiety attack? I used to think anxiety was just a cop out for people who couldn't handle adult responsibilities. I think I might be wrong here. It's real.

I try to recall the name of that therapist I saw when my mom died. The one I told to shove his anxiety medication up his ass. Maybe I should apologize and ask him for a new prescription?

It was fifteen years ago, but he could still be in business, right?

"Fuck," I groan, laying my head back against the headrest. "What do I do? It says here I have twenty days to file a response."

Frank sighs. "Okay, um… can you drop it by my office?"

"Sure." I say this with a tone similar to the one you use when someone asks to cut in front of you in the grocery line. You're never thrilled when they do it, and admit it, the only reason you agree is because you don't want to act like a total asshole in front of your kid.

"Look, don't panic. I'm sure there's a perfectly good explanation. Have you tried talking to her?"

He must not know me at all.

"I tried to call her and I'm sitting outside of West Bay, but she won't answer, and they say she's with a client." The panicky feeling returns and I start to sweat. Mostly because it's fucking hot outside and I'm sitting in my car without it running, but still, this shit is heavy. Divorce. That's huge. I'm not my father. He's been divorced like four times. Divorce isn't something I can handle.

"Get me the papers and I'll call her lawyer." Frank snorts. "And here I thought I was her lawyer. Is there a name on it? Like a lawyer's name?"

Scanning the papers, I read through it.

IN THE SUPERIOR COURT OF THE STATE OF ARIZONA IN AND FOR THE COUNTY OF MARICOPA

MADISON J. COOPER, PETITIONER
AND
RIDLEY D. COOPER, RESPONDENT

PETITION FOR DISSOLUTION OF A COVENANT MARRIAGE WITH MINOR CHILDREN

And then the words, *Self-represented* stand out to me. Okay, so I've got that going for me. Might just be the only thing at this point but let's just put a point on the board for me here.

"She doesn't have a lawyer."

"All right, that's good. Let me look into this. For now, bring the papers by and I'll see what we can do."

"I'll be right over," I tell him, starting the truck up. I'm certainly not wasting any time here.

I welcome the rush of cool air that blasts my face when the air kicks on, but it doesn't help much. I'm still having that anxiety attack because I can't get a hold of her and probably can't force myself inside the room she's in without getting arrested. Believe me, I consider the getting arrested part for answers. It wouldn't be the first time. I was once arrested because my college professor gave me an C- on my midterm and I thought it was necessary to break into his house for an answer as to why.

If he didn't answer the door, why wasn't it acceptable to go through the window if it was open?

Or maybe it wasn't open. I don't remember.

2

THE WAITING GAME I DON'T PLAY

Have you ever wondered what hell feels like?

I actually haven't. I never really had the desire to find out.

By noon, I'm pretty sure I know exactly what it's like. I can see it at least. And let me tell you, it's awful.

Think of the worst day you've had, then multiply that by a hundred. That's hell. I'm teetering on the edge of hell, balancing the tightrope and hoping I don't fall off.

After I gave Frank a copy of the petition to dissolution of marriage, I headed back to the office to check on Kennedy and maybe see if by chance Madison called there instead.

My office is in downtown Phoenix. For a while, Brantley and I worked out of my house, but it got to be too chaotic once Callan started walking so I rented a space on the first floor of a fancy high-rise. I'm cheap. I don't like to spend money where I don't need to, but when your toddler son begins taking work orders and construction plans to use as his personal coloring pads, it's time to move your office.

I'm also glad I did because once Noah was born, there's no way in hell I could have imagined trying to work in the same house as that little monster.

"Is the inspector finished up at the Aster house?" I ask Kennedy, our office manager.

We call her the office manager strictly by her request. I don't pay her office manager pay. She's the only one in the office. How can you manage an office if there's nobody else in it?

That's a conversation for another day.

"No. Didn't show."

"What do you mean he didn't show up?"

Kennedy barely looks up at me, her stare strangely focused on her phone. Nothing new there. I swear it's glued to her hands. "That's what I'm saying, Ridley. The inspector didn't show up. B and Trey stayed there all afternoon."

It's noon. How that adds up as all afternoon isn't right, but we don't pay Kennedy for her math skills. We pay her because she can file paperwork, answer the phone politely and actually schedule appointments without fucking it up. You'd be surprised with today's workforce. Or maybe it's just me who's completely blown away by the lack of accountability in today's youth.

I once hired a kid to do tile work, and he showed up to the jobsite and wanted to know about health insurance his first day. That wasn't so weird. Me catching him making a family of snowman out of grout, that's weird.

Wanna know the worst part?

He laid the tile all right. Guess what his design resembled?

A dick. A big fat dick made of mosaic tiles. Luckily we were able to fix it but I swore off hiring anyone for like a year. I'll admit though, the dude had talent to be able to do that.

"Hey." Kennedy finally glances up from her phone, popping bubbles with her gum. "Can I have Friday off?"

Never mind the fact she's popping her gum, and she knows I hate that, but how can she possibly think I can function enough to contemplate three days from now? Doesn't she know what I'm dealing with?

Right. No. She doesn't. Unless Brantley told her, which he wouldn't. Brantley's secretive and for no reason whatsoever. If there's ever anyone you can trust not to tell your secrets, it's him.

I glance at Kennedy. "Did Madison call the office today?" Since I left the salon, I've been dealing with the city of Scottsdale on some building permits I filed three weeks ago, and they're giving me the runaround about them. But I know for a fact Madison hasn't called my cell phone.

Kennedy shrugs, pushing her glasses up her tiny nose. "No, I don't think so."

Kennedy's attractive. Not in the way you'd think. She's kind of awkward in a sense. Nerdy even. A petite girl who wears these thick black-framed glasses, jet-black hair she usually has up in a bun, I've frequently had to kick Trey out of the office because he fantasises about her playing naughty teacher to him.

Before you go thinking I have a thing for my secretary, knock that shit off. She's nineteen. I'm not a creep. I'm twenty-eight. I have rules. And also—this is kinda up in the air right now—married and have morals.

Speaking of being married, guess who still hasn't answered their phone?

Yep. Madison.

I've called fifty-two times.

How can she still be with that client? It's been like what… I'm not the greatest at keeping track of time here but I'm pretty sure it's been three hours. Who pays for a massage that's three hours long?

I bet Derek Jeter does.

I'll shove his bat up his ass if he's trying to round home plate with my wife. Listen, I have nothing against Derek Jeter. And he's probably never even seen my wife, but I'm just using him as an example. I'd use David Beckham, because I bet he's the type of guy Madison would go for, but wrong sport. We don't see many soccer players in the desert.

I take a step toward my office behind Kennedy's desk only to have her groan and smack me on the shoulder with a set of building plans. "Hey, dude, day off? Remember?"

"Oh, right." I wave my hand around. "Yeah, sure. Take it off. I don't really care." Believe me when I say my voice is completely dejected. It's almost pathetic.

Kennedy stands up, her hand on my forehead. "Are you sick?"

I stare blankly down at her. She's like five one. Being six one myself, I won't ever be eye level with her unless I'm sitting down. "No, why?"

"You just told me I can take the day off. Last time I asked for a day off, you asked my mother to fill in for me."

I expect people to be at work. I don't understand the need for a day off during the week when you have weekends off. You don't see me taking a day off during the week, do you?

Before you answer that, I didn't take today off. I simply took a couple hours to find out why my wife suddenly filed for divorce.

"I'm fine." I step into my office. "Let me know if Madison calls and call the electrical inspector and see where he's at."

Sitting down in my chair, I scan my desk for my cell phone I tossed down somewhere on this mountain of paperwork a minute ago. I find it next to my wedding photo.

A stabbing sensation hits my heart. Leaning forward, I rest my elbows on my desk and stare at the photograph. We're standing facing each other, nearly kissing with her arms wrapped around my shoulders. She looks happy in that picture. I remember the day like it was yesterday and the way nothing else mattered but us and the adventure we found ourselves on.

We were still in college when Madison got pregnant with Callan. Not long after we found out, I proposed. Marriage seemed like the thing to do. I wanted to marry her. I did, I still want to be married to her. Would I have asked had she not gotten pregnant our junior year of college? Probably not for a while, but I did, and I don't regret it.

Wasn't she happy? I always thought she was. Or had I been so focused on my business I didn't realize we were slipping away?

I mean, isn't that what every country song's about? Wife leaves him, then the dog? We don't have a dog so at least I have that going for me. We do however have kids, and if she takes them from me too, she might as well rip my fucking heart out and toss it to the wolves.

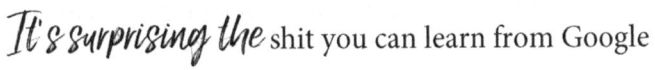

It's surprising the shit you can learn from Google when doing some research.

Did you know women file for divorce twice as often as men do? Don't believe me? Google it. First thing that pops up.

Want to know the number one reason as to why they ask for a divorce… per Google?

#1 Infidelity.

I've never cheated on her. Ever. Wouldn't even think about it. Look at her. That's like marrying Jennifer Aniston and cheating on her. Brad Pitt, you're a dumbass. I'm sorry, loved you in *Ocean's Eleven*, but you're pretty fucking dumb.

Next one?

#2 Incompatible.

Okay, well, that's just bullshit. We're compatible. Remember the shower?

#3 Drinking/Drug Use.

Um, can we pass over the drinking? I don't do drugs but is it wrong to drink a six-pack in one night three days a week? Maybe don't answer that just yet. Let's move on.

#4 Grew Apart.

I wouldn't think we've grown apart, have we? *Again*, remember the shower?

#5 Personality problems.

That could be debatable on my part. Around the third day of every month, she turns into a completely different person and as we call it, "shark week" takes over.

#6 Lack of communication.

Do we have to talk so much? Why can't I come home from work and just sit and watch TV? I mean, I'm not rude or ignoring her. If she asks a question, most of the time I answer it the first time. Or maybe the second? Surely not the third.

#7 Physical or mental abuse.

I've never in my life laid a hand on her. Let's clarify here, in anger. Because sex doesn't count on that one, right?

#8 Loss of love.

Had she fallen out of love with me? How could that be possible? She fucked me in the shower this morning.

#9 Not meeting family obligations.

I admit, I could improve my score on this one. I work a lot.

#10 Last one? Employment problems.

I run my own business and I'm the most sought after custom home builder in Maricopa County. It's a business that gives her freedom. One where she only works because she's bored during the day. Pretty sure my income isn't the problem here.

You see that guy? The one with his head in his hands contemplating his next move?

He's in hell. I'm sure of it.

My phone beeps beside me. I scramble for it, pushing aside plans and paperwork only to see it's a text message from Brantley.

Brantley: Everything ok?

No. It's not okay. Today's been like being on an airplane and knowing the world just went to war and you can't check anything. You can't obsessively sit in front of the television while we show our military power. Instead, you're stuck with no Wi-Fi and are 30,000 feet in the air hoping you're not about to be shot down.

Me: Can't get a hold of her. Did the inspector show up?

Brantley: No. I tried calling him but he didn't answer.

What's with people and not answering their phone today? Is it national "Do Not Answer Your Phone Day?"

Brantley: Sent Trey to the ER. They took the nail out but he'll be off work the rest of the week.

Great. Just fucking great.

Remember my phobia with hiring people? Well, I need this job on Aster Drive by the end of the month which is why I hired Trey in the first place. The last thing I need is a laid-up trainee.

Brantley and I started Cooper Custom Homes right out of college. My trust fund financed the initial start-up of it, but it's been just the two of us for eight years. Occasionally we contract out for certain aspects of the jobs we do. For the most part, it's just us, and we like it that way. I take pride in knowing we built a home from the ground up.

Me: Call me when the inspector shows up. Drywall is being delivered tomorrow.

I check the time again. 2:46 p.m.

Picking up my phone, I select Madison's name again. This time it doesn't even ring before it goes to voicemail, so I finally leave a message. The fifty-third call, I leave a fucking message.

"Hey, it's me. Your husband. *Still* your husband as the state of Arizona will say for the next…." I scan the paperwork where it says I have twenty days to respond, but the parties can't advance with divorce proceedings for sixty days. "Sixty days. Is this a fuckin' joke, Mad?" I seethe into the phone, practically spitting the words out. "You send me divorce papers, and then you don't bother to check your phone at all today? It's bullshit, you know?"

Okay so if I wanted to get her attention, do you think I have it now?

Probably not. This is Madison we're talking about. I once couldn't get a hold of her when she was pregnant because she was at the grocery store and couldn't hear her phone ringing. I was in the parking lot when she got out, leaned against her car expecting a reason as to why she didn't answer. I mean, she was nine months pregnant with Callan and ready to pop any day. Of course I was concerned, and she didn't answer her phone?

The nerve of her, right?

Am I over the top?

Probably.

It's who I am.

And what did she do when she came out to find me leaned into her car?

Rolled her eyes.

I'll tell you a secret. I once took a shot of lighter fluid. Wait, no. I take that back. That's not a secret, just a fucked-up story. But my reasoning here, sometimes I think I'm mentally unstable. Maybe it's from the lighter fluid. It once got so bad that when I was thirteen, I went a whole year thinking I had schizophrenia because my cousin Josh told me so. If you look at the symptoms—personality changes, increasing withdrawal from social situations, irrational, angry or fearful responses to loved ones and inappropriate or bizarre behavior—you get a little paranoid.

Turns out I was going through puberty.

Anyways, I had a point to this story. All those feelings I dealt with while going through puberty were incredibly stressful for me. I do not like not knowing what's going on with my body. If I have a cold or the flu, I demand to be treated that same day.

See where I'm going with this?

No? Well, you should. I don't like being in the dark. So this shit Madison is pulling today just isn't working for me.

I check the time once more. 3:25 p.m.

I don't know what time Callan gets out of school, but I do know one thing, Madison picks him up, which means she'll be at the house and I can get some answers, right?

Yes. The answer should be yes.

Grabbing the crumpled-up papers from my desk, I head out the door.

3

GIVE ME ANSWERS, WOMAN

Since I leave the office shortly after three, it doesn't take me long to reach our home in Cave Creek. Have you seen those housing developments where all the homes look the same, and everyone in them does too?

It's where I live. Suburban hell.

I paid cash for this house when I was twenty-four. My mother died when I was fifteen and me being her only child, she left me her trust fund she'd received from her rich oil-drilling father I couldn't stand. No really, I couldn't even be in the same room as that man without wanting to shove cotton balls in my ears so I didn't have to hear his constant complaints. He died a couple months back, and I couldn't even bring myself to attend his funeral. That's really shitty of me, isn't it?

I was born in Houston Texas where my grandfather was someone everyone hated. He was that guy who thought because he was rich he could park his Rolls-Royce in the middle two parking spots and not give a shit.

If you ask me, he was a real son of a bitch. My parents divorced when I was five and we moved to Phoenix where her sister lived. Though mom had her trust fund, she never touched it. Refusing to live off her father's money, she put the money aside and worked two jobs to give me a decent upbringing but I think that's where I learned my work ethic from.

I never knew about the money growing up. It wasn't until a few weeks after she passed that I found out. At first, I was pissed at her. Why'd we struggle so much just because of her pride? The older I got, the more I understood the lesson she wanted me to learn. It's far more rewarding to work for what you want than to be handed it.

Anyway, my point. I may have been given a trust fund, but I work hard for everything in my life.

A year ago, Madison and I decided it was time for something a little bigger. With two boys, we were rapidly outgrowing our 2,000-square-foot home, and I wanted the hell out of this neighborhood.

Being a custom home builder, the obvious choice was for me to build us a house. Have you ever heard of that saying the mechanic can't keep his own car running because he's constantly fixing other peoples?

Works the same for a home builder. I started our house in Granite Mountain Ranch Estates, you know, the part of town no one can afford?

Brantley and I got it to the framing stage and had all the plumbing and electrical installed, but unfortunately it's been patiently waiting for me to finish hanging the drywall for the last four months. It's not like I meant to put the house on the back burner, but with my business growing, I don't have time. I work seven days a week, usually fourteen hour days and most weeks it's still not enough.

Some would say I need to loosen up and hire out for more aspects of the building process, but I fear in doing that the quality of work is lessened. That's like fucking your wife and her not getting off too. I'm very thorough when it comes to sex. It's a process for me: I put in some moves, she comes a few times and then I can have my fun.

It works the same with business. Take care of your customers first. But what the fuck do I know, right? My wife just asked for a divorce out of the blue so this just in, I might not know everything there is to know about life. Clearly this curve ball slipped passed me.

Speaking of my wife, do you see that white Lexus LX570 parked in my driveway?

It's ugly. I've never cared for the way the grill looks, but that's Madison's car. A little pretentious, don't you think?

Do you really think she has any grounds for divorce when she drives a car like that?

Yeah, me either.

Sure, I drive a brand-new Ford Raptor, but it's my work truck. I'm in my truck more than my bed some weeks so I splurged and bought something I loved. And like I said, we're not hurting for money.

Snatching the papers off the seat next to me, I head in the house with determination. Punching the buttons to the alarm, I can hear Callan talking to someone in the kitchen. Following the voice, I'm lead through our home with its southern pole barn feel you wouldn't expect someone like Madison to like. She's surprising when it comes to her décor she chose for the house. Me? I couldn't give a flying fuck how she decorates our house as long as my bed is comfortable.

I'm very particular about my sheets too. Thread count is important whether you want to believe it or not.

You see that boy at the table? Not the one on the floor drinking water out of a bowl. The younger looking version of myself with the baseball cap on backward reading the *National Geographic* and dressed in black-and-red shorts and a matching tank top?

That's Callan. I'll get to the one on the floor in a minute. Before you judge Callan on reading the *National Geographic*, understand he's not like other six, almost seven-year-olds. Most parents like to say their kids are gifted. In their eyes, the kid is the smartest at everything, plays every sport with the best ability and the best looking.

Callan? He's awkward. I say that in a loving way, I really do. To say he's gifted is an understatement but with it comes a personality that's difficult at times.

There's nothing in this world I love more than my boys. Sorry, Madison. They replaced her as that number one spot. And I'd hope she has the same feeling.

That's not to say I don't love her and wouldn't gladly take a bullet for her any day of the week, I'm just saying your kids come first, right?

Hiding the papers in my back pocket, I move past Callan to sit in the chair across from him. "Hey, guys."

Bright blue eyes that match his mother's lift from the magazine. "Ridley."

I know what you're thinking. What six-year-old calls their dad their first name?

Don't get me wrong, it's not like he calls me by my first name all the time but it seems he does it just enough to remind me he's smarter than me. And just wait. It gets worse.

There's times when I've honestly thought to myself, my son will either cure cancer someday, or he will rule the world. And not in a good way. No really. I'm being completely honest here. I once asked him, "If you could cure cancer or rule the world, what would you do?"

Guess what his answer was?

Lex Luther all the way. He said, and I'm quoting him here. "I'd rule the world. I'll hire someone to cure cancer."

I like the way he thinks, but honestly, he scares the living shit out of me sometimes.

Now for Noah. Do you see the boy on my lap now? The one wearing a Superman cape and a Batman mask with brown hair that hangs in his face?

That's Noah, our youngest who's obsessed with Wolverine. You'd think by looking at him it's either Superman or Batman, right?

Nope. Just wait.

"Hey, Noah. How was your day?"

"Grr!" he yells, holding my face by my cheeks. "I am Wolverine!"

Same answer every day.

When Noah was a baby, the only way to get him to sleep was gangster rap. You had to sing it to him every night. Sometimes—judging by his personality—I wonder if that was a bad idea. Although, because of his awesome taste in music, I can now sing every line to "Hypnotize" and honestly, I rock the shit out of it. Brantley likes to tell me I'm not a gangster and shouldn't be rapping, but he doesn't know what the fuck he's talking about.

I look at Callan and set Wolverine on the floor to resume his water. "Where's Mommy?"

He shrugs, his eyes finding the magazine again like I'm annoying him by my very presence in the room. It's then I notice the title: "Your Brain. 100 things you never knew."

"Probably upstairs," he mumbles, flipping to another page.

Clearing my throat, I stand up and ruffle his hair. "Good talk."

I probably should have paid attention to him a little more, asked how his day was or at least double-checked what he's reading. For all I know he could have had a *Playboy* magazine stuffed inside there. Doubtful.

There're two staircases in our house. I've never understood the point of it. At least 600 square feet of this house is wasted with stairs.

I take the stairs in the kitchen because they're closest. No sense in wasting time. Down the hall and to the left is our master bedroom.

See that woman standing in front of our king-size bed folding laundry? The one with the long brown hair, perfect skin, perfect tits, just fucking perfect... that's Madison.

And guess what? She's fucking calm like she didn't serve me with divorce papers today.

"Hey, honey," I say, slamming the bedroom door behind me. "How was your day?"

She jumps at the sound of the door, her hands on her heart. "Jesus Christ, Ridley. You scared the shit out of me!"

I laugh, and it's sarcastic. I lay on the bed, right over the clothes she's folding and sprawl out, my arms behind my head. "You know, I had an *awesome* day. You should check your messages, I told you all about it after I called you fifty-three fucking times." Then I hold my hand up and repeat the numbers with my fingers whispering. "*Five... three.*"

She glares at me, a pointed look I receive, oh, you know, like at least once a day. She's only glaring because some of the clothes that she folded are now wrinkled.

She's a perfectionist like that. And if I had to guess, she'll iron them later. "I guess I missed your calls." She turns, walking into the bathroom with an arm full of towels.

I turn myself over and roll off the bed, taking with me all the clothes she folded. "Really? Fifty-three of them?" Taking the papers from my back pocket, I slam them down on the lava stone countertop knocking over her perfume bottles cluttering it. "What's *this*?"

She doesn't even look at me. "What's it look like?"

"Looks like a fuck you." Crossing my arms, I turn and lean into the counter. "Which is interesting to me because you see that shower right there?" I point to it, and she even looks. "I literally fucked you against the tile this morning, and you certainly didn't seem like you were upset. So one would wonder, what changed from you moaning my name to you not wanting it anymore?"

Madison rolls her eyes when the word moaning comes out of my mouth and walks past me into the bedroom. "Don't be so dramatic. You can't seriously be surprised this is happening. Did you even read it?"

"I don't need to. The title says it all. But you know, since we're focused on that, when did we become irreconcilably different?"

"I can't remember the last time we weren't, Ridley. Just because we have good sex doesn't mean we get along enough to make a marriage work."

The last time we weren't? Those five words rattle around in my head. So this is an ongoing thing I should have seen coming? I don't miss the good sex part because let's face it, it's amazing, but I'm not focused on it.

"What the fuck are you talking about? Now who's being dramatic, Madison? What the fuck are you talking about?"

"I'm talking about *you*, Ridley. I'm talking about you not being a part of this family and me being a single parent to these kids. When was the last time you ever came home at three in the afternoon? The only reason you did today was because of those papers. You know nothing about us anymore."

I can't believe what she's saying. Okay, a small part of me can, but I'm not about to let her think she has the upper hand here. She's had the upper hand all day long with this not answering her phone thing.

"That's not true." I flop myself back on the bed when she reaches for the laundry again.

She rips a shirt out from under my head. "Okay… what's Callan's teacher's name?"

You see that guy staring at his wife blankly? He has no clue. He doesn't even know where the kid goes to school. Don't look at me like that. I'm not a bad guy. Well, that's debatable on who you ask today. Don't ask my wife.

"Who's his best friend?"

More staring on my part. I try to recall that kid I saw two weeks ago at my kitchen table one morning. He had blond hair, right? Now if I can think of his name….

Madison's eyes narrow into tiny slits. "What's the name of his soccer team?"

"He plays soccer?" And why'd she let him play the dumbest sport? Couldn't she have enrolled him in football?

"This is my point. You know nothing about our family." That's not her entire point, and I know it. It's in the subtle way her eyes won't meet mine and dance over my features, never landing. Madison almost never says what she's really thinking. I'm sure of it. Something in her blue eyes tells me she's lying, or at the very least, omitting the partial truth. She thinks she's clever as shit. "I bet if you had to put Noah to bed tonight, you wouldn't know the first thing about what to do or what he sleeps with."

"He sleeps with his cape and mask." I'm guessing here. I have no clue.

She shakes her head. "Wrong."

"You can't be mad at me for that." But she can, and she is. See that woman frantically trying to distract herself with the laundry, she's mad. Oh yeah, she's fucking pissed at me. "And when did Callan start soccer?"

She turns to me with a raised brow and her eyes appraise me from head to toe. Well, I'm lying down so that's a little hard but still, she's definitely appraising me. "This is my point. You know, this is exactly how Kip warned me you'd react."

Kip? That's a guy's name, right?

Her declaration breaks me out of my shock, and I jump to my feet. "Kip? Who the fuck is Kip?"

"I don't have time for this." She's avoiding my question now. Reaching down to her feet, she picks up a pile of socks I knocked over and sets them on the bed again. "I'm so tired of this and as much as I would love to stand here and argue with you all afternoon, Callan has soccer practice in twenty minutes. And since you seem to think this is completely out of the blue and we don't have problems, I think it would be a great idea for you take him."

"Fine. I'll take him." Shoving the papers in my back pocket, I get to the door before I look back at her. I'm not sure what look I thought I'd be met with, but the one I get surprises me. She's facing the bathroom, her back to me. The problem with her snub is she doesn't realize I can see her face in the mirror above our dresser. And she's crying.

My heart races, a feeling of desolation rooting inside of me and I desperately want to go to her, wrap my arms around her and beg her to tell me everything. Bottom line is, for a moment, I forget how to breathe staring at her. You're probably wondering what's stopping me from wrapping my arms around her now? A little thing called pride. And it's like a goddamn elephant standing in front of me.

The elephant sways when I notice her left hand. Do you see that diamond ring she's wearing?

Me either. She probably hawked the son of the bitch the moment she filed these papers.

Have you seen the movie *Gone Girl*?

I have and it's fucking disturbing. I don't know why but that entire movie is replaying in my head, and I'm thinking maybe I should check the bank account and credit cards or see if she's hiding shit in the garage I don't know about to set me up for her murder.

Downstairs, Noah's in the living room watching his iPad and Callan's still at the table, his magazine in his hand. "Hey, buddy, I'm gonna take you to soccer practice."

I'm pretty sure this is the first time he's ever heard these words out of my mouth because his eyes widen in surprise. "I'm not in the mood for jokes."

Me either, dude.

I'm expecting him to be excited or at least show some sort of emotion.

He does neither.

He's so much like me it's ridiculous. I give a nod to the garage. "I'm not joking, let's go."

"Oh yeah?" Setting down his magazine, he looks at me, a hint of smugness set on his six-year-old face. It's rather alarming how well he can pull said look off. "Do you even know where my practice is at?"

I play it cool. "Of course I do, but the question is, do you know?"

He rolls his eyes, clearly not amused with me. He and his mother have something in common. "It's at the community center."

"Well then, let's go." I hold my keys up. "What time do you have to be there?"

You know those looks you get when someone stares blankly at you, and for a split second, you feel kind of dumb? It's like being back in school and you were talking in class but the teacher called on you, and you're left wondering what the right answer is?

Well, that's me.

Callan, he's the teacher right now and the look I'm getting, if he had a ruler in his hand, he'd probably slap it to my forehead.

"Practice starts at four."

I glance at my phone. "We better go."

Mostly because I have no idea where the community center is, and it's going to take me a while to find it.

Okay, let's just stop for a moment because I can see the judgmental look on your face. You think I'm a bad father, don't you?

I'm not, I swear. I love Callan. I just don't have a lot of time and going to soccer practice I didn't know he even had wasn't one of the many things I had to get done on any given day.

Just as we're by the door to the garage, Madison comes downstairs like nothing happened and hands Callan his cleats with Noah on her hip as she's struggling to get the jogging stroller out of the garage. "Bye, baby. Have fun tonight."

"I will, Mommy." They hug and then Callan glances at me. I kiss Madison good-bye every time I leave, and you know, this time *won't* be any different.

Stepping toward her with a smile, I can tell she wants to back up. Her eyes say "fuck you" while her body language remains relaxed in front of the kids.

Drawing her into a hug, I kiss her flat on the lips with intention. Christ, she fucking hates me. Do you see the way her body turns rigid like a corpse? When I pull back, I whisper in her ear, "We're talking about this tonight," because she needs to know I'm not letting this go.

Noah pushes me away about a foot still clinging to Madison. "No, Daddy."

Madison's lips press together in a tight line, and her expression turns serious. Her muscles tense, but she says nothing and smiles down at Noah and Callan who are watching us curiously. It's not often Callan acts his age, but he is right now, innocent looking and probably sensing more than we want him to.

"See my boys tonight," Madison says, untangling herself from me. She wants to punch me in the face. I can see it.

But Callan doesn't move, his stare fixated on his mom. "What are you going to do, Mommy?"

She gets *Mommy,* and I get called by my first name?

Madison kneels to his level, straightening out his tank top. With the garage door open, the afternoon sun shines down on her dark hair making the hint of caramel highlights shimmer. She touches the side of his face when she says, "I'm gonna take Noah for a run while Daddy takes you. Is that okay?"

Callan shrugs. "I guess so."

4

THE "OTHER" DAD'S

Soccer? Really? I don't understand soccer. I mean, yes, I understand the premise is to kick the ball into the opposing teams net, but honestly, as a sport, it makes absolutely no sense to me.

As I stand here watching a bunch of six and seven-year-olds chase each other around the field, I can't help but ask myself why my son CAN'T play a normal sport that has a purpose? You know, something like football. Now there's a sport. You've got designated plays with the intention of scoring a touchdown. That's the problem with soccer; there are no designated plays. Just a bunch of kids running after a ball with the hopes of one of them making it in the net. Where's the strategy in that?

Don't get me wrong, I'm sure when some people look out to the field they see a game of skill and athleticism. I'm just not one of those people.

What kind of person am I? You see that guy standing on the sidelines near the bleachers? The one with the baseball cap on backward, hands buried in his pockets with stiff shoulders? The one with the puzzled look on his face who keeps looking down at his watch hoping time will suddenly speed up? That's the kind of person I am.

That's a dad who clearly doesn't understand a damn thing this coach ten feet away from him is explaining to his team. He's got a clipboard, and he's handing out something called "pennies" while throwing down miniature cones yelling something about sharks and minnows. What the hell? Can someone please just kick the damn ball so we can get on with it?

There are eight kids surrounding the coach as he splits them into two teams. Each one runs enthusiastically in the direction that the coach points them to and then there's Callan.

You see that kid sitting inside the goalie net? The one who bears a striking resemblance to the man with the stiff shoulders? The one *still* reading the *National Geographic*?

That's my kid. Bright side, at least he's not the kid eating dirt and picking his nose.

"I don't know why Coach Bennett lets that kid play," a man two feet from me grumbles, shaking his head voicing his disgust that a boy would be reading during practice. "He just sits there."

I remain quiet but shift my position so that I'm facing them. Immediately they have my attention because they're talking about my kid. I'm holding my tongue because it's probably for the best I don't say anything. You may find this hard to believe but, I think most people are fucking idiots, and I have to keep my mouth shut, or 90 percent of what I'm thinking could land my ass in jail. Or punched in the face. Both have happened. Not pretty.

The guy next to him laughs, like this guy's observation is funny to him. Probably is. It's not his kid they're talking about. "You know damn well why he lets him, Jeff. It's because Madison's his mom, and Bennett just wants to stare at her tits and ass every Tuesday and Saturday."

I eye them assessing their build and whether they can kick my ass. Over the years, I've become pretty good at assessing whether I can win a fight.

These guys are strong maybe. It's hard to tell for sure. They're big but they look like the only weight they've been lifting is their own fat asses in and out of a fast food restaurant booth.

They kind of remind me of those football jocks in college. You know the ones I'm talking about…? They have muscles but you know most of it comes from playing offensive lineman, and they couldn't throw a punch if they had to. Me, on the other hand, I can throw and land a punch. I work out at least four days a week, despite my long hours and run twice a week. I'm in shape. Always have been. Fitness is important to both Madison and me, and I don't think these two have seen the inside of a gym in years.

"Who are you talking about?" I ask, stepping forward to include myself in their conversation whether they want me to or not.

The taller of the two speaks first but doesn't look at me when he says, "Callan's mom. She's got great fucking tits and ass." And then he examines me when I'm in his eyesight, his hand coming up to shield the sun. He eyes me up and down. "Who are you? We haven't seen you around before."

I'm always up for a little game of fuck you. My lips pull into a grin, my arms crossing over my chest in what can only be displayed as intimidation. "Callan's dad."

You know those looks you get from people when they're so shocked they can't form words for a few seconds, but their mouth continues to move? The whole fish out of water effect? I'm getting that right now. And then he asks, "Really?" And he laughs like he's amused. I'm clearly not. "Well, shit. We assumed Callan's dad was some kind of deadbeat."

Well you know what they say about those who assume, it makes an ass out of them and makes me want to break his jaw. I wonder how this guy feels about a broken jaw?

I snort, and in case you couldn't tell from my reaction just now, I'll just come out and say it for you: I have no respect for this douche digger or his booger eating kid who just kicked my son's magazine out of his hand and then turns to wave like we should applaud or something. Didn't think I noticed that, did you? Yeah, well, I notice everything. Not if you ask Madison, but I do. I want to grab that little fucker by his neck and make him pick the magazine up. It'll have to wait though because first I have to deal with this asshole in front of me.

I stare blankly at the man.

When I don't say anything—because forgive me, I'm trying to decide what to say—his buddy asks, "How long have you and Madison been divorced?"

Divorced? They're really trying to piss me off, aren't they?

A whistle's blown in the background but neither of us look, we're locked in a stare. And as I look at these guys, I realize they *really* want to know. It's like they're trying to gather enough information so that they can offer her a strong shoulder to cry on while staring at her tits.

"We're *not* divorced." Not yet anyway. And as far as I'm concerned, we *never* will be. I don't care what those papers now stuffed under the seat of my truck say. And I'm certainly not telling shit for brains she filed for divorce.

"Do you work out of town or something?"

Raising my hand to my jaw, I scratch the side of my face. Not that it itches. I just do it. "What did you say your name was?"

The man gives me a "what the fuck" look. "I didn't, but it's Kent. And you are?"

I smile. I can't help it. "I'm Ridley. And no, I'm not *usually* out of town."

"So you're not divorced, and you don't work out of town. How come we've never seen you at any practices or games?" He's smiling like he's trying to make me out to be a bad father for never being around. Little does he know he's too late because today I already feel like a piece of shit. But there's still no chance in hell I'm going to let them see any chinks in my armor.

While all this is going on in my head, he's still talking. What the fuck is he saying?

Right. He's pointing out to me what a bad father I am.

"I run my own construction business. I can't usually make it to things like this because I work for a living." Do you see that look on my face? The one that screams sarcasm?

I'm glad you see it because by the blank look on their faces they don't.

Look at them. It's obvious they don't know what hard work is. Without one callus to show for a hard day's labor, they're probably pencil pushing accountants. Both of them. I bet they've never had dirt under their fingernails.

"Well, that explains a lot. Callan's a bit of a mama's boy."

What the shit? A mama's boy? My kid?

Well yeah, okay, I guess he is a little bit closer to Madison than me. But that's beside the point. What the fuck does that have to do with these guys questioning me like a round of speed dating?

The guy Kent, the one asking all the questions, gives a dismissive nod toward who I assume is the coach of this team. "It also explains why Bennett is always giving the kid extra attention." And then these two bag of dicks look at one another and exchange a knowing glance. There's an inside joke between the two of them and they start laughing.

Ask me if I care?

Nope. Not even a little bit.

Okay, that's not completely true. I mean nobody likes to be laughed at or about but when I really think about it, if this is what these two find entertaining, I feel bad for them.

Sadly, this is probably the highlight of their day.

I mean look at them. Their lives are a shit show. Just look at their kids. One's picking his nose and eating it, and the other has his hand down the back of his pants digging for God knows what.

Just as I'm contemplating dragging Callan off the field to try and explain to him the finer points of any other sport, another whistle blows and the coach yells, "We're done, boys!"

I walk forward and bump Kent's shoulder with mine, purposely. "And you're right, my *wife* does have great tits and ass."

I don't look back at him. There's really no point to. I walk toward my son with the purpose of getting the hell out of here. When I spot him, I stop.

See that kid walking toward me with his ripped magazine in hand and a troubled look on his face?

That's a kid who's beginning to realize he's not like the other kids. It makes me want to punch these two guys in the face on pure principal for saying he shouldn't be on the team. Just because my kid doesn't think his boogers are an afternoon snack shouldn't mean he can't play. It's fucking soccer. It's not like it's an actual sport. Might as well be playing kickball.

I kneel to his level as he drops his bag at my feet. "You okay, bud?"

"I'm fine." His answer's short, his cheeks flushed. "Can we go now, Ridley?"

"It's Dad," I tell him, grabbing his bag and following after him. I do give Dumb and Dumber one last look to see them high-fiving their Olympic nose-picking athletes. "Hey, listen, bud, do you even like soccer?"

Don't get me wrong. I wish the answer was that my son loves playing all sports, but the reality is it's more likely he hates it, and as a parent, why in the world would we make him play something he doesn't enjoy?

I mean, if it's reading he wants to do, let him. I get he needs physical activity, but this kid, the one staring at his magazine like someone just ripped his heart out, he doesn't seem like he's enjoying this. I could be wrong here, but I doubt it.

Callan stops and looks at me curiously, the setting sun shining on his face. "I guess so. I mean, it seems like the thing to do." And then he shrugs. "I'm hungry. Can we have pizza?"

The thing to do? I'm not liking that answer, but I let it go for now.

"Yeah, sure."

It's when we're in the car, I can't let it go. He's sitting in the backseat staring at his ripped magazine. He's nervous. He might even be scared. Of what I'm not sure.

"You don't have to play if you don't want to."

"I know, but all the other kids play sports. I feel like I should play. Dylan plays football."

Ah, yes, I remember now. His best friend's name is Dylan Conner. By the way, Dylan's dad is a tool. Are you surprised I think this?

Probably not.

I focus on the important part of what he said. He feels like he should play?

I'm not sure what to say to him because I can tell he's doing this to please others and you know, it pisses me off. He's doing it to fit in. He's a child. He should never feel like he has to fit in.

5

THE COLD SHOULDER

I take Callan out for pizza, and the kid eats three pieces. I'm impressed. For someone his size, barely fifty pounds, three pieces of pizza is like me eating an entire pie myself. Not that I'm complaining about him eating. He's a growing boy. It just surprises the hell out of me.

We don't talk much through dinner. I suppose both of us have a lot on our minds. While I appreciate the time to think, I can't help but notice the crease in Callan's brow and the tense expression on his face. I know the look. It's the same one I get when I'm stressed out. It's certainly not a look I want my six-year-old having though.

I knock my knuckles on the table as he chews on a piece of crust. "Hey, bud, is there something you want to talk about?"

He shakes his head. No words, just a dismissal.

I know I should keep asking, push him to open up to me because it's obvious something is bothering him, but to be completely honest, I'm scared his answer might be more troubling than I need to know.

And before you say it, I know what you're thinking. What kind of parent would let this go?

Well, if you knew Callan at all, you'd know it's best to let him come to you. If you push him to talk when he's not ready, it'll be weeks before he tells you what's going on. And most of the time it has to do with insane questions like, "Is there any evidence that a thermonuclear device exploded over Hiroshima?"

He asked me that two weeks ago when I got home at midnight and he was pacing the hallway. *That's* the kind of shit that keeps this kid up at night.

When we get home, Madison is in the kitchen with a glass of water, her nightgown on already. "Hey, buddy." She's not talking to me. She won't even look at me and fixes her stare on our son. "How was soccer?"

Callan shrugs, wrapping his arms around her. "It was good, Mommy."

Sometimes, judging by the way he acts 90 percent of the time, I forget Callan's age. He's still a child regardless of the way he thinks. I watch the two of them for a moment, locked in an embrace, my smile tugging at the corners of my mouth. For a split second, the papers she sent me today don't matter. For the one at her feet, we have to make this work. I see myself in Callan, and I promised, no, I *swore* my kids would never have a life like I did. One with an absent father.

So how'd I let it get bad enough Madison wanted out?

Looking around the kitchen, I expect to see Noah on the floor drinking water or running around like Wolverine, but I don't see him. "Where's Noah?"

"In bed." Madison hugs Callan to her side. "How about Daddy gets you ready for bed? I'm gonna go take a hot bath."

Callan shrugs again, as though this might just be the only action he's good at. And after tonight, I'm kinda convinced it might be.

But let's backtrack here a second. She wants me to get him ready for bed. I don't care either way. I'll do it since I'm, you know, his father and I should be doing this kind of thing, but I can't help but wonder if this is a trick to ignore me. I know it is for sure when she refuses to make eye contact with me as she slips into the other room and upstairs, leaving me alone in the kitchen with Callan.

He stares at me but this time doesn't shrug. I think we're making progress. "Is she mad at you?"

He's perceptive, isn't he?

I roll my eyes following him up the stairs. "How'd you guess?"

"She made you take me to soccer and now you're here alone with me."

He acts like we've never spent any time together. And I know that's not entirely true. At least I don't think it is.

"Let's go get you ready for bed. You have school in the morning."

I have absolutely no clue what my son does before he gets ready for bed. I did when he was younger, but the last two years, I guess you could say I haven't been around much. Needless to say, we stare at one another in the hallway.

I know the usual, the things most kids and adults do like brush your teeth, but does he shower before bed or in the mornings?

This is Callan we're talking about. The kid might take two showers a day knowing him. It wouldn't surprise me one bit. I remember when he was a baby, bath time was his favorite and if I ever needed to calm him down, I'd sit him in the tub for a little while.

"What do you do before bed?" I finally have to ask, feeling sweat drip down my back. "Do you have a routine?"

He gives me this look that says, "I can't believe I have to explain this to my father." "I wouldn't exactly call it a routine." And then he scratches the back of his head and nods to his bathroom. "But I brush my teeth and go to bed."

Moving past me, he disappears into the bathroom separating his and Noah's rooms and brushes his teeth. I take that moment to sneak into Noah's room and kiss him goodnight. By the way, he sleeps in his mask. It's a little weird kissing Batman goodnight, but that kid has so much damn personality it's unbelievable. He's been that way from day one, always crazy.

"Night, Wolverine," I whisper, kissing Noah's forehead and pushing his hair away from his mask. He doesn't stir. The world could end in a ground-shaking earthquake, and there's no way in hell Noah would wake up. Callan, on the other hand, if you even sigh in his room, he's wide awake.

I meet Callan back in his room where he pulls a pair of pajamas out of his dresser drawer.

I bury my hands in my pockets, unsure what to do next as he gets dressed, but go with, "Okay, so should I read you a story?"

"No. But I do have a question."

I sit down on the edge of his bed. "Okay."

Do you sense the apprehension in the "okay?" You should because what comes next makes me feel stupid and wonder if I'm just that dumb, or my kid is a child genius and I'm not really his father. It's not the first time I've thought this. I've often wondered if Madison slept with a science geek who looked like me and just told me I was the father.

Sitting with his hands in his lap, he stares at me with what can only be described as pure confusion. Or maybe it's me. "What went on at Three Mile Island and Chernobyl? Were they different?"

Do you see that guy sitting on the bed? The one blinking rapidly like his contact lens fell out? Well, one, he's not wearing a contact lenses and two, he has no idea what Chernobyl is. I know what happened at Three Mile Island. "Um, uh, so Three Mile Island was a nuclear power plant that had a cooling malfunction and it caused part of the core to melt the reactor and destroy it. There was a little radioactive gas released, but it didn't kill anyone."

He nods like he knows this already and I'm not at all surprised he does. "And Chernobyl is what *could have* happened then?"

My eyes widen. "Yes?"

Callan grins just a little. "You don't know what I'm talking about, do you?"

I sigh and pull back his blankets so he can get under the comforter. "No. I don't."

"Chernobyl is in Ukraine. Can we go there? I read that it's like a tourist town now. Well, part of it anyway."

"Really?" There's no way I wanted to go to Ukraine, but I wasn't telling Callan. He seems, I don't know, almost excited to be talking to me about this, so I don't want to let him down. I was never one to promise what I couldn't deliver. My dad pulled that shit when I was a kid so when I became old enough to know better, I swore I'd never promise Callan anything I couldn't give him. Now I see exactly why parents did it.

"Yeah, in 2011 they opened up a sealed zone around the reactor. I want to go there."

You're laughing, aren't you? I see the humor in the way Callan is. It's funny. But that's because he's not your son and you're not living with him and wondering, what the fuck? This isn't normal, is it? Should we be concerned? Madison laughs his behavior off, but I see that he's not like the other kids. He's different. He reads at something like a fifth-grade level and his math skills… don't even get me started on that.

"What if you turn into The Hulk?" I tease, raising my eyebrows as I tickle his ribs.

He squirms away from me, his hands over mine to push them away. "I'm being serious, Dad. I want to go to Ukraine for my birthday next month."

"Buddy, we can't go to Ukraine next month. Besides the fact that you don't even have a passport, I don't think your first out of country trip should be to a nuclear reactor war zone."

"It's not a war zone, Dad."

"What do you want for your birthday?"

His eyes light up. "I want to go to Ukraine."

"Besides that."

"Well, how about a book on Chernobyl?"

"Do you have one in mind?"

He nods and hands me a note beside his bed. "It's called *Voices from Chernobyl. The Oral History of a Nuclear Disaster.*"

I think I should be worried about his obsession here.

And then he seems to lose focus about Ukraine when he looks at my wedding ring that catches his eye in the dim lighting of his room. And then he stares at me like he's waiting for me to tell him no completely, or that I have to work so going out of the country for his birthday isn't an option. I can see the questions on his face so I decide to change the subject.

"Does Mommy have any boys that are friends?"

That catches him off guard. "Boys that are friends? Like Uncle B?"

"No, like boys I don't know."

"Pedro?"

"Who's Pedro?"

"I don't know. He's Pedro. He cleans the pool on Thursdays."

We have someone who cleans our pool?

I don't know why I didn't know that. You'd think I would. I'll have to look into this Pedro guy. "Does he come in the house?"

Callan shrugs and turns over onto his side like he's ready for bed now. "Sometimes."

Nodding, I pat his head and then lean in to kiss his forehead. "Night, buddy."

"Dad?"

"Yeah?"

"Are you going to be home early every night?"

I realize then how odd this looked to him, me coming home so early and taking him to soccer, two things I've yet to do in years. I swallow, feeling like my throat is dry. "Probably not," I tell him, honestly. "But I know I need to make more of an effort to come home earlier, don't I?"

"I liked it."

And the look on his face, the one where he finally shows me today he's the almost seven-year-old boy and not some kid who needs to be studying nuclear reactors reminds me I still need to be a dad, regardless of running a business. It's not his fault I don't trust anyone to hire them out for bids.

I'm feeling like shit as I walk down the hall to the bedroom where Madison is, half expecting the door to be locked.

Surprisingly, it's not. There's hope then, right?

Maybe. And that's a slim fucking maybe after today.

She's there, lying on the bed with a book in hand. I don't bother looking to see what book because it doesn't really matter. What matters is what she looks like lying on our bed. Fucking stunning. I'll never get over how naturally beautiful my wife is.

Look at her.

Her hair is down, framing her face like a curtain, her skin perfectly tan with the right amount of glow. For a second, I want to lie down beside her, brush my knuckles over her cheek and tell her I love her. But I don't. Maybe it's my pride again, but I stay rooted in place by the door contemplating what I'm going to say to her. She filed for divorce today. I know she gave me a bunch of reasons earlier but that's not all. There's something more to this and I'm going to find out what it is.

As I stand there in the doorway of the bedroom, she's unaware of my presence in the room. Part of me wonders how long I could stand there and watch her before she notices me.

Clearing my throat softly, her attention moves from the book to me.

"Is Callan asleep?"

"Yeah." Our eyes lock, and I'm curious what she'll do. Nothing. I nod and fold my arms over my chest. "By the way, he wants to go to Ukraine for his birthday."

She laughs. She's probably heard this all before.

Her laughter ignites my smile, and I shake my head. Focus, Ridley. Get some answers.

I kick the door shut, much like I did earlier today but softer this time because I don't want to wake up Callan.

"Why are you having him play soccer? It's pretty obvious he doesn't even like soccer, Mad."

Rolling her eyes, she acts like even being in the same room as me annoys the everliving fuck out of her. "It's good for him to do something that helps him fit in with the other kids."

"Why are we trying to make him be something he's not. Let him be who he wants to be, not what's socially acceptable. He's almost seven. If we start telling him who has to be now, what's that teaching him?"

"He asked me to play soccer, Ridley," she says with a light bitterness to her tone.

"Well, he spent the whole practice reading his *National Geographic.* And I met some of the other dads. They seem like fucking tools if you ask me." I smile and believe me when I say it's condescending, and I've fucking perfected that smile. "Who's Kent?"

Madison shrugs and I kind of believe the shrug. "I don't know, some other dad."

"What about that Kip guy you were talking about? Who's he?"

This look isn't as believable. Kip is someone I *need* to look into. "Nobody."

There's a sourness in the pit of my stomach. Has she turned to someone else? "Nobody my ass," I mumble with a regretful shake of my head as I push away from the door. "I'm not leaving here until you give me some answers."

I'm given a stare I don't like very much. Do you see that lift of her eyebrow and the pressed-together lips? She's pissed at me. "So now you want answers?"

I attempt to offer her a similar look, but I'm not sure I achieved it. By the way her expression doesn't change, I'm sure mine did nothing to faze her. "Well, yeah, you served me with divorce papers."

"Maybe you should stop focusing on the actual papers and the fact that I gave them to you and think about why."

"What's that supposed to mean?"

"It means that just like I said before, when was the last time you were home at three in the afternoon? Never. And the only reason you came home was because you didn't get answers and wanted them. Well, I want things too. I want a husband who actually gives a shit about me and our sons."

I know what you're thinking. If your wife filed for divorce because you're never around, why not just change it and spend more time at home?

The truth is, I love my wife and I love my kids. I don't work long hours because I *don't* want to be around them. I work them to provide a life for us, one where they enjoy the comforts I never had being raised by essentially a single mother.

I had a relationship with my dad, but I didn't live with him. Until my mom died and I was forced to. Up until then, it had just been my mother and me, and I swore, fucking swore Madison would never live like that.

"How can you say I don't care?" I take a seat on the bed, facing her. "You have more than enough money, and you never have to ask me for anything. If you want something, you know I'll give it to you."

"You're hardly home anymore."

"Because I'm working and providing for you and our boys!"

When she lifts her eyes to mine, pain clouds them. "I *never* asked you to marry me, Ridley."

For a moment, I freeze, my mouth open and my eyes wide with shock. Did she really just say that to me? I know what she's referring to. Madison got pregnant with Callan when we were in college, and by most standards, he was an accident. "But I did, marry you," I tell her, hoping she understands I didn't do it because I had to.

She's somewhat quiet, but if her thoughts were spoken, she'd be screaming at me with the look I'm getting. "And now you're married to your job."

Do you see that guy on the bed? The one where his blood pressure is through the roof and he's about ready to explode on his wife? That guy is losing it. In a matter of seconds.

"You're so focused on running your business you've forgotten about us, Ridley." She sits forward and it does nothing for my focus because I have a clear vision of her breasts hanging out of her nightgown. "And I'm not doing it anymore. So yeah, I want a divorce. I'm not sure I'm in love with you anymore because the truth is, I don't even know who you are. And I bet you don't know me anymore either."

I should be insulted, really. "That's not true."

"Really? You don't think so?" The look on her face makes me want to kiss and strangle her at the same time. If there's any woman who's ever gotten on my nerves more than anyone else, it's Madison.

"No, I know you." I look at the ceiling, pretending to be deep in thought but I'm not. I'm thinking about her tits and wishing my dick was between them.

"Okay, what do I eat for breakfast every morning?"

Well shit. Could she have picked a more complicated question? Don't answer that. She could have. "Eggs?"

"Exactly my point. I'm allergic to eggs, Ridley."

"I meant *not* eggs," I say, trying to backtrack. I knew she was allergic to eggs but it was the first thing to come to mind, and I panicked. I don't even know what I'm saying. I'm not even sure I'm making any sense.

I'm not entirely sure what to do or say next because there's certainly some truth to her words I hadn't seen until now. So I take my shirt off and throw it on the floor, intending on getting into bed completely naked. I don't take my shorts off just yet; instead, I raise my brows suggestively and flop myself on the bed. She's flustered, and I'm high-fiving myself. "How about I show you just how much I know you?"

Madison loves to be controlled in bed. What woman doesn't from time to time? They want you to treat them like a fucking lady but every now and then, they want you to grab a fist full of their hair and pull it like you fucking mean it. I'm ready to do that if it means she'll forget all about this divorce bullshit.

Still avoiding eye contact, she grimaces slightly and stands near the bathroom door. "You're not sleeping in the room with me. Go sleep on the couch."

I knew that was coming.

Before she's out the door and into the bathroom, my voice stops her. "Mad?"

She turns to me, her eyes questioning.

I point to myself. "I'm not giving up."

Then she meets my gaze full on. I don't smile because part of me knows what she's about to say. It's written on her face long before the words are spoken. "Ridley... Didn't you hear anything I said?" Her eyes drop, leaving me with inexplicable emptiness. "I don't...." she pauses and then continues, her tone sinking as I listen with rising dismay, "love you anymore."

Fuck, that stings. Way to curb stomp my heart. I really wish you wouldn't have heard that part. Look away next time. Save me some fucking dignity already.

My jaw tenses, my grip on the pillow tightening. "Did you ever love me?"

She lifts her chin, meeting my icy gaze straight on. "Pre-business owning Ridley, yes, but I don't know this guy in front of me... anymore."

I clench my jaw tighter before saying, "I suppose that's all I needed to know. Good night, Madison."

Just like that, Madison Cooper has me at her mercy, but I tend to think she doesn't know what the fuck she's talking about. How is it possible for her not to love me anymore?

It's not. At least not in my eyes. Remember that college professor who gave me the C? Ask him how determined I am.

So the way I see it, I have a few options. I can give her the divorce. I can tell her no and string this out with lawyers and make her life miserable, or, I can make her fall back in love with me.

Guess which one I'm going to pick?

6

GAME PLAN

When I wake up in the morning on the couch, I'm sore. I remember exactly *why* I don't like sleeping on the couch. It's not at all comfortable and remember, I like my bed and more importantly my hot wife in it, both of which I don't have this morning.

Before I open my eyes and remove the pillow over my head, I recall what Madison said to me last night.

I don't love you.

Pushing my own ego and pain aside, I refuse to believe it's the end. I have a plan. Not a good one, but it's a plan nonetheless.

I'm going to make her fall back in love with me. Easy enough, right?

Let me clarify this before you tell me that should be easy. I'm attempting to do what every man forgets about once he lands the girl. If we knew we had to work harder once we were married to get some ass, a lot of men wouldn't get married. Half the fun of being married is being able to have sex whenever you want, right?

I know what you're thinking. How'd this go from making your wife fall in love with you to sex?

I'm a man, and I'm just being honest here. Everything leads back to sex. The ones who tell you it doesn't are full of shit or are better men than me.

As I'm lying on the couch, my phone vibrating underneath me, I realize I'm more than likely running late this morning and that's just not an option for me. Attempting to remove the pillow from my head, it's more difficult than I expect. Mostly because someone is sitting on my head.

Raising my hands from my sides, I feel around to find two legs and two arms. Little ones, which means Noah's sitting on my head, naked. Well, he's got underwear on but still, mostly naked.

"Get up, bud."

"Shhh," he giggles, smacking my hands away. "Daddy sleep."

Laughing, I sit up and reach out to catch him when he falls off my head and into my arms. "Gotcha."

Noah doesn't like to be held. Never has. Even when he was a baby, if you picked him up, he screamed. Unless it was Madison. He'd hang on her hip all day long every day and you know, I don't blame him one bit. If I didn't have to work, I'd like to hang out with my hands on those hips all day.

He slaps my hands again. "No touching Wolverine!" And then he growls at me, takes the GI Joe in his hand and stabs me in the ear with it.

Rattled and wondering if my eardrum has been ruptured, I grab my ear and throw a pillow from the couch at Noah as he runs away from me. "That wasn't nice, Noah!"

Like he fucking cares.

Tenderly touching my ear to check for bleeding, I notice Callan staring at me curiously. "Did you sleep on the couch last night?"

Still trying to process what just happened to my ear, I don't answer his question and ask, "Where's your mom?"

He shrugs, midbite of his bowl of Captain Crunch he's holding. "Work?"

"Don't you have school this morning?" I glance down at my watch. It's 6:45. I can't believe she didn't wake me up and tell me she was leaving, and another thing, who the hell is she massaging at 6:45 in the morning?

"Yeah, I have school. Mommy usually takes me."

Digging my phone out from underneath me, I check my messages. None from Madison but three from Brantley asking how last night went. They were sent at like three in the morning, which means he was probably out at the bar. No surprise there.

Callan disappears inside the kitchen dressed in his school uniform while I text Madison.

Me: So I'm taking him to school? What do I do with Noah?

Remember yesterday when I called her fifty-three times, and she didn't answer?

Guess who answers right away this time?

Yeah, Madison.

Probably because we're dealing with the boys this time.

Madison: Yes, take him to school. I had to work early. Drop Noah off with Trisha.

I actually snort as I read the text. Work earlier? Likely excuse.

Me: Doing what?

Madison: I do have a job, Ridley. Can you please handle taking Callan to school and Noah to Trisha or is that too much to ask of you?

Can she be any more of a bitch?

Yes, she probably can and will.

I don't reply either. Let's see how she likes being ignored.

Peeling my sore self from the couch, I rush upstairs, take a world record speed shower, knock all Madison's perfumes and lotions off the counter because I fucking feel like it, and then I'm loading Callan and Noah in the truck.

Callan flips down the DVD player immediately. "Do you still have the *Cars* movie in here?"

"Probably. Nobody watches that but you."

And right then I pray to God that *Cars* DVD is in there because my statement was only partially true. Over the summer there was one instance where Brantley thought it'd be funny to watch a porno back there. I'm pretty sure I took it out since then. I've never been so happy to hear that Pixar music.

As I'm sitting in the driveway, I'm reminded I have no idea where Callan's school is. All I know is it's a private school, but I couldn't tell you where it's located. "Hey, buddy?"

"Yeah?"

I turn to look back at him after I start my truck. "Can you remind me where your school is?"

He shakes his head but doesn't look at me. He's fixated on the screen in front of his face, and I'm strangely glad he's not reading for once. "El Dorado on 76th street."

Jesus, that's in Scottsdale.

Checking the time, it's now nearing 7:30 and it's going to take at least forty minutes to get there. "What time do you start?"

"8:50."

Okay, I got this. I can do *all* of this and prove to Madison I can help.

Noah is so excited to see his babysitter, Trisha, he rushes in her house without so much as a good-bye. I don't have time to talk to her, so I rush inside, sign him in, kiss his cheeks and then I'm out the door and back in the truck, thankful to be dropping off the little beast with someone else today. I know that's bad to say, but forgive me, he did stab me this morning.

Ten minutes into our traffic-filled drive to school and that damn movie, I'm wishing Callan would go back to reading. I'm not used to listening to anything but my music on the way to work. I guess maybe I've been a little bit selfish in that manner.

My phone rings beside me in the cup holder I have it in, but I don't answer it through the blue tooth. Mostly because it's Brantley and he's not one you can ever put on speaker phone.

"What's up?"

"Where are you? The drywall is here."

I gasp. Of all the days for West Ridge Drywall to be on time, it's today when I'm running late. And I don't do late, just so we're clear. I once, in elementary school, gave a tardy slip to my teacher for not starting class the exact minute it was set to begin. You can probably sense my mood today based on that information right there, and the fact that my wife of the last eight years told me she didn't love me last night.

"I'm dropping off Callan at school and then I'll be there."

Brantley's quiet for a minute and then chuckles. "So I take it last night didn't go well?"

"I'll see you in an hour," I tell him, hoping he can sense Callan's in the truck with me, given I just told him that, but this is Brantley we're talking about, and he's sometimes not so bright on the hidden messages.

"Fine. Stop by the office though and pick up the electrical permits there."

"Why? They should be at the jobsite already."

"They *were*, but Steve never showed up last night, and I accidently took them back to the office and forgot them."

Damn it. "Fine. See you in two hours then."

Tossing the phone in the seat next to me, Callan's laughter floats through the truck. He's always had the cutest laugh to the point when you hear it, you immediately smile. Doesn't matter if you're running late.

I smile at him in the rearview mirror, watching his eyes light up as he watches his movie. I don't know why, but I think back to the day Madison told me she was pregnant with him.

We were still in college, actually just starting summer break before our senior year when she came knocking on my door, red faced and crying. I knew immediately something was up but her being pregnant definitely wasn't what I was thinking. We'd been seeing each other since that Halloween party, but had yet to move in together or even take our relationship past dating and fucking.

It changed that day when she said, "I'm pregnant." Actually blurted it out while giving me a blow job and handed me the pee stick.

From then on, my plans changed. I knew I'd have my own business and I wanted to be with Madison, but once she told me she was pregnant, I asked her to marry me. No way did I want her raising this kid alone or thinking she was alone. Like I said, my mother was constantly alone and I wouldn't have Madison going through that too.

Obviously she said yes and in November, after being together a year, we got married. In February, Callan was born, and three years later, we had Noah.

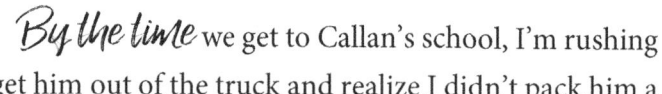

By the time we get to Callan's school, I'm rushing to get him out of the truck and realize I didn't pack him a lunch. Shit. Was I supposed to?

I stop as we're walking into the school, moms surrounding me and I'm almost embarrassed to ask. "Wait, what do you eat during the day?"

He looks up at me with those wide blue eyes. "I usually eat what Mommy gives me, but I can eat school lunch too. Just tell the office lady."

I look around. What office lady?

Callan nudges my hand. "In there, Dad." He then points to the door that clearly states Office. At least they keep it simple around here.

"Okay." I glance down at him. "Thanks."

He starts to walk away from me, up the hall to where I assume his class might be when he turns and smiles. "Thanks for taking me to school."

"Anytime, buddy." Kneeling, I motion for him to come back over and he does. It's not as awkward as I expect it to be, but I wrap my arms around him. "Have a good day."

"I will. You too."

I doubt my day will be good, but I'm not about to tell him that. I know he can sense my apprehension and the sadness on my face. He's too perceptive.

Callan jets the other way, his head down and never looking up at any of the other students around him. Turning, I open the door to the office only to have three women staring up at me. "Can I help you?" a younger one asks, only to flash me a beaming smile and her cleavage. Not only does she actually fucking pull down on her blouse, she leans in as if to give me a better view.

It's the craziest fucking shit. Want to pick up chicks? Guys, listen up. They're not at the bars. They're at the elementary schools.

Drop your kid off at school. If you don't have one, offer to take the little shit down the road who keeps egging your car. Make him work for you.

And when you get to the school, act depressed. They'll run to you.

"Can I help you, sir?" Here we go with the sir again and from a girl barely old enough to babysit my son.

I pull my wallet out of my back pocket. "My son needs lunch."

Another woman to the left of the jailbait walks over and puts her hand on the counter. "Are you a substitute teacher?"

I give her a look of confusion. “No. Do I look like one?”

The lady who strangely resembles Mrs. Doubtfire shrugs. “Not really, but I’d gladly be your student.”

What. The. Actual. Fuck?

Is she flirting with me?

Another woman, even older than Mrs. Doubtfire, approaches the counter. “Do you have a child who goes here? I’ve never seen you before, and I know all the parents.”

I’m not surprised this lady knows all the parents. She’s like a hundred years old. She probably has them all in that ancient brain of hers.

“Callan Cooper.”

The ladies awe at one another. “Awe, little Callan is such a sweetie.”

While I’m glad he’s a sweetie as they call it, this only confirms those douche bags at the soccer fields theory last night that my son is, in fact, a mama’s boy.

After putting twenty bucks in Callan’s lunch account, I rush to the office to get the permits and then to the jobsite where Brantley and the inspector are.

“Jesus, you look like shit.” Brantley laughs, staring at me with wide eyes as he’s leaning against the counter eating a bagel.

“Yeah, well…” I take a drink of my coffee and lean up against the counter beside him. “I feel like shit. Noah stabbed me with a GI Joe.”

“Man, that kid is a little baller.” He laughs. Brantley claims Noah’s going to grow up to be his hero. He literally takes shit from no one.

Never ever think you’ve one-upped my youngest. He remembers everything. He had to get shots one day when he was something like two, and Madison took him. Afterward he wouldn’t even acknowledge her for two days because she held him down. Big grudge holder that one.

"What took you so long this morning? You're usually here before me?"

He's right. I hate to be late. I don't do late. It ruins my whole day if I'm even a minute late.

"Had to take Callan to school." And then I remember all the looks I got this morning. "Dude, you know how you're always going to the bars to hook up with women, I think you need to get a kid. You wouldn't believe how many chicks hit on me while I was there."

"Well, I'd entertain the idea of a kid, it usually comes with problems, as *you* can attest to. And I'm *never* getting married. They say marriage is like a prison sentence. It's why you wear rings. They're tiny shackles. Besides that, Grady seems to be as much as I can handle."

He's talking about Madison's best friend's kid. They're not important right now. I'll explain later.

"True."

"So what did she say?" Brantley asks, flipping through a book of tile samples he has in his hand. "She give you a reason?"

I tell Brantley everything. Always have. If there's anyone who knows me, it's Brantley. We spend fourteen hours a day together. It's safe to say he knows me better than anyone.

"She said she doesn't love me anymore." Do you hear the dejection in my voice? You should. It's pathetic, and even I want to slap myself.

"Well, that's just stupid." He sets down the tile book and turns to face me as he runs his hand through his golden-brown hair. "Of course she still loves you. Maybe you need to do something to get her attention? I once knew this guy who had a star named after his girlfriend.

My cousin, he named a black hole after his mother-in-law. You could do that too."

Sighing, I glance at the inspector approaching us. "My life is a black hole."

Around noon, Madison sends me an invite on my calendar. A meeting at Callan's school. Immediately I call her because I have no idea why she'd send it to me, or what I'm supposed to do with it.

"What's this meeting with his teacher?"

I wish I could see her face because just the tone of her voice is telling me something I should listen to. But I can't, and I don't.

"Apparently his teacher needs to see us."

While I'm not wild about taking off in the middle of the day when I have the plumbing inspector meeting me here in an hour, I know this is what Madison was talking about and if there's ever a test, this has to be it, right?

So the good husband and father I'm trying to be would go to the school conference, wouldn't he?

"Yeah, I'll make it work. Should we be concerned? Does he usually have parent-teacher conferences?"

She pauses, the line quiet for a moment. "Well, no, he doesn't." I can hear talking in the background, mostly women, I think. "His teacher made a special request to meet with the both of us today."

"All right. About last night—"

And she cuts me off with, "I have a client in fifteen minutes."

"A man or a woman?"

"Ridley, I don't have time for this."

"I'm just asking… man or woman?"

"Woman."

Is she lying? Probably, but I'll let her slide for now. What was I going to do, drive to her work and wait outside her door?

Well, I thought about it, but I can't today. I have drywall to be hanging and a compliance inspector up my ass about not meeting electrical codes.

7

ARE YOU SMARTER THAN A 7-YEAR-OLD?

Take a look around.

Do you see those parents sitting nervously in the classroom? The ones *not* talking to one another with an unspoken void between the two of them?

I don't think there's a void, but I know she does. When I look over at her, I feel it radiating from her. I don't think she's telling the truth about not loving me; she still does, even if I have to prove it to her, but there's something else there I intend on finding out.

"Where's Callan at?" I've never been to a parent-teacher conference, and I don't remember having them as a kid. I remember plenty of student-principal talks. Surely that's not what this is because we've never even had to punish Callan. We won't talk about Noah right now.

"He's at Trisha's house. She watches him on Wednesdays because I usually run late with clients."

It's apparent, a maybe partial grounds for her rash and totally uncalled for decision yesterday, that I know nothing about my family's schedule.

"Thanks for coming on such short notice," a woman who seems old enough to maybe babysit my son says, sitting down in a chair meant for first graders, not adults. What's with this school and hiring kids? Do they just wait for them to get out of sixth grade and offer them teaching jobs?

Just so you know, I'm miserable and completely uncomfortable. Look at me squeezed into a chair meant for a child across from the teacher. Not only am I wearing work jeans and a shirt that's covered in grout and I look like Shrek in the chair with my knees up around my elbows.

The teacher looks at me. "Are you Callan's uncle?"

What the fuck?

"No." I glare at Madison because after last night and the soccer dad's, does she mention me to anyone or do they just assume she had a sperm donor? "I'm his father."

If you just repeated *Star Wars* in your head, I'm high-fiving you right now.

Focus though. His teacher is somewhat attractive, if you're into eighteen-year-olds. We discussed this already. I'm not, but I can bet your ass if Brantley was here with me, he'd be asking this girl out.

Anyway, you can't miss she's pretty, and I can see why Callan loves her so much. She's nurturing in a sense, but not in a way I want to put my head on her tits and hug the shit out of her like I do with Madison. Nurturing in a way I'd probably let her read me a story while I took a nap on the floor in this very classroom.

She's talking now so I better pay attention.

I straighten up in my mini chair meant for Umpa Lumpa's and listen in.

"As I'm sure you both know, Callan's incredibly talented and gifted not only as a first grader but a child. I can't tell you what a pleasure it is to teach someone who has such a thirst and desire to learn. When we spoke at the last parent teacher night, I informed you Callan was taking it upon himself to visually act out his feelings toward the assignments we were taking on as a class. This usually ranged anywhere from a loud, deep sigh accompanied by an eye roll or could escalate to a deep groan that ended with him dropping his head onto his desk and pounding his fist exclaiming "Oh for the love of Stephen Hawking are you serious?"

I look to Madison. Our son does this shit? That's odd, right?

I don't ask this, but I'm certainly thinking it. You've met him. Does this seem normal for a kid his age?

Madison straightens her back, taking on the posture of a mama bear about to protect her young. "After our last conversation, I had a long talk with Callen about keeping his thoughts about those things to himself. He assured me he's stopped his disruptive behavior. Are you telling me that's not true?"

Ms. Sadie waves her hand around, which she does a lot when talking. I've nearly been smacked upside the head twice now. "No, no, Mrs. Cooper, that's not what I'm saying at all." She lays her hands on the folder and folds them. At least I don't have to dodge her hands anymore. I silently wonder if you were to tie her wrists together, would she stop talking? "Quite the opposite actually. I just wanted to review where we stood last time we spoke so that I could share with you that Callen has taken great lengths to not outwardly display any displeasure with the lesson plan."

At this point, I'm thinking to myself this is good. These parent-teacher conferences are a breeze. I don't know why parents complain about this shit.

Guess what? I'm wrong. As usual.

"He has, however, not completely given up his crusade to express his distaste." With every word, I fight the urge to roll my eyes. "Instead of disrupting the class with his dramatic enactments of frustration, he has taken to drawing his displeasure for my eyes only." And then Ms. Sadie opens a folder filled with what looks like assignments and worksheets. Each one she sets before us has Callan's name at the top and a pretty simple, but to the point, comic strip at the bottom. Each one shows a stick figure student sitting at a desk with his head down exclaiming either the word "Seriously? Ugh!" or the phrase, "Please, Lord, take me now." "Most of my students can't even read those words let alone write them like Callan can."

I can't help the laugh that escapes me. This shit is funny. He's also an amazing artist for almost seven. I look back up at the teacher, smiling, and Madison, and it seems I'm the only one who thinks so.

Ms. Sadie clears her throat and turns from Madison to me. "Please understand I absolutely adore Callan. He is truly a one in a million student, and I know in my heart he is destined to accomplish great things. My concern, however, does lay in the fact that I fear Callan's less than desirable behavior stems from boredom. He's just *so much more* advanced than the other kids. I would suggest him skipping a grade, but I'm afraid because of his age, that wouldn't be the best course of action for his emotional wellbeing."

Madison again speaks before I have a chance. "So what would you suggest then?"

"Well, I was hoping maybe you both would be open to Callan possibly attending Primrose Academy. It's a school for gifted students and Callan would be in a classroom with other likeminded children."

"When you say like minds, what exactly do you mean?" Madison asks.

I've always known Callan was gifted, but I was thinking more along the lines of he may just be able to access nuclear codes or some weird shit like that.

"Well, as I'm sure you know Callan, has a far more advanced thought process. His interests and likes are usually more developed and thought out than most of the other students in his grade."

"Are you saying he can't relate to the other kids in his class?" I ask because I've sensed this already just at the one soccer practice I went to.

"I wouldn't say he can't relate to anyone. I would say he has a harder time relating to the boys in the class over the girls."

Probably cockier than I need to be, I chuckle leaning to the side in the chair. "So he's a ladies' man?"

Madison may not sense my humor, but Ms. Sadie smiles, steely blue eyes entertained. "Basically, yes."

My confidence soars to a new level. I grin at Madison and wink, draping my arm over her chair. "He takes after his father."

Madison rolls her eyes, her lips thinned with irritation. She pushes me back in my seat next to her. "Stop it. This is serious."

While I'm giving myself varying mental high-fives and fist pumps, Madison looks more concerned.

"Is it a problem the girls like him?" I can't miss the concern in my wife's voice, and I think maybe I should be taking this more serious than I have been.

Ms. Sadie considers Madison's question and then shakes her head. "Well, normally no, but since we're on the subject, it seems the girls have taken on a very possessive relationship with Callan. They are constantly competing with each other for his attention." She's back to talking with her hands. "During recess, Callan and the girls tend to gravitate toward the picnic benches where they have started a sort of origami club. It seems that the girls have taken on the task to try and outshine the other with more creative origami shapes in an attempt to impress Callan. There have been *several* incidents of sabotage."

Sabotage? I don't know about you, but I'm picturing little girls with pigtails boxing next to the flag pole over my son's attention. I guess maybe I don't know anything about little girls.

"These are first graders doing this? Shouldn't they be playing tag and swinging?" You have to admit you were thinking it too. What kind of six- and seven-year-olds act like this?

"And it's not Callan's fault the girls like him," Madison notes.

"No, not at all." Ms. Sadie smacks my head. "Oh, I'm sorry. I get a little excited when I talk."

Ya think? Jesus. I rub the side of my head and stare at Madison. She probably paid the teacher to hit me.

Madison snorts, her laughter contained and waits for Ms. Sadie to explain. "You were saying?"

"I wanted you to be aware Callan has been asked to give his account of certain incidents, and while he has been honest, I can tell that it stresses him out when this occurs," Ms. Sadie explains, finally folding her fucking hands on the table with a gentle sigh leaving her lips. "He just wants everyone to be happy and get along."

And there you have it. While our son is far more advanced than other kids, he cares. He wants everyone to get along, including his mother and me.

"Does he get along with the boys?" I ask. After what I saw last night, I'm worried he doesn't have any friends.

Ms. Sadie frowns. "It's not often I see him with the boys. They tend to gravitate to the ones who play sports at recess and Callan doesn't seem to have any interest in joining them. I think it's easier for him to relate to the girls. They're thoughtful and creative just like him."

So he doesn't have any friends but girls. While I wouldn't necessarily describe this as a problem, I get why Madison and his teacher would be concerned.

I'm staring at Madison wondering how I can make this right when she glances over at me, and then turns her attention toward the teacher. "Well, thank you for your time."

Ms. Sadie hands Madison a brochure on the school she suggested. "I just want you guys to consider it. I haven't talked to Callan about it. I wanted to meet with you first, but I think you should look into it. Maybe take a tour and speak with their guidance counselor."

Madison and I stand, together, and make our way silently to the parking lot. When we're beside my truck, our eyes meet. "Is he weird, Ridley?"

She's concerned and worried, and I don't blame her. You don't set out to have a child who's different from others. It's hard, and you feel bad for the child because they can't relate to anyone, sometimes you included.

Thinking this is one of those times she wants me to comfort her, I lean in and pull her into a hug. She lets me, but her muscles tense. Maybe it's the concern weakening her distaste for me but she lets me hold her, the hot Arizona sun beating down on our faces. "Yeah, he's weird but that's okay. He owns it and I think it's to be admired."

And then I laugh. "Now Noah, he's got issues. He stabbed me this morning."

Madison jerks back. "With a knife?"

"No." I silently wonder if stabbing is something he does often. The look on her face tells me this isn't the first time. "With a GI Joe. It hurt."

"Oh, well I'm sure you're fine." She blows me off like my ruptured eardrum means nothing. "He stabbed Nathalie on last week with a pencil."

Nathalie is Madison's beside from and I don't have any sympathy for her or that she was stabbed by my son. In fact, I intended on high-fiving Wolverine when I get home tonight. You'll understand when you meet Nathalie. Until then, I don't even want to discuss her. It'll just piss me off.

"Callan's not weird, Mad." I lean back against my truck, my hands falling away from her. "He's special, and we have to make him understand it's not something he did wrong."

She nods as though she agrees, tucking her hair behind her ear. My eyes are drawn to her neckline, my thoughts then moving onto what I'd like to do to that neckline with my mouth. "I'm going to be late tonight. Can you pick the boys up from Trisha's house?"

I'm no longer thinking about Madison's neckline. I'm sweating in fear.

Remember how I said I rushed into daycare this morning and right back out?

There's a reason for that, and it actually had nothing to do with me running late. Okay, it did, but there's another reason.

Fear of Trisha. Just wait until you actually meet her.

Have you ever seen *Alice in Wonderland*? You know the Queen of Hearts lady, right?

That's what Trisha looks like. I'm not lying. Every time I look at her, I have this fear she's going to say, "Off with their heads!" and chop my head off. Before you label me a pussy here, I had a bad experience one time on a subway in New York where this lady, who was kinda sorta dressed like the Queen of Hearts, offered to give me a blow job when I was seventeen. I was seventeen and it was a blow job. I still said no though because she looked fucking crazy.

Turns out, I was right. She was crazy and proceeded to lick my shoulder for an hour on the subway, and when I told her to stop because it was making me sick to my stomach, she tried to cut my throat with a plastic knife and said, "Off with your head!"

I never returned to New York and never will.

"Why do you have her watch them? She's crazy."

Madison waves me off. "Just because some cat lady who looks like Trisha tried to cut you with a plastic knife doesn't mean Trisha's crazy."

"I don't trust her."

She reaches into her purse as if my concerns for our children's safety means nothing to her. "She nearly killed me."

"Who?"

"The Queen of Hearts lady."

"Oh my God, you're such a baby." Her smile tugs at her lips, and I feel like I've at least accomplished something here. Opening the door to her car, she gets in, and I push myself away from my truck to stand closer. "Can you pick them up or not?"

"Yes, I can." I stand with my body in the door of her car so she can't shut it. "Can we talk tonight?"

It's not hard to miss the way her smile fades and the panic sets in. "Sure."

Sure. She gave me a sure. That's a start, right?

Backing away, I allow her to shut the door because I have to get back to the jobsite, finish with the plumbing inspector and attempt to get at least a start on hanging drywall.

The entire way back to the jobsite, I keep thinking of the way she said sure. Like she wasn't sure, but wanted to. I can't help but think she doesn't want the divorce. She couldn't, could she? We're perfect for each other. We get along, we laugh, we have great kids and similar upbringings.

Part of what drew Madison and I together was our similar childhoods. A father missing from the picture.

And then I think, is that why she wants a divorce? Because she thinks I'm missing from the family?

Well, I admittedly gathered that much last night, but I keep going back to the fact that she said she didn't love me. I have to show her that love is still here.

My ideas range from bringing home flowers to maybe a gift, but would anything material convince her I loved her? She knew I'd buy her anything and everything I could. And she knew I loved her so it had to be more.

Chocolate cake? She's a sucker for flourless chocolate cake. Baking it myself would probably score me the most points, wouldn't it? Too bad I can't cook. The last time I tried I caught the microwave on fire. In case you're wondering, if you make cup of noodles, remember to add water to the cup.

When I'm back at the jobsite, Brantley's hanging drywall in the living room with Trey, who I thought wouldn't be back for a few more days.

"What are you doing here? I thought Brantley said you were advised to take a few days off."

Trey pushes his black hair from his face, nervously watching me. He mostly talks to Brantley and not me. Though he's never said it to my face, he thinks I'm intimidating. I don't know where he gets that from. I'm a pretty easy going guy to talk to, right?

Maybe don't answer that.

"Um, I know they did, but I need the money and I can't miss out on work."

I can understand his drive and need to work. I've been there before. But… I follow rules. Most of the time and Labor and Industries isn't someone I'm about to fuck with.

Turning to the counter, I grab my drywall saw, and he backs up. "You can't until you get a note from the doctor that says you're cleared for work."

Does he think I'm going to stab him with this? By the way he backs up another step, he must think so. "I know, but I thought maybe you could make an exception for me."

Doesn't he realize I don't make exceptions for anyone? Apparently not. "Can't, man." I wave him off. "While I appreciate your work ethic here, you gotta have clearance first."

Trey grumbles something I can't hear and rolls his eyes. "Fine. I'll go get clearance." And then he limps away.

"You could have let him stay," Brantley notes, wheeling the drywall lift over so we can get started on the ceiling first.

Snapping on my tool belt and grabbing my screw gun, I shrug. "I know, but with the way my week's going, I'm not about to piss off LNI too." I motion to the sheetrock. "Let's get this done. I need to pick up the boys in a couple hours."

Brantley stares at me. "You're going to leave work early two days in a row?"

I stare at him because he can't see it. I'm not even sure I understand what's happening either. It's similar to when my mother died. Not as bad because her dying was pretty fucked up, but I remember when we found out she had cervical cancer. It was a Tuesday. Ten weeks to the day, on a Tuesday, she died. I was numb for days, motions and words, everything around me was almost robot-like. I attempted life, but inside, I wasn't there. I feel that way today.

And it's not lost on me yesterday was a Tuesday. It's officially the worst day of the week. Monday, you're good now. Tuesday? Fuck. You.

"I have to," I tell Brantley. "If I'm going to convince Madison she still loves me, I have to make an effort to be more present in their lives."

His brows scrunch together in confusion. "Did she tell you it's because you're not around?"

"Yeah, something along those lines. She said a lot of things I might not have heard, but one was me not being around, and the last one was her not loving me anymore."

"Well, that kind of shit doesn't just happen overnight." Brantley reaches for the other end of the sheetrock, and we lift it together onto the lift. "Maybe you're just not seeing how much you actually fight or disagree."

I try to think back to our last disagreement. Sure, we have arguments but nothing that stands out as a fight. I'm also not a yeller. If something's bothering me, I usually stay quiet.

Don't look at me like that. You think judging by the way I need answers, I'd be one to get in your face and yell until my point's across. Am I right?

Well, you'd be wrong. Sure, I want answers, but if something's really bothering me, the kind of shit that sparks the heated arguments where words are screamed and bounced right back, I don't do that. I grew up with a father who yelled at my mom, me, everyone. He'd yell until he was red in the face, but not a damn thing ever made any sense to me.

In turn, I don't yell at Madison so I wouldn't consider any of our arguments to be fights.

Now she may have a different theory on this, which, apparently by the papers in the glovebox of my truck would attest to, she definitely thinks differently.

"I wouldn't say we've been fighting." Reaching for the handle of the lift, I begin to crank it up as Brantley steps on the ladder to screw the ceiling boards up. "You know since we took on multiple homes in the last three months, I haven't been home much, and when I am, I'm sleeping."

"She can't really blame you for that though. It's not like you're fucking around on her. You're working."

"I know." As I say that, I'm not sure I believe what I'm saying. I see it one way, but I know she sees it another. "She said we could talk tonight so I'll head home early, pick up the boys and then see if we can talk about it."

Brantley nods, but I'm not sure he gets it. He's a bachelor, never been married and I doubt he ever will. He has women he hangs out with, and he fucks around with Nathalie a lot, but being tied down is not for him. He's always been that way too.

"Ask her out on a date," Brantley suggests, his arms above his head screwing in the drywall as I hold the crank steady.

"What do you mean? Like take her to dinner?"

"Yeah, but actually ask her instead of just taking her to dinner. Make it her choice."

He has a good idea, doesn't he? If this was me trying to get a girl to fall in love with me, I'd ask her out and attempt to make her see just how great of a guy I am before I take her to bed to seal the deal.

I could ask her out, get a babysitter and make her feel special but not because it's a birthday or an anniversary but because I made time for her out of the blue.

I knew there's a reason as to why I'm friends with Brantley. He thinks like a guy trying to get pussy every night of the week. And not just any pussy. He wants the variety pack which means he has to work a lot harder to collect all the different flavors there is to offer.

Now, how to ask her out?

8

NOAH THE CAT KILLER

Do you see the woman with the red hair and blue eyeshadow?

Scary, isn't she? And she strangely resembles the Queen of Hearts, doesn't she?

In your head, you're totally picturing her saying, "Off with your head!" aren't you?

And to think Madison willingly leaves our children with this nutball during the day. It's ridiculous.

As soon as I walk in the room, I spot Noah on the floor lying on his stomach with his ear to the floor like he's listening for something. I'm not entirely sure what he's doing, but this is Noah we're talking about. He also likes the floor, if you couldn't tell. For a month, he slept on the floor because he said it was more comfortable than his bed.

Give the little guy a break. When I told you he's three, I meant newly three. Like his birthday was last week so let's go easy on him.

"Hey, buddy," I say. His head snaps up at the sound of my voice.

Crawling to his feet, he runs to me, his arms locked around my neck. Don't worry, I made sure to check his hands first for GI Joes. "Daddy home."

"No, I'm here to pick you up." I level him a serious look. "This is *not* your home."

"Madison said you were picking them up," Trisha says, leaning into the wall with a baby on her hip. "I didn't think she was serious. Have you ever picked them up?"

Jesus, harsh much? What's with people these days? They act like because I work during the day and don't have time to do these types of things, I'm not present in the world at all. Was this the way it was for men in the thirties and forties when women couldn't work and were forced to just be housewives? Did society just assume there wasn't a man at home?

I don't look Trisha in the eye. I can't. It scares me, and the last time I looked her in the eye I had nightmares about New York subways for three nights. "Yeah, well, I am. Where's Callan?"

"Right here," he says from behind me, his backpack on his shoulder. "Why are you picking us up?"

"Mom's running late tonight." I smile, but it's more uneasy than pleasant. "Just us boys for a little while?"

Do you hear the fear in my voice? And did you notice my words came out like a question?

Callan does, and his eyes widen a bit, but he corrects the look before I have time to ask what he's thinking. I probably don't want to know.

Noah refuses to let go of me, so I carry him outside like a gold chain wrapped around my neck.

"I'm hungry." Callan opens the door to the truck as I open the other side to put Noah in his car seat. "Can we get dinner?"

"Yeah, what do you want?"

He thinks for a moment climbing into his booster seat. Tapping his finger to his chin, he then shrugs and reaches for his seat belt. "Can we have McDonald's?"

I laugh. "You remember how Mommy was upset with me last night?"

He nods.

"Well, if I get you guys McDonald's, she'll probably kill me."

"Why?"

"Something about their nuggets being poison." Rolling my eyes, I hand Noah his Batman mask he dropped on the floor of the truck. "I don't really know. How about hamburgers from that roadside place you like?"

Noah lifts his fists up in the air and I flinch, thinking he's about to hit me again. "Yeah! Boogers!"

Callan chuckles at Noah and turns on the DVD player. "You mean burgers, Noah."

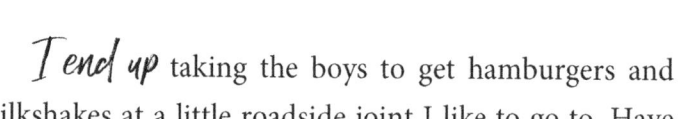

I end up taking the boys to get hamburgers and milkshakes at a little roadside joint I like to go to. Have you seen a three-year-old amped up on a chocolate milkshake?

It's pure insanity. I've never seen him this crazy, and you saw what happened this morning with the GI Joe.

Take a look around the front yard. Do you see that tiny kid about the size of a one-year-old? It's Noah. He's small for his age. He's trying to make friends with the neighbor's cat by dragging him out from under my truck by his tail.

I hate to break it to him but judging by the look in that cat's eyes, friendship isn't in their future.

"Noah, don't do that to the cat. He's going to scratch you." I no sooner get those words out and what does the cat do?

Scratches him. And not just once. It's like a bitch slap that just keeps coming. He even gets on his back legs and tries to run after Noah.

Callan shakes his head beside me. "That cat hates Noah."

I can see why if that's how he treats animals. Can cats sense evil? Or is that horses?

Either way, it ends in tears and loud screams. "Cat stupid!" Noah screams, holding the side of his face.

He runs to Callan and hugs him, which isn't surprising, but I'm curious why he didn't run to me first since I'm his father. Kneeling in the grass, I reach for his hand to pull it away from his cheek. "Look at those battle wounds, Wolverine."

His tears slow when I say that, and he sniffs but makes eye contact with me. The green in his eyes stands out, a reminder this kid looks more like me than Madison. "Grr," he growls and then his eyes shift behind me to the cat walking away.

Do you see the look in my son's eyes? The one of resentment for the animal who clawed the shit out of him?

Remember that look in about five minutes.

Callan runs inside and then returns with a wet washcloth and hands it to me. Gently, I clean the blood off Noah's face and see it's not as bad as it initially looked, but he has about six scratches, one really close to his eye.

Fuck. If Madison sees this, she's going to think I can't handle my own kids. Awesome.

"Can I ride my bike?" Callan asks, pointing to the garage.

Nodding, I take Noah by the hand, hoping scarface loses focus on the cat. "Want to ride your bike too?"

"Yeah, yeah! Brother bike!"

Noah has his own bike, but he refuses to ride it. Instead, he rides this old big wheel we got for Callan when he was younger.

There's a big difference between Callan and Noah, and it's apparent when they're doing physical activities. While I struggle to think Noah will ever live up to Callan academically, it's obvious Noah's a natural athlete. Walking, running, riding bikes, kicking a ball around, he's never struggled with any of that, even from the beginning.

While I'm watching Noah do donuts, slide jobs around corners and racing up and down the street on the big wheel, I notice that damn cat lying in the street. You'd think he would have run away after the tail incident.

Remember that look on Noah's face? The one where I said pay attention?

We're back to that.

Check it out. He's about I don't know, maybe fifteen feet from the cat, eyeing it like he remembers. I shit you not, he even raises his hand to his cheek and then glares, his hands tightening on the handle bars.

If you're a cat lover, you might want to close your eyes for what happens next.

With a sudden sense of determination, Noah takes off on his bike heading right for the cat, and I even scream at the cat to get him to move, only he doesn't. He stares at Noah as if he senses his impending doom and deserves it. I don't like cats, as you know, but I still don't want to see what's about to happen.

"Noah, stop!" I yell and attempt to run after him, but he runs right over the cat before I can get to him. I don't know why, but I kinda blame the cat here because Jesus Christ, why didn't he move when he saw the bike? Don't cats usually run away from moving objects besides a ball of yarn?

"I can't believe he just did that," Callan says with wide eyes.

Yep. He did. Ran right over the cat with his big wheel.

Just keep your eyes closed if you want because I'll let you in on a little secret. The cat didn't make it. His nine lives were up.

Noah glances back over his shoulder, a pointed glare at the cat. "I am Wolverine," and then rides away on his bike. I blink a few times, trying to decide if that really happened and if I'm standing over a dead cat.

Remember how I said Noah's a grudge holder?

Clearly this was a grudge-murder. I'm still in disbelief this actually happened.

"He's like Al Pacino in *Scar Face*."

I raise an eyebrow. "You've seen that movie?"

"Yeah, on Netflix. Rest in peace, Mr. Poppy." Callan pets the cat's head softly and then stands next to me watching Noah still riding away. "It's like the ending of a movie, and he's riding away in the sunset."

Mr. Poppy? Who the fuck names their cat Mr. Poppy?

"Let's hope he comes back. Your mom would miss him," I tease, attempting to draw a little humor to the situation, though I know this isn't the time. My toddler son just murdered a cat.

Sure, you could laugh and say, "Oh, he's three, he didn't mean to," but let's be honest. You saw the look in his eyes. He totally meant to hit him.

There's no blood or anything, the cat went peacefully, at least that's what I'm telling myself. Staring down at him, I have flashbacks of my own cat slaughtering experience when I was younger. I'm not ready to share that dark part of my life just yet. It'd be too emotional right now.

Let's focus on the bigger issue here. The fact that I have a dead cat on my hands and a son who's showing no remorse. Should I have him tested?

I got one kid who could potentially arm nuclear weapons and one killing animals. Isn't killing animals a sign of a serial killer? Are we going to look back on this moment years from now and say, "There were signs?"

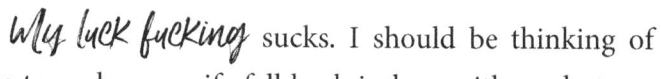

My luck fucking sucks. I should be thinking of ways to make my wife fall back in love with me but no, I'm attempting to bury my neighbor's cat without him and my wife knowing.

"What are you doing with that shovel?"

I jump at the sound of Madison's voice and attempt to hide the shovel behind my back. I'm not sure why. It's obvious she's seen it since she asked. At least I don't have to worry about her now. I only need to hide it from the neighbor.

Can you see how much I'm sweating? Christ, it's embarrassing. It's like the time I had to bury my neighbor's cat when I was a kid. It was a very traumatic experience. I'll tell you about it later but it's why I can't stand cats. "I'm burying George's cat."

Her eyes widen and then she notices the black plastic bag at my feet. "Why?"

"He scratched the shit out of Noah earlier tonight so Noah ran over him with his big wheel."

"Oh my God," she panics, her eyes wide and darting from the bag to me and then back to the bag. "What do we do?"

I raise an eyebrow and then lean down to pick up the bag. "Bury it?"

"Shouldn't we tell George?"

"No."

And now she's staring at me like I've lost my mind, but then she bites her lip. Fuck, that's hot. She doesn't do it often, but it gets me every time. "What if the cat comes back?"

Let me tell you something here. Madison hates scary movies about as much as I hate cats. She once watched *Pet Cemetery* when she was seven-months pregnant with Callan and already paranoid as shit. Pregnancy hormones do strange things to her. Anyways, she forced me to sleep with the light on in our room for three nights and made me swear we'd never get a cat. Like I'd fight her on that one. Though on the fourth night, I was done with it. I made her turn off the light and sleep like a normal person because that shit was getting out of hand. We still have our no cat pact though.

"This isn't *Pet Cemetery*, Mad. He's not going to claw his way from the ground and sit on your chest in the middle of the night meowing."

She shivers at my detail. Maybe I'm a shit, and maybe this is why she wants a divorce, but the boy inside of me senses my opportunity, and I act like I'm going to throw the dead cat at her.

Madison jumps, her hand on her heart. "You son of a bitch!" And then she scurries inside the house.

Maybe I shouldn't have done that because now she might not talk to me and the chances of us having sex tonight are slim.

With the bag in hand and amused with myself, I sneak out to the corner of the yard and then it hits me. The guilt. I can't bury the cat without telling George, our neighbor. I just can't. Call it my conscience, but it'd eat me alive if I knew I had his cat buried in my yard and didn't say anything.

I've also seen *Pet Cemetery*, and while I enjoy giving Madison a hard time about her paranoia, I'm not at all wild about having a dead animal buried in my yard.

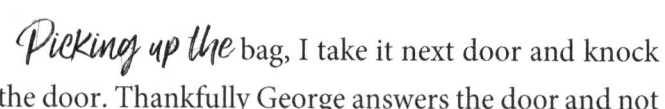

Picking up the bag, I take it next door and knock on the door. Thankfully George answers the door and not his bitchy wife who hates me for starting my truck early in the morning. It's not my fault she likes to sleep until eight in the morning. I *wish* I could sleep that late.

"Hey, Ridley, what's up?" George is a friendly man, or at least he always has been and waves every time I see him, which is about once a month with my crazy schedule. But I'm not sure how friendly he's going to be when he Wolverine killed his cat.

Though I should, I don't feel as bad about the cat as I should. Mostly because he leaves footprints all over my black truck. There's nothing worse than a black truck with dusty cat prints all over it. Pisses me off.

"I've been better." Raising the bag up in the air, his eyes lower. "I'm really sorry, but Noah accidently ran over your cat."

"Mr. Poppy?"

"Yeah."

He laughs. Actually fucking laughs. "Thank God."

Is he for real? Is this really happening?

George tips his head, his stare focusing on the bag and then me. "At least he's out of his misery."

Have you seen *Christmas Vacation*? I want to laugh at the irony of this, but I don't and manage to ask, "Misery? For what?"

George laughs again, and I'm beginning to think he's crazy. More so than Noah. It's one of those laughs that reminds me of, you know, the Queen of Hearts. "Poor bastard had ball cancer. You know, like your junk."

I back away a few steps. I know what he's referring to, but George is a retired air force instructor. Did he really just say junk to me?

"Cats can get ball cancer?"

He nods. "Yep. It was all over his body. He should have been dead months ago." And then he takes the bag from my hand. "I'll take care of him. I swear it was like he was trying to commit suicide. He'd lay under my car every day right under the tire. Even ran out in front of cars, but somehow they always missed him."

"Well, his nine lives were up today."

George takes the cat inside and strangely I don't feel nearly as bad as I did. If he had cancer, it was for the better. Noah actually did him a favor, in a harsh way, but still.

When I get back to the house, Noah and Callan are watching television in the living room. Well, Noah is and Callan's reading another *National Geographic* book. This one's *Three Mile Island: What could have happened.*

At least he's doing his research, but I am wondering how I'm going to take him to Ukraine someday.

I'm not sure if I should say anything to the little serial killer in training on the floor or not. Do you punish three-year-olds for this kind of thing? Would he even understand?

I gotta do something. He can't go around killing animals. Stabbing me is one thing but animals are another story.

"Noah." I kneel next to him on the floor.

He looks up at me, adorable green eyes waiting for me to say something. He blinks a few times, waiting. "Daddy." And then he crawls on my lap.

Callan peeks around his magazine at us and rolls his eyes like he knows what I'm doing won't work.

I turn Noah to face me. "You hurt that cat."

He remembers all right and raises his hand to his check and the deep red scratches. "Bad cat."

"I know he scratched you, but you can't run over animals just because they hurt you." Because if that was the case, then Mr. Poppy would have been dead years ago when he first started using my truck as a red carpet.

"Yes. I'm Wolverine!"

"No. You can't hurt animals."

He shakes his head, grinning now. "I'm Wolverine," he repeats like I should know.

Okay, this isn't working.

I set him back on the floor so I can go find Madison.

I find her in the kitchen cleaning up. She doesn't notice me at first, and I take the time to watch her in silence, wishing I could read her thoughts and what it is she's looking for. She filed for divorce for a reason, damn it. And sure, she's giving me some reasons—some valid ones—but there's more to it. I want to know why.

I don't love you anymore.

But that can't be it. How could she have fallen out of love?

Had I really been that blind I didn't see it? I know I keep asking myself the same questions, but my mind just keeps going in circles.

And then I remember Brantley's suggestion. Ask her out on a date.

I can't just blurt it out.

I should be flirting, shouldn't I? And then I can naturally lead it that way.

Women? We're not good at flirting once we're married. It all leads back to the fact that we get regular sex and don't see the point anymore unless we're trying to get said sex.

I know. What a bunch of lazy bastards, right?

I'm just being honest here. I'm not saying it's right.

So guess what I'm trying to think of?

How to flirt again. It's like I've lost my touch.

When I was in college, it was easy. All I'd have to do was smile, wink, maybe say, "What's that you're drinking?" and it was over. They'd spread their legs.

As Madison's standing there loading the dishwasher, I'm leaning into the doorway watching her, admiring just how beautiful she is when the last little bits of daylight shine through the kitchen window and highlight the auburn in her hair.

She catches me, gives me a once over and rolls her eyes. "Why are you staring at me like that?"

I push away from the door and stand next to her so our shoulders are touching. "You're beautiful. That's why."

"Did you tell George about his cat?"

"Yeah. Turns out the cat committed suicide. He had junk cancer."

"Junk cancer?" She glances over her shoulder at me.

I grab my dick through my jeans. "Yeah, like his balls had cancer in them."

Her cheeks flush but the corners of her mouth twist, her gaze moving lower to where my hand is. There, right there, she's fucking lying when she says she doesn't love me anymore. It's subtle, by the desire in her eyes, that can't be mistaken for just desire alone. There's familiarity there. She remembers my humor and the way it makes her feel inside, like she knows me and knows I can make her smile, even if it's just for a split second.

I move to stand behind her, my hands on her hip, my mouth exactly where I've wanted it to be for hours. Her neck, collarbone, shoulder, anywhere she'll let me for about five seconds when she sighs. "Ridley, stop it."

"Why?"

"Because."

I could literally do this all day long. Noah gets it from me. "Because why?"

"Because I have dishes to finish, laundry to start, laundry to fold, kids to get bathed and then eventually get some sleep tonight because I have to work in the morning."

My heart beats a little faster. She said we could talk and now it just seems like she's making excuses. "You said we could talk."

"If you want to talk, then get the boys ready for bed, that way we have some time."

I did it last night. I can do it tonight too.

Do you see the amusement in her eyes? Why is she looking at me like that? It's like the time I was in the delivery room when Callan was born, and the doctor asked if I wanted to see the baby crowning. Being a soon-to-be father, I had no fucking clue what crowning meant so I looked to Madison and she gave me a half grin, much like this one, and said, "If you want to."

"Why are you looking at me like that?"

Now she full-on grins. "Because."

"Because why?"

She turns back to the dishwasher. "You're wasting time. Go get the boys ready for bed."

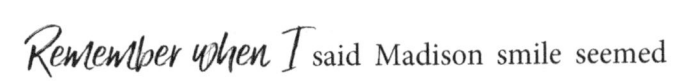

Remember when I said Madison smile seemed off?

Yeah, well, it fucking was. I'm beginning to think I was set up for failure tonight on all accounts. Look at how my nights went so far?

Dinner?

Disaster.

Playing with the kids?

Epic failure.

Bath time?

Take a look around and you'd probably get an answer.

Have you ever bathed a three-year-old?

There's absolutely nothing easy about it. I think I'd rather bath a cat who was clawing the shit out of me. No offense, Mr. Poppy.

Do you see the gallon of water on the floor and the dad on his knees trying to soak up all the water with towels?

That's how my night's going.

"Noah, stop it with the water." Raising my hand up, I push my hair from my face only to have it soaking wet now because just as I say, "Keep it inside the tub," he takes a cup full of water and splashes me in the face.

"Spash, Daddy!"

It's illegal to punch a toddler. I actually tell myself this a few times.

Callan stands at the doorway and hands me a clean towel. "Mom's going to *kill* you."

I wipe my face off. "What's his deal?"

"Well for starters, you shouldn't have given him a cup." Callan pushes past me to the tub and rips the plastic cup out of Noah's hand. "And second, don't fill the tub up so high. The less water he has in there, the less that ends up on the floor."

Where was he when we started this bath-time fun?

Reading.

I hand him a dry towel I find under the sink. "Can you help me clean this up before your mom sees it?"

"Too late," Madison says from the hallway, her arms folded over her chest.

Groaning, I look to Noah instead. "You got me in trouble."

He laughs like this is funny.

I can't look at Madison's face. I don't want to because I know I'm going to see disappointment. If I can't handle bathing our kids, how can I save our crumbling marriage?

Attempting to stand, I don't take into account the wet floor and end up right back on my ass on the tile floor.

Noah, Callan, and Madison begin to laugh. And then so am I but my stare locks on Madison because it's been years since I've heard her laugh like that, the kind of laughter where nothing else matters but the scene before you.

Our eyes meet, sincerity in hers. She knows I tried here, and I'd like to think it's scored me some points, but there's also an unmistakable pain present underneath her smile.

With my hands supporting me against the counter, I stand up again, my body brushing against Madison's. "I hope that was entertaining for you," I say, my voice kept low and somewhat gravely because I want her to be affected by my words.

And she is. It's in the weakening of her posture and the way she watches me walk past her.

Despite being soaked, an accessory to murder and limping, because I think I twisted my ankle in the fall, I'm feeling pretty good about today. My plan might work after all.

Told you my dedicated side would pay off.

Were you actually doubting me?

9

SHE'S USING YOUR DICK

When I enter our bedroom after taking a quick shower, Madison is reading the same book she was reading last night. I want to take it and rip it from her hands when I notice the title. *The Best of Me* by Nicholas Sparks.

I hate romance novels. They give women unrealistic expectations of romance and relationships that men can't live up to. I bet that's why she's doing this. She thinks I need to be more romantic.

You know what really pisses me off about them? I bet if I was reading *Playboy* or watching porn she'd be pissed, yet here she's drooling over men and detailed sex scenes, and I can't say anything?

Drawing in a deep breath, I push the bedroom door closed behind me and lock it.

Lying down on the bed, I take the book from her hands, toss it aside and straddle her legs. She's in her nightgown again, the one where the spaghetti straps fall off her slender shoulders.

"My legs are sore from my run. Can you get off them?"

I do as she says only I push her thighs apart so she's spread-eagle before me. And then I smile. "Better?"

"No." And then her eyes move down my chest… and lower. Did I mention I just took a shower and didn't bother to put on clothes?

It's all part of my plan. Seduce my wife, make love to her and make her realize how much she still loves me.

Her breathing picks up, and her eyes find mine again when I lean forward. Surprisingly her fingers raise and trace my lips. My mouth presses against hers, my tongue begging for entrance. When I attempt to lay on top of her, Madison has other ideas, and she pushes me on the tops of my shoulders until I'm on my back.

I'm thinking, fuck yeah, I'm about to get some, but then she gets up and goes to leave the room.

What the fuck?

I'm not having it and grab her hand before she can get away. "I don't think so. You're not running away from me." And then I have her back on the bed and underneath me.

I don't know why but I grind my semi-erect dick into her.

"And *deep* down"—I push forward once more emphasizing the word deep by whispering it against the shell of her ear—"I don't think you want away from me."

Her body relaxes, her hands moving from beside her to my shoulders. "Ridley, not tonight."

"I'm not saying we have to fuck. I just want to talk." Complete lie on my part. I want more than anything to fuck her, but if she's going to talk and give me some answers, then I'll take that over having sex. We can fuck after we talk.

I'm not sure if she's wanting to avoid talking to me but something in her changes, or it's the fact that I'm hard now, like rock-hard and sliding my dick against her wet center. She wants me. It's obvious judging by the heat between her legs and the way her body's trembling beneath mine.

Her head relaxes against the pillow, her neck arching as my chest presses into her firm breasts. My mouth makes its way to her skin, sucking and biting as I move along her curves, my hips beginning a rocking motion against her.

That's exactly what she wants because she moans in my ear, the gentlest sigh leaving her parted lips and I know I've won this round. I also have to work quickly in case she changes her mind.

Madison doesn't say a word when I enter her. She's certainly not pushing me away by any means. The feel of her around me is almost painfully intense, but better than anything. I could probably lie here for hours and not even move, just enjoy the heat and the tightness.

Madison has other ideas and is suddenly frustrated by my hesitation. Arching her back against me, she forces us together deeply.

Jesus Christ… it's my turn to gasp at the flood of sensations.

I have to keep it together no matter how badly my body wants to let go—moving, rocking us together as gently as I can.

Clutching my upper arms and digging her nails into my flesh ineffectually, trying her best to ensure I don't go anywhere, don't pull away, our bodies slide together with desperate movements.

I want her to look at me, but her eyes are closed as her lips part, and she moans my name and rocks her hips into mine, searching for her need to be relieved. Her expression is astonishingly erotic, utterly unguarded and confident in the way she moves. Hands down, Madison is beautiful when she fucks. If I was good at sharing, I'd tell her to be in the porn business because men would pay to see this woman come every day. I'd probably become a habitual masturbator and never leave the computer like I did when I was fifteen.

The pressure inside me builds quickly, that ever-present tingling in my balls becoming more apparent, and I don't want to stop, the sensation driving me forward.

I won't last long, but I take comfort in knowing I will be ready again within minutes if I need to be. That might be a lie. I am approaching thirty.

I won't finish without her, though. I can't take this much pleasure from her body and not give back. Drawing back, albeit against Madison's attempt for me to stay, I reach between us, circling the spot I knew so well. It takes about another minute before she's shaking beneath me, her lashes lowered, breath gasping.

What can I say? I'm pretty good at this.

Watching Madison in the midst of an orgasm I gave her is a fascinating sight. It's my own breaking point, and I can't stop myself. Determined to find my own release, I drop my weight against her chest again, my hands darting to underneath her ass. Pushing myself into her deeper, my body jerks in time with my release.

"Jesus Christ," I say, blowing out a breath into her neck. Her hands fall from my back like she's attempting to shut off her emotions the moment I slide out of her. I don't like that one bit, but I ignore it for the time being.

When I can think and move again, I collapse beside her, but she won't look at me.

Is she disappointed?

Madison and I used to have sex a lot, even with the long hours I work. I'd come home at two in the morning, wake her up and she was ready to go and into it. None of this just lying there waiting for me to finish, she was fucking into it.

Where did it go?

We had Callan and Noah, and it became harder to squeeze time in. It wasn't all because of the kids. I can't blame them for the lack of sex because we got comfortable. Words and motions became familiar and before I knew it, weeks would go by before we had sex. Weeks! That's something I *never* thought would happen.

All right, let me put it to you this way. You know those couples who have sex all the time?

Yeah, me either. I don't know many who are married and actually have sex on a regular basis. Most men I know, like the guys at poker night, they complain about not having enough sex. Believe me, it's never enough for us men unless it's like once a day. Twice would be nice too but you know, I'll try not to be greedy.

Anyways, my point… I have one. You know in the beginning, it's hard to get enough of each other. It's the whole, "I can't wait to be inside you" and her screaming my name at the top of her lungs.

The reality is that part of the relationship doesn't last and slowly the newness slows to a comfortable pace. You can't have sex all the time. But here's the thing… when the newness wore off for Madison and me, that's when I fell in love with her. For the record, she said it first.

Here, go ahead and take a look at that afternoon it was said for the first time. A little background, she's pregnant here. About four months.

Do you see us there in bed, you know, the younger version of us in bed, blankets on the floor, sheets tangled around my waist with my head between her legs?

Her hands fist in my hair and she arches her back against the white sheets. "I love you."

Did you hear it? I mean, it was moaned, but I made the words out clearly. You know when someone tells you they love you.

Smiling, I wink at her. "It's about time. Your eyes said it months ago."

"When did you see that?" She slaps the side of my head as I crawl up her body, trying to get her to kiss me, only she won't have it and turns her head. Remember where my mouth was? I don't understand why girls don't like the taste of themselves. It's only the best taste in the world, aside from beer in my opinion.

"When you were screaming my name." I waggle my eyebrows and settle between her legs letting the sheet fall away completely. You're welcome for the view. I have a nice fucking ass, and I can admit that with confidence.

Blinking slowly, her arms wrap around my neck bringing our chests together. "What about you?"

Me? I've been in love with Madison since I first laid eyes on her, remember?

But back to the moment. Look at her. She's wanting to know if I love her too. But you know me by now and I say, "I love me too. I'm a loveable guy."

You see that glare but the smirk on her face? She loves my witty personality. "Just tell me you love me, you pussy."

I don't, yet, and raise her thigh higher up on my hip to enter her. My mouth moves to her shoulder and then neck, kissing my way to her mouth. "You're so dirty, baby," I growl against her jaw before my lips find hers. I kiss her once, twice, three times and then say, "I love it…

and I love you. Since the day I first saw you wearing that Catwoman costume, I knew I was in love."

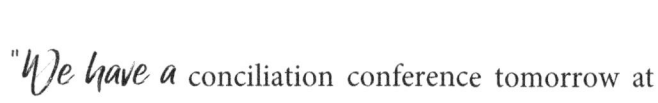

"We have a conciliation conference tomorrow at one," she tells me, righting her nightgown.

Pulling on a pair of shorts, I sigh, standing at the end of the bed staring at her. "Madison, I can't just take off in the middle of the day again. I have a job to do, you know."

I'm trying here, I really am, but how can she think I can just stop working and deal with all this shit when I own the business. If I don't do these things, Brantley has to, and building custom homes isn't a one-man job. She knows this. She understood it when I started the business, but now it's all of a sudden changed?

"And what the hell is a conciliation conference?"

"The state requires you to go when you file for divorce. It's to work out a parenting plan and custody I assume."

I do not like the words parenting plan and custody. In fact, I fucking hate them. I heard those words a lot growing up and swore I would never make my kids go through it. Sitting down on the edge of the bed, I face the wall, afraid to look at her because I know what's coming. Maybe her reasoning, but more so, the realization that this could end the way I don't want it to. Could I really be a weekend dad?

My heart pounds in my chest as I stare at the wall. "If you were serious about this, why didn't you hire a lawyer?"

Her voice is quiet, the bed dipping beside me as she moves to sit next to me. "I thought we could work everything out ourselves and it'd be less messy for the boys."

"Is that so? And how do you suppose we do that if you're not willing to talk to me?"

"I *am* talking to you. Right now, I'm talking to you, and I talked to you last night. You hear what you want, Ridley."

That's untrue and unjustified as far as I'm concerned. I don't believe that for one second. I've heard what she's saying to me. Remember? She said she didn't love me. *How* could I have forgotten that?

Swallowing over the insanely huge lump in my throat, my brow pulls together, and I twist to face her. Raising my hand, I cup her cheek hoping maybe that might convince her. "How can you honestly say you suddenly don't love me anymore. It doesn't just happen. Just five minutes ago, what was that? Sure seemed like you loved me then?"

I sound so fucking pathetic I want to punch myself in the throat so I can't talk anymore.

"That's *all* you heard last night?" She stares at me, ignoring my comments, the sadness returning. Her lashes flutter, tears welling up. "Us growing apart.... It didn't just happen, Ridley. It's been going on for years, and you're blind if you can't see it. The busier you get at work, the more you ignore what's happening here. I don't even know you anymore. It's like you're a roommate. Sure, you provide for us, but we *never* see you. You leave the house before the boys are up and by the time you get home, they're either in bed or supposed to be in bed. Up until the last two days, I bet you hadn't seen them for more than five hours. It's not just me, how do you think it makes them feel?"

She's right on that one, but still, I work. I can't help that I'm trying to provide for them.

My stare catches her wedding ring she finally has back on, and I wonder if she takes it off when she leaves the house. "Madison, I meant what I said when I gave you that ring. I did. And the way I see it, I have two options here. I can walk away, but I don't think it's what you want. Or I can stay and show you I can be different."

I can see it in her eyes, what I'm saying, the way I'm saying it, she's thinking about dropping all of this because deep down, this isn't something she would do. The Madison I know wouldn't resort to something so drastic, but then again, do I know this woman at all?

"You should move out," she says, delivering the earth-shattering blow straight to my heart.

I stand up immediately, my temper rising. Remember when I said I didn't yell? I didn't until now. "What the fuck? No, I'm not because this is my house. This is fucking bullshit, and you know it. I'm trying here, and you're giving me nothing and acting like it's already over between us before I have a say in any of it."

"That's because it is over. You just refuse to see it," she retorts with cold sarcasm.

"Maybe I didn't see it, before… but I see it now. I see *you*. And I'm not giving up without a fight."

She says nothing.

"I think I should get a chance to at least prove to you I can fix this."

She tosses a pillow at my face. "Sleep on the couch."

"Maybe she's sleeping with someone else?" Brantley suggests, and I want to punch him for saying that because the pain it sends to my heart makes that heart attack feeling return.

I'd kill the motherfucker she's sleeping with, if that were the case.

"She's still fucking me," I mumble, taking a drink of the beer in my hand. I left the house when Madison told me to sleep on the couch. I would eventually end up there, but I couldn't stay there and not demand she tell me the exact moment she began thinking of a divorce. So I went to the bar.

Leaning back, I dig my cell phone out of my pocket to send her a text message. If she wasn't going to talk tonight, I'd text her and demand answers.

Me: Are you in love with someone else?

Brantley raises an eyebrow, lifting his beer to his lips. "Like since she asked for a divorce?"

"Yep." I set the beer back down on the table. "Right before I called you."

He laughs, as though it's entertaining to him. "Dude, she's using you."

I never thought of it that way. Was she? She wants a divorce but not from my dick?

I text her again.

Me: Are you using me for my dick?

Still no answer.

Most men would be all over that. Not me. I love my wife and my boys.

Me: I love you.

That's romantic, right?

She still doesn't reply. Maybe she's sleeping already? It is like what, midnight?

Yeah, midnight. Fuck. I should be at home. Sleeping.

Me: Are you sleeping?

"Get her pregnant," Brantley suggests, his eyes glued to the sports highlights on the television above our heads. "I had a girlfriend who once poked a hole in the condom. I caught her and she became an *ex-girlfriend* but maybe try that?"

I roll my eyes. "That's dumb."

But then I think, what if that's what she wants?

Me: Do you want another baby? I can totally knock you up.

"It's an idea. Not a good one, but an idea," Brantley mumbles, glancing over his shoulder to watch a blonde walk by.

"This is serious, B. I *like* being married."

It's his turn to roll his eyes. "And that I will *never* understand but, dude, come on." He nudges my elbow with his. "You're looking at her asking for a divorce as a bad thing."

I raise an eyebrow. "It's not?"

"No. It's a good thing. It'll be like college again. Different chick every night."

"I didn't like college for that reason."

Me: I don't want to be with anyone else. I love your pussy.

Was that too much?

I'm a man of repetition. I eat the same thing for breakfast every morning. Eggs, scrambled, and a slice of wheat toast. I have the same cup of coffee on the way to work. Americano. No cream. When I run, I run the same five-mile loop every time.

And you know, I like fucking the same woman. Mostly because I'm comfortable. I don't have to worry about whether I'm going to find her fucking the neighbor and I know exactly what to do to make her come.

In turn, she knows what I like. There's something to be said about that, and after a very traumatizing experience freshman year of college, I'm not open to experimenting anymore.

"What's your plan then?" Brantley finally asks, probably wondering why it's a Wednesday night and I'm still at the bar at midnight.

Just as I'm about to text Madison again, finally she responds to my messages.

Madison: Stop. Texting. Me. I'm trying to sleep.

I raise my beer. "Thinking of becoming an alcoholic. Maybe start an arrest record." Then I shrug. "After that, I'm not sure I have a plan."

"I thought you were going to ask her out on a date. What happened to that plan?"

"My plan?" Sighing, I shake my head. It's like the universe is against me. "I had it all figured out. I was going to flirt with her like I did in college and then ask her on a date. But then Noah killed a cat and then decided to flood the bathroom. When we were finally had a chance to talk, it turned into us fucking and then her yelling at me. All I gathered from everything that happened is that Madison thinks I'm a bad husband."

He snorts and takes the fresh beer the bartender handed him. "And you wonder why I don't want to get married and have kids." And then he motions to me while looking at the bartender. "Can you get my boy here a shot?"

I wave him off. "No, I don't need one."

Brantley stares at me and then knocks my cell phone out of my hands. It's probably for the better at this point. "*Yes* you do." His eyes shift to the bartender. "He's getting a divorce."

"It's not official," I mumble, still holding onto the fact that it's not final yet.

"Pretty official," Brantley says, chuckling. "She filed."

"Yeah but I still have sixty days, or something like that."

Brantley reaches for his beer and shakes his head like I'm the stupidest motherfucker alive for believing this. "Uh huh."

The bartender then hands me whiskey. "Looks like you need this."

He's right. I do.

Have you ever seen a jackhammer ripping up concrete?

That's essentially how I feel when I pry my eyes open the next morning. The bright light pouring through the front windows is similar to, I don't know, pure agony exploding behind my eyes.

Rolling over, I take a pillow and cover my face with it, hoping maybe it suffocates me.

You know that feeling you get when you know someone's watching you? I'm getting it right now, so I peel the pillow back to see Callan standing over me.

"What?"

He blinks. Twice. "You're alive? For a moment I wasn't sure."

I toss the pillow at him teasingly. "I'm not sure if I am or not."

"You're talking, Dad. You're alive." He snorts and tosses the pillow back at me. "Did you make Mom mad again?"

"Probably." Groaning, I attempt to sit up, my stomach rolling as I do so. Never again.

Immediately I'm reminded of *why* I'm on the couch again.

Since last night didn't work for asking her out on a date, I'm should try a different approach, shouldn't I?

My muscles are feeling a little tight from two nights on the couch. I think I need a massage, don't you?

Callan sits down beside me. “You’re going to be late.”

Fuck, he’s right.

10

I'D LIKE TO MAKE AN APPOINTMENT

I know I mentioned this before—okay, you watched me charging into her work, so I know you know—but Madison is a massage therapist at West Bay. She didn't start out to be one, but the job came about not long after Callan was born and it allowed her to just work three days a week and have some spending money.

I'm actually jealous she got a job doing it because when she was going to school for her certification, I was given massages every night. Couldn't complain there. And then it stopped once she got the job.

So what's my plan for asking Madison on a date to convince her she loves me, not just my dick?

I'd trap her where she couldn't get away from me.

The salon. In a closed room with the door locked.

If she wasn't going to talk to me at home, I'd schedule an appointment to have a massage, right? Maybe one with a happy ending?

When life kicks some people down, they stay down. Not me. I will straight up donkey kick my way back up.

Thankfully it's a different girl working at the counter Thursday morning when I make my way into the salon. You're probably wondering why I'm not at work?

Well, the permits got held up for the compliance inspection and Trey finally had medical clearance to work again. Believe me, I'm feeling bad about not being at work today, but I had to get her to see I cared and hopefully, I still have a business once she agrees to stay married to me.

I grin, flashing a sideways smirk at the young girl behind the counter. Women fall all over themselves for smirking. It's like we're trying to lead them on with it, and guess what? We know it.

You know how I got Madison to sleep with me that first night we met at the Halloween party? You'd be surprised. It wasn't my vampire costume, although I looked fucking amazing in it. And yeah, I did ask to suck her blood, but it was the smirk that sealed the deal.

"How can I help you?" the girl asks, tucking her jet-black hair behind her ears.

"I'd like to schedule an appointment with Madison Cooper." I wink. "I hear she's the best."

Did you notice I didn't say what I wanted to see Madison for? This will come back to bite me in the ass. Believe me. Just wait.

"She has an opening at ten this morning. I can put you in there."

I look down at my watch. That's in twenty minutes. Perfect!

"And your name?"

Fuck! I panic a little internally, but I'm quick to say, "Jeff Westin." It's the name of one of my clients, but Madison will never know.

She types away and then smiles up at me. "Great!"

Jesus, that was easy. Why didn't I think of this Tuesday when she wouldn't answer her phone?

"I can get you into the room if you'd like." The girl, whose name tag reads Lindsey, points down the hall that's lined with floor-to-ceiling windows overlooking a Camelback Mountain.

I follow her down the hall and into a private room with no windows and a table.

Lindsey smiles tenderly, but her eyes drift lower to my waist. Is she looking? Nah, she can't be, or can she?

Christ, this place is full of weirdos. I'm not sure I want Madison working here.

"You can undress all the way, or however you feel comfortable and get under the blanket."

I nod and go to close the door behind me, but she stands there staring at me like she wants me to invite her in.

"Thanks," I say and then slam the door shut.

As I stare at the dimly lit room around me, I'm not sure what to do. Should I keep my clothes on… or… undress and let her be surprised when she notices it's her husband?

I decide to undress all the way but leave my boxers on and lay face down on the table. She might not even notice it's me, aside from my back. She'll probably notice that because guess who has scratch marks on his upper arms from his wife?

This guy. Proudly.

It's another ten minutes when there's a soft knock at the door and Madison enters the room. "Good morning, Mr. Westin," she says, her voice just above a whisper.

I don't say anything in reply because once she hears my voice, she's going to know it's me, right?

Maybe not.

"Oh, it says here you're in for waxing? Why don't you turn over and we'll get started?" I peek one eye open and see her moving around the room toward what looks to be hot wax.

Waxing? You have to be shitting me. For the love of all things holy, why didn't I specify what I needed?

No wonder Lindsey looked at my junk.

"Um, I think I made a mistake."

"Oh my God, Ridley." Yep. Told you she'd know my voice. "What the hell are you doing here?"

"I'm feeling a little sore. Can you give me a massage?"

"No. I can't." She blinks rapidly, stepping back away from me as if she's trying to make excuses. "I have appointments."

"No, you don't." Twisting around on the bed, I sit up and let the blanket fall away. "I made an appointment, and I'm a paying customer."

Her brow furrows just slightly, like she can't decide if she should be angry or amused I schedule myself with her. I feel myself smiling. "I think this is against the rules…."

"Well, the girl at the counter didn't say anything, so here I am. But I think she likes me, and I also lied about my name."

"You could really get me in trouble for this. And Lindsey flirts with everyone. Don't flatter yourself."

"Oh."

She nods to the hot wax. "Well since you're here and you weren't paying attention and scheduled to have your balls waxed, guess you're going to have some smooth balls."

"No fucking way." My hands fly to my balls cupping them with care. "I asked for a massage."

"Nope. You didn't. You should have been paying more attention instead of flirting with Lindsey."

"I wasn't flirting with her." Groaning, I flop back against the table. "I didn't ask for a wax, did I?"

"You did." She smiles, taking a wooden stick and stirring the steaming wax. "Take your boxers off and lay back, husband."

I do as she says because any time I get to take my clothes off in front of my wife is a good day. But I didn't miss this part. She said husband, didn't she? Did I hear that correctly?

One point for me but when that fucking wax hits my nut sac, I lose every point I've even gained in the last two days when I scream.

My legs tense when she applies it. "Fuck, that's hot!"

Madison laughs, clearly entertained. "That's just the wax, you big baby."

I can feel my balls tightening in preparation as Madison takes my dick in her hand and moves it to the side. I'd be lying if I said I didn't have a semi already, because I totally do. Hello, my dick's in her hand. Oh, the possibilities.

I raise my head up, my arm supporting my neck behind my head. "Does this come with a happy ending?"

She snorts out a laugh. "That's against the rules, *sir.*"

Why is it hot when she calls me sir?

She's waiting for the wax to cool, I assume because there are seconds of downtime after the wax is applied and my dick remains in her hand like she's cradling him. And then I think shit, does she hold dicks in her hand all day?

It's official. She needs to quit.

"How often do you do this?" I ask, raising an eyebrow.

She looks up at me and then shrugs. "Maybe once a month."

"And you hold their dick in your hand?"

"Well no, I make them do it."

"So you're holding mine because you want to?"

She doesn't answer me. Instead, she pulls the fucking wax strip off my balls and pain shoots through them immediately. It feels like someone has taken a branding iron to my nuts. She might as well have kicked me because the feeling is somewhat similar.

It's emasculating to have your wife waxing your balls and having you scream like a girl. I don't like it.

When she's finished with the second strip, I sit up and hold my sore burning-like-lava-has coated-them balls. My breath comes out in short gasps. "No more. Stop that."

She's raising her hands from me, laughing like this is the funniest shit she's ever seen.

"*Goddamn*," I scowl at her and then struggle not to bite through my bottom lip. "Why are you laughing?"

"Because you're being such a baby about it."

A fiery stabbing sensation rushes through my crotch and I dream of tea-bagging and a brick of ice for relief. "Well, you wax your clit, and we'll see how you feel."

She reaches for the wax again and pushes me back with her hand on my chest. "My clit doesn't have hair on it, smart ass. And, I have waxed my lady bits before and didn't scream at all."

"Well, give you a fuckin' medal." I stare at her, my heart pounding. "Who waxed you?"

If she says a man did, I'll kill him.

"Lindsey does it on occasions."

Thank God.

The last strip she applies and rips off like it's just a piece of tape is by far the worst. I can't even explain what it feels like except it's similar to when you rip off a toenail. I'm 90 percent sure she took off my first layer of skin.

Madison can't stop laughing when I fly off the table and yank my jeans on. "No more! I can't handle it." I'm pacing the tiny room, and it makes it look like I'm going in circles. "I don't care if you have more to do, leave it like this."

"It's done." She raises her hands, still laughing hysterically and I can't remember the last time she's laughed this hard. Probably last night when I broke my ass on the tile floor in the bathroom. And then her laughter dies off, and her eyes move to my crotch. "I have to say, it looks nice."

Say what?

I didn't look. My balls feel like they're on fire right now and I don't want to look but my curiosity gets the better of me, and I peek inside my jeans.

Moving my dick aside, I see red balls. Bright red balls that are screaming "fuck you, motherfucker" at me as tiny pin-drop sized blood coats the skin. I'm fucking bleeding. Told you she took off skin!

But they're smooth and strangely make my dick look bigger. Not that I needed any assistance in that department, just so we're clear, but, I see the advantages.

I shake my head. I think I'm… I don't know… upset with myself? Disappointed maybe? "I can't believe I did this."

"Neither can I," Madison says, watching me carefully as I button my jeans and reach for my shirt. We stand there staring at each other when she asks, "Why did you make an appointment?"

My throat tightens and I swallow, attempting to push away the pain raging in my pants to what I came here for. Her. To ask her out on a date. I'm a little mad at her at the moment for skinning me. "I came here to ask you out, and I didn't know how to do it."

Her brow pulls together. "What are you talking about?"

"On a date."

She sighs, her shoulders slumping. "Ridley, just face it. It's over and we just need to make this less painful."

Fuck her. Less painful? My balls have been skinned for her. But do you see her face right now? Look really close because there's something in the way her lashes flutter and her eyes sadden.

I drop to my knees before her so we're eye level as she's sitting on a stool. My palms frame her face. "Tell me right now to my fucking face you don't love me. At all. That you want this divorce, and I'll walk away and give you what you want."

She says nothing and blinks, slowly.

"I'm fucking trying, okay. Maybe I've been blind for a while, but you can't dismiss that once you told me how you felt I've been trying."

Again, she says nothing because she knows it's the truth.

"Then go out with me. Let's try to make this work and if in these fifty-something days I have left, I can't make you see you're still in love with me, then I'll give you the divorce."

Her eyes search mine, darting to my lips and then my eyes. "So you're going to make me fall back in love with you?"

I pull her toward me, my breath blowing across her face. "No. I'm going to *remind* you why you fell in love with me. Because, honey, you and I both know you haven't stopped."

She can't argue with me, and she knows it.

"Have dinner with me tonight. I'll get a babysitter."

"We can't tonight. Nathalie's coming over with Grady for dinner."

Ah, yes, Madison's best friend, Nathalie, and her devil child. You think Noah the cat killer's bad, wait until you meet Grady. He makes Noah look like an angel.

"Fine. Friday night."

"Callan's birthday party is the next day."

"So? Doesn't mean we can't go out."

She raises an eyebrow at me. "Well, his birthday is Friday so that'd mean we're going out alone on our kid's birthday?"

Fuck. "You're right. Sunday then?"

Madison stands and grabs onto my shoulders to make me stand with her. She twists me around so I'm facing the door. "Fine, Sunday I'll go on a date with you. Now, will you leave?"

"Yes," I say proudly, forgetting about my burning nut sac for a split second. "But, can you apply some lotion to these tonight?"

She rolls her eyes. "No."

I may not be getting my nuts massaged tonight but still, I had a date and time to at least work this out. That's progress, right?

Walking awkwardly back to the counter, Lindsey is all smiles. "How was your wax, Mr. Westin?"

Do you think there's a reason as to why she didn't ask me what I wanted to see Madison for and just scheduled me in?

I grunt my reply, which is a "fuck off" muttered under my breath and hand her my credit card. It's then I notice Madison is standing behind the counter now too, smiling.

Of course she's smiling. She got to inflict pain on her husband she's trying to divorce.

Apparently, this is funny to them. I don't even pay attention to what I'm signing and hope I wasn't charged more than five bucks to have my ball skin ripped off.

Madison waves to me, still all smiles. "Have a nice day, Mr. Westin."

Guess what? She's wearing her wedding ring. I can't help but feel pretty good about that. But the feeling disappears when I attempt to walk.

I look back over my shoulder. "You too, *Mrs.* Cooper."

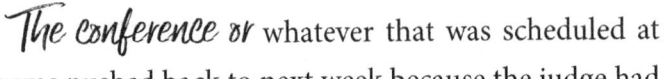

The conference or whatever that was scheduled at one was pushed back to next week because the judge had a scheduling conflict. I'm excited because that not only allows me to get some work done but maybe by the time next weekend arrives, she'll have forgotten all about this divorce nonsense.

It's around seven that night when I finally make it home after hanging the rest of the drywall in the house and taping. With the burning sensation below my belt, all I want to do is sit on a bag of ice. I'm certainly not ready to see Nathalie and her devil child, so I invite Brantley over for dinner.

He groans when he sees Nathalie's Trailblazer parked on the street. "You didn't tell me she was going to be here."

"Whoops."

He glares and opens the door. Just so you know, Brantley and Nathalie met about the time Madison and I did. We were all at the same party that night. They hated each other. Like couldn't even be in the same room together without wanting to kill one another.

Nathalie thinks he's a pig who uses women, and he thinks she's a bitch. They're essentially both right, but I have to defend my friend here. He's always honest with women, and they know ahead of time he's just in it for the sex.

About a year ago, at our annual New Year's Eve party Madison and I have, they fucked. And no, in case you're wondering, the child she has is not Brantley's. He's product of another drunken night Nathalie had with some other guy. She makes a habit of getting drunk and spreading her legs. Hypocritical don't you think? Anyways, from what I gather, they still fuck on occasions. I don't ask and Brantley's never been one to talk about it.

And Madison can't understand *why* I don't let her go out with Nathalie to the bar.

Anyway, Grady's dad isn't part of his life now, which is sad. The little fucker needs a man around to set a good example for him.

Walking inside the house, I smell steak. Madison is an amazing cook. Throws down the best meals at the drop of a hat.

Brantley walks in behind me. "I'm starving."

We're still dressed in our work clothes, trudging through the house in our boots, covered in a thin white dust from hanging drywall. Madison frowns when we come around the corner into the kitchen. "We should eat outside."

I grab a beer from the fridge and one for Brantley. "Okay. Do you need help?"

For a second, she's taken back by my willingness to help. "Uh, well," she reaches for a bowl on the counter with what looks to be pasta salad in it, "you could find the boys and tell them it's time for dinner."

"Okay." I'm not excited by this. Mostly because Grady will probably be with them and he hates me more than his mother does. I think she tells him to.

"Sorry for intruding," Brantley says, wrapping his arm around Madison as I walk outside to see if the boys are in the backyard.

"You're always welcome here, B."

Upstairs, I find all three boys in Callan's room. He looks stressed out sitting on his bed with a book on Ukraine while Noah and Grady are playing with GI Joes on the floor. They pay me no attention when I sit down next to Callan. "Hey, bud, how was school?"

He shrugs, flipping the page in his book. "Boring. But I got a book from the library today."

I point to the one in his hand, reminded of the parent-teacher conference we had the other day. "This one?"

"Yeah. I really want to go to Ukraine. Will you take me?"

He's not going to let this one go. Maybe he does have a little bit of my personality in him?

"We'll have to talk about it sometime. That's a big trip for a kid and more than likely not that safe."

"It's not Rio De Janeiro, Dad."

I feel really dumb right now. "What's wrong with Rio?"

"Their crime rate is ridiculous. It's a third world country."

Show's how much I know. I ruffle his hair. "Dinner's ready. Let's eat." Peeking over the bed, I toss a pillow between Noah and Grady. "Dinner's ready. Go downstairs."

Do you think they listen to me?

Nope. It's like I'm not even there.

I leave them up there and pass Nathalie in the hallway. "Tell your kid it's time for dinner."

"Why didn't you tell him?" she asks, putting her hand on her hip. Nathalie could be pretty if she wasn't such a bitch. She has long blonde, super curly hair that's always sticking up all over the place. It's wild and like I said, would be considered cute, but her personality ruins it for me. "Didn't Madison send you up here to do that?"

I stare at her, the two of us standing in the middle of the hallway as Callan rushes down the stairs when he hears Brantley's voice. There's something off about the way she's watching me, and I know this is my wife's best friend and she more than likely knows more about me than I want her to. But is she withholding information? I could tackle her to the ground and sit on her head until she tells me what she knows, but I won't. Instead I try more of an asshole approach because it's what I'm good at.

Leaning in, I whisper in Nathalie's ear, "Just because you're happy being single and fuckin' my best friend, doesn't mean you have to talk my wife into being part of your slutty single mom cult."

Harsh? Oh, just wait until she starts in.

"Oh, please." She pushes me into the wall with a quick jab to my shoulder. "I'm not talking her into anything. *You've* done this all on your own."

Why do people keep saying that?

"Well, she agreed to go on a date with me," I say, half tempted to stick my tongue out.

Nathalie rolls her eyes. "I'm sure you'll find a way to fuck it up." She sticks her head in the bedroom. "Boys, dinner's ready."

And then they both come running.

Nobody listens to me lately.

"So I heard you got your balls waxed, Ridley."

Choking on a mouthful of steak, I shoot Madison a glare. "You told her?"

Luckily the boys aren't at the table with us. They're in the backyard playing basketball. Well, Noah and Grady are. Callan's sitting by the pool with his feet in the water reading his book.

Madison smiles, her eyes lighting up and you know, it's been a long fucking time since I've seen this smile.

I turn to Nathalie and force a grin. "Fuck off, Natalie."

"It's Nathalie."

"I don't care."

Brantley stares at me, a slow smile creeping across his face. "Is that why you were walking weird?"

I nod, not knowing what else to say. I fucking knew she was going to tell everyone.

"Does it, you know, make it look bigger?" he asks, laughing now.

I refuse to look at any of them and cut into my steak again. "Stop talking about this. It's not appropriate."

"Ha!" Nathalie laughs. "You're *never* appropriate."

She's right, but I refuse to ever agree with her. "And neither are you so shut the fuck up."

Madison kicks me under the table. "Ridley, knock it off."

I know what you're thinking, geez, you're in a bad mood now.

Yeah, well, have you had your ball skin ripped off? No? Then don't judge me.

Grady walks up to us, takes my steak from my plate and throws it on the ground. I want to take my steak knife and stab his hand for doing that. But I don't.

Instead, I glare at Nathalie. "Control your kid."

She laughs. "He doesn't like men."

It's not even that he doesn't like men, which she's partially right. The only man he's ever tolerated is Brantley, but I think Nathalie secretly tells him what a jerk she thinks I am.

Did you know at mine and Madison's wedding, Nathalie objected to the wedding? Yep. Fucking stood there and said, "Don't marry him!"

Can you also believe she was her maid of honor and shitfaced?

I can.

I don't react to Grady taking my steak, but I do glare at him only to take a foot to my other shin when he kicks me. "Son of a bitch!" I scream in pain because it's like he's wearing steel-toed boots. Grabbing my beer off the table, I take a long drink, hoping to talk myself down from drop kicking this child. "Stop that. You're lucky I don't stab you with this knife."

Grady is two years old. And doesn't talk. I'm positive he doesn't understand when you talk either.

Nathalie throws a piece of bread at my head from across the table. "Don't talk to my son that way."

I set down my beer with a loud thud on the wooden table. "Teach him some manners then."

Have you ever heard the term resting bitch face? If not, just look at Nathalie. She has the look perfected to a fucking art. "Yeah, you're one to talk."

With a grin of satisfaction, Grady takes off toward the pool.

Remember when I said he's a devil child?

Clearly, I knew what I was talking about.

I don't say anything more to Nathalie but I glare. I'm hoping my glare might make her head explode. If only I had super powers.

After everyone leaves that night, Madison's in the kitchen cleaning up and I can see she's tired and wants to go to bed. What do I do?

I should probably help her but I'm more focused on trying to seduce her again so I lick the back of her neck. She doesn't find this sexy and slaps at my head. "Stop it."

"Why?"

Subconsciously I think I'm annoying her to get her to yell at me because that meant talking instead of ignoring, right?

She turns to face me, wiping her soapy hands on a hand towel beside the sink. "You want to know what upsets me?"

I smirk. "I'm *dying* to know."

"Just once I'd like to come home for you to have actually done something around here. I get it, you run a business and have little time for anything else but would it kill you to put your dishes in the sink and not on the counter. Or better yet, in the dishwasher?"

"I'm never sure if the dishes in the dishwasher are clean," I say, attempting to defend myself with humor. "And I don't do the dishes because what if I break one?

Remember that time I broke that plate your grandma gave you? You didn't talk to me for an entire day."

"At this point, I wouldn't care if you broke every dish we have as long as you made a damn effort. Or when you see that I've picked up the house and put away all the laundry, why do you have to leave your pants on the floor in our room? Do you not see everything else is nice and clean and it'd be nice if you helped me keep it that way?"

I blink a couple times but I don't say anything right away. I'm not sure I know what to say. For an intuitive and observant person, she was painting me to be oblivious to what was happening to us. Had I really turned my back on her for that long?

I scrub my hands over my face, leaning back into the counter. "I'm... I just don't understand any of this, Mad. I thought you were happy. Why haven't you said anything to me until now?"

"I have said things, Ridley. I've asked for your help but it was apparently not what you wanted to hear at the time. You don't seem to get it. By the time I get Callan ready for bed, you're already asleep or still at work. And when you are home, you think I should give you all my attention, but you know what, you're just like having another child."

I am *not* a child. "What's your point?"

Do you see that look I'm getting? The one where she looks strangely like she might be constipated? I think I shouldn't have said that.

She throws her hands up in the air, reaches for the door to the dishwasher and then slams it shut. "My point is when you are here, you're not! I feel like a single mom most of the time. We've grown apart."

We've grown apart? She thinks that?

And my first thought is, I should have seen it coming if we'd grown apart, right?

"Ridley, I was so in love with you. I was, but now, I just don't know what's happening anymore. I want to make it work, but I'm scared all this, you being here, trying, I'm scared it's just a phase, and a couple months go by, and you'll go back to what it was like before. I don't even know how this happened. We went from being these two people who couldn't get enough of one another to this, barely talking in passing. That's not a marriage. It's not even a life. I refuse to be married to someone like that. I deserve a husband who wants to share his life with me, not one working all the time."

Do you see that guy, the one with itchy balls and a confused expression on his face?

He needs to up his fucking game for sure.

11

DEE THE REPTILE AND RODENT LADY

It's the morning of Callan's birthday party when I notice Madison in the kitchen, making food and doing all the things she does as a mother without ever being asked to do them. I get this sharp pain in my chest when she sighs and stares at the plate of veggies. She's attempting to make it perfect, because it's in her nature to do so, but she's unsettled with it, or me.

In the last few days since she agreed to let me try and prove to her that she still loves me, I've been sleeping in the bed again. It's much more comfortable.

I can't say we're okay yet because if I'm being honest, I'm starting to see there's some truth to everything she said in the kitchen.

"I was so in love with you. I was, but now, I just don't know what's happening anymore. I want to make it work,

but I'm scared all this, you being here, trying, I'm scared it's just a phase and a couple months go by and you'll go back to what it was like before."

Those words, the way her hurt ripped in me, I knew then this was serious. She had a reason for doing this. I may not agree, but she had her reason.

Madison notices me watching her, does a double take and sighs, like she's remembering something she forgot. "Hey, listen…"

I don't like conversations that start like that. My heart pounds in my chest waiting for her words.

"…my mother is coming today…." And then her voice trails off because she knows how I feel about her mother.

Jenna Adams is a fucking bitch, like if I could slap my mother-in-law in the face, I would.

"I'm sorry she's coming. Nathalie invited her, and I wasn't sure what else to do."

I know what you're thinking, do I like anyone? I do, sometimes but not Madison's mother and trust me, you won't either. She's a drunk, uses Madison for money and basically tells Callan to his face, be less weird and people will like you.

"I don't care if she's here, but if she says anything to me or upsets Callan, I'm going to say something."

Her brows draw together, rawness and pain evident in her features. She doesn't want her mother here either. "Don't make this more complicated today, please."

"How would I complicate things?"

She raises on eyebrow.

"Define complicated.'"

"You." Her voice shakes around the words. "You're complicated."

Of course she'd say that. I sigh heavily and reach for a carrot from her tray of vegetables. "I won't say anything to her or be mean, *but* if she says something to you, or our kids, I'm not going to remain quiet like I did the last time."

Guess what? Her mom hates me too. And I'll be honest here, I think Jenna, her mother, only disapproves of me because I provide for Madison, something her own husband never did. He left town when Madison was two and nobody's seen him since then.

Madison catches my eye and my thoughts. She's wearing a royal blue dress that shows off just the tops of her breasts, her hair curled in soft waves. God, I hope she gives me a chance because I can't stand to think of not having her for the rest of my life.

I know what you're thinking. If you feel that way, why not tell her what you're thinking?

Women?

Our brains don't work like that. We may think something and never say it. And believe me on this one, you might not want to know everything we're thinking. Mostly because I'd say 85 percent of the time it has to do with one of two things. Sex or getting you to *have* sex with us.

I'm just being honest.

Watch. Here's my attempt at telling her what I'm thinking.

"You look…" I breathe in, watching Madison move around the kitchen. "…pretty today."

"Thanks," she mumbles, keeping her distance from me.

"Do you need help?"

"No, I think I got this, but can you make sure Noah has pants on? He didn't earlier, and I don't want people showing up when his pants are off."

I chuckle and itch my balls by sticking my hand right down my shorts. "I wish I didn't have to wear pants today because you know, my balls still itch *so bad.*"

I know what you're thinking, gross, right?

Just wait. I do this on purpose because the moment I stick my hand down my pants, Madison's eyes follow as if she can't help but drag her eyes there. She's just about to say something when Nathalie walks in carrying a box of what looks to be cake. "That's disgusting! Wash your hands!"

Madison laughs and shakes her head as I remove my hand.

Moving past Nathalie, I'm behind her about two feet and then lunge back at her, my ball sweat hand covering her mouth. "You were saying?"

It's really paybacks for her son ruining my delicious steak the other night.

But here's the thing, I should have looked at what she had in her hand when I did. Whatever's in her hand makes contact with my junk. Hard. I don't even know what was in her hand, but it hurts.

I may never father another child, and I'm pretty sure I can't breathe.

Yep. Can't breathe.

Falling to the floor, I curl into a fetal position. Madison walks over to me, shakes her head and then steps over me like she holds no concern for me and my pain. "Go find Noah and his pants."

Nathalie, on the other hand, is gagging in the kitchen sink and washing her mouth out with soap.

"I hope you get diarrhea," I mumble when I can breathe again.

She spits bubbles at me. "I hope you die of blunt force trauma!"

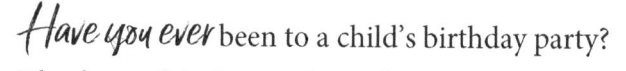

Have you ever been to a child's birthday party?

They're awful if you ask me, but no one does today and I'm glad they don't. Mostly because after two beers, I'm afraid I'll give them my honest opinion.

Guess who I meet at the birthday party?

Pedro. Remember the pool guy? I'm very excited about this because I want to see if there's anything going on with him and my wife, and I know I'll be able to tell when I see them together.

I motion for Callan to come over when I see a darker-skinned man appear with what looks to be his son and he's staring at the pool. "Who's that guy?" I ask Callan when he's next to me, kneeling to his level.

"Pedro."

He acts like I should know him, and I sorta feel weird that I don't. "Who's he?"

"He's the pool guy. You hired him, Dad."

I raise an eyebrow and stand up. "I did?"

"Yeah." And then Callan walks away probably thinking I'm crazy. Which really wouldn't be a surprise.

Intending on asking Madison about Pedro, I walk inside the house to find her arranging the cookies on a platter as kids rush around the house.

"Why are these cookies shaped like rats?"

Madison hands me a white rat cookie. "Because it's a reptile and rodent party."

"What's that?"

"It's a theme, Ridley," she says like I know nothing about birthday parties. Mostly because I don't. "I hired this lady named Dee, The Reptile and Rodent Lady.

I snort. "Her name is Dee, The Reptile and Rodent Lady?"

"Yes. She's really popular with the kids. We're lucky I was able to book her."

Lucky huh? I don't feel so lucky as I stare down at the rat-shaped cookie with cinnamon drops for his eyes and black licorice for the tail.

I don't like rodents of any kind. When I was about Callan's age, my mom thought it would be a good idea to get me a pet. Since divorcing my dad and not having a man around most of the time, she wanted to teach me some responsibility. I was all for it because, at seven, everything seems like a good idea.

Well not long after this talk about getting a pet, I come home from school and there's a small cage sitting on my dresser in my bedroom. Needless to say, I was beyond excited. I had plans for this pet. I didn't know what it was, but it was going to be awesome.

As I walked up to the cage expecting a lizard or even cooler, a snake, I was hugely disappointed to find nothing in the cage. My mom came out of her room at that moment and had a huge smile on her face. I looked at her like "what the hell are you smiling at?"

"Hey, babe, I didn't hear you get home. What do you think of your new pet?"

"Um, Mom, there's nothing in there."

She stared at the cage, curiously looking around it. "What? Oh no. It must have gotten out. Crap. The pet store clerk said that could happen. Well, we'll just have to keep our eyes out for it and put it back in the cage. It'll show up eventually. Everything has to eat sometime, right? We'll just leave a bowl of food out next to the cage in your room tonight."

This was my mother's logic. It'll show up sometime. And I'm the one who needed to learn responsibility?

"Mom, I don't even know what I'm keeping an eye out for?" I asked, hoping she'd give me a clue.

"It's a guinea pig."

Somewhat disappointed I didn't get a lizard, I stood there for a second not really knowing what to do next. Did I start to look for it or did I just wait for it to come to me? This was all unchartered territory for me, so I decided that I would keep an eye out but wait and see.

After dinner, Zeke—the name I decided to give my new pet—still hadn't shown up. When I asked my mom if she thought maybe he got out or what we were gonna do if he didn't show up, she reassured me it would all work out. After all, it had to be getting hungry so it would probably start looking for food. Satisfied with her answer, I just went to sleep.

Sometime in the middle of the night, I felt a weight on my chest. When I opened my eyes to see what it was, there he was, my new pet, Zeke, staring at me. My mom didn't tell me Zeke was an albino guinea pig. Have you ever seen an albino guinea pig? They're pure white with blood-red eyes. BLOOD-RED EYES! Like the fucking devil. Seeing how it was in the middle of the night, and I had just been woken up by the Satan of guinea pigs sitting on my chest, I wasn't exactly calm in my next move.

Jumping out of bed, I sent it flying through the air, and it landed on the floor. Scared of me I supposed, he got up on his back to feet and started making this squealing noise that only scared me more so then I started screaming and ran into my mom's room while Zeke took off under my bed.

I see no cuteness in a rodent, nor do I understand what would possess a sane person to think any sort of rodent would make a good pet. They're gross and their eyes glow red in just the right light. As a general assessment, I usually steer clear of anyone with red eyes. Animals included.

"So what exactly does this Dee the Rat Lady do?" I ask, pushing the cookie away from me.

Madison rolls her eyes and continues to put out all the reptile and rodent-themed party shit she must have picked up this week. I look at the wall. Pin the tail on the rat? Seriously?

Fanning out black napkins, she perfects her arrangements on the table. "It's Dee The Reptile and Rodent Lady," she says, correcting me. "And she brings over an assortment of snakes and like mice or something. I'm not really sure, but she's who Callan wanted."

I'm actually surprised by this based on our conversations about Ukraine lately. I thought for sure he'd want a party based on nuclear reactors or some crazy science project.

Madison finishes what she's doing and looks at me. "He's really excited you're here for this."

I fight the urge to sigh and roll my eyes. "I've been at every one of his birthday parties, Madison."

Her expression is sharp and accessing. "Have you? Have you actually been *here* or standing next to your buddies drinking beer while the kids play and I cook and take care of everything?"

Did she slap me in the face because it certainly feels that way?

My gaze moves to Callan outside with his friends, and I realize she's right.

Dee is exactly what you would expect a woman who makes a living playing with snakes and rodents to look and act. She's dressed straight out of *Crocodile Dundee* movies, complete with the khaki shorts, matching shirt, and knee-high socks paired with boots and a desert hat. You know the kind that has flaps that cover your neck, so you don't get burned as you cross the vast plains of Phoenix? Yeah well, she's wearing that right now, in my house, out of the sun.

She also can't stop talking about all her adventures trapping rats and mice. Apparently, aside from her lucrative gig as a party host, Dee is a rodent trapper. "If you think you have a rodent problem, don't wait and see, just call Dee."

That's her slogan. Catchy, isn't it? What? Not impressed? Me either.

This woman literally makes a living out of my worst nightmare. She and I will never be friends.

The kids are having a great time though. Callan and the other kids are completely taken with Dee and her tales of snakes and mice.

Watching Madison as she laughs with the kids surrounding the snakes, it's obvious Madison is a hands-on parent who prefers to be a part of everything the kids are doing.

It's not just Callen who has a big smile today. Madison seems truly happy for the first time in I don't know, months, years? My heart swells when I see Callan wrap his arms around her neck, kissing her cheek.

I've always known Madison does everything in her power to make sure our boys are safe and happy, but to see the look of satisfaction on her face when they're enjoying themselves too, nothing compares to that. She's not only the love of my life, but she's also the best mom I could ask for my boys.

Speaking of which, where the hell is Noah? I haven't seen him since I put pants on him earlier and he promptly took them off the moment I left the room.

Turning to look around, I don't see him anywhere and decide to check outside in the backyard. Brantley's out there with Nathalie's son, trying to teach him how to throw a baseball, something he probably shouldn't be doing. The last thing Grady needs to know how to do is have an accurate aim with a weapon.

"Hey, man, you seen Noah?"

He stops throwing the ball and looks around the yard. "Noah? Nah, man, I haven't seen him." He cringes, his body shuddering. "Isn't he in the house with the snakes?"

As much as I don't like rodents, they don't necessarily scare me. I just hate them. Plain and simple. Brantley, on the other hand, he doesn't just hate snakes. He's completely and utterly scared shitless by them. I'm not really sure why. Some childhood trauma he won't share, but whatever it was has scared that man far worse than any baggage I carry from my ordeal.

I think it's kind of bullshit that he won't tell me what happened since I poured my heart out to him and shared my satanic guinea pig story, but whatever.

"No, I looked there first and didn't see him. Maybe he's upstairs."

Just as I'm about to turn around and head back into the house, I hear a woman scream from inside.

Running inside, I see Madison holding Noah with one arm and is trying very hard to calm down Dee by patting her back.

"What's going on? Why is she screaming?"

"Noah took the tops off the albino mice and red rat snake cages," Nathalie tells me with wide eyes.

I relax a little that there's no blood and everyone seems to be okay. "All right, so why is she screaming?"

"They got out," Dee shouts. "All of them!"

I panic, my eyes drifting to the cage with the rats. "When you say all of them, how many are we talking?"

"Four albino mice and two red rat snakes."

"This is awesome!" Callan says, smiling, but I don't miss the way he's sitting on the kitchen counter and not standing on the floor. He's probably scared too. He high-fives Noah, who Madison sets next to him on the counter. "Good job, dude."

Noah points to his own chest and shakes his head. "No dude. Wolverine."

I'm more focused on the loose rodents. It's like some damn rat god decided to fuck with me today. Not just mice, but *albino mice* with devil eyes, and on top of that, not just any snake but a red *rat* snake!

Suddenly Dee turns and lunges for me, fisting my shirt between her hands and bringing our faces within kissing distance. "You have to find my babies. Hewey, Dewey, Lewey, and Norman are my life! If Sampson and Saul get to them first, there won't be anything left to love!"

This lady is batshit fucking crazy if you ask me and needs a toothbrush. "Okay, okay. First, stop touching me." Only she doesn't. "And second, isn't catching mice kind of what you do?"

"Yes, yes, of course, but I'm compromised." Yes, she said that. Compromised? What a nut job. "My emotions are taking hold of me, and I can't think. Please, you've *got* to help me. We need to spread out and search every inch of this house. Also, we need someone to keep an eye out for Sampson and Saul."

Madison walks over and gently removes Dee's hands from my shirt. "Okay, Dee. You need to calm down. I'm sure we'll find everyone in no time, but you have to remember not to panic. Panicking will not help the situation."

Another surge of pride races through my chest. See what I mean? Not a better woman.

Madison leads Dee through some deep breathing exercises and then looks at Brantley and me. "Why are you guys just standing around? Go find those damn mice."

I can't help the look of complete shock that crosses my face as I stare at my wife. Madison knows about Zeke, and yet she's telling me to go find them? Remember what I just said about her being the best. I take it back. She's a backstabbing traitor!

As Madison takes all the kids outside, I grab Brantley and drag him into the kitchen. "We have to find the mice."

Brantley shakes his head as if I'm asking him to commit murder with me. "Nope. No can do. What if I run into Sampson or Saul?"

"Where are your balls?"

"Hairy and attached," he jabs, glaring at me. "Unlike yours."

What an asshole. I'm tempted to revise our contract for our 70/30 percent ownership. Not really, but still. Jerk move. "You know… you're being a real dick." I shove him away from me, annoyed everything I do lately turns to shit. "I thought you were my best friend."

"Fine." He sighs and reaches for a beer in the fridge. "But I swear to fucking God, if I find one of those snakes, I'll never come over here again."

Brantley begins to look through the couch cushions and on top of the entertainment center while I check under the furniture and inside the first-floor closets.

After twenty minutes, we meet back in the living room to discuss our next move over a beer. Sticking my hand in a bowl of chips on the table, that's when I feel something furry. It's a fucking mouse.

Screaming, I toss it at Brantley who jumps back in shock, loses his footing and falls on the ground where guess who's at his feet?

Sampson or Saul, I'm not sure there's a difference between the two and don't actually care. All I care about is they were found, and I intend on finishing our house because I no longer want to live in this one.

12

MONSTERIN-LAW

Callan's had seven birthdays and until today, I can't remember ever giving him a present that was just from me. It's always come from Madison and me but this one, it's from me. Only.

The book he wanted about Chernobyl.

When he opens it away from the other kids at his party, his eyes light up like they did the other night.

Standing in the kitchen, alone with me, his arms wrap tightly around my neck, the book on the counter. "Thanks, Dad. It's the best present ever." My arms move around him, holding him to my chest.

Madison's near the back door, watching us from a distance as tears sting my eyes. There's been a few times I've been brought to tears by our children. Mostly out of pain at the hands of Noah, but there're these moments when they make you proud or happy, moments like this when I know I've given him exactly what he wanted.

My stare catches Madison's and she mouths, "Thank you," to me.

I wink and then pull back to hold Callan at arm's length. "You like it?"

"I *love* it!" Reaching for the book, he opens it to flip through the pages.

You see the man standing in front of his son, the one where nothing can ruin his day now?

His day is about to be ruined.

"I thought you said you'd have wine here?" a voice asks from behind us, and I don't even have to look to know who it is talking to Madison. My good feeling is gone, out the fucking door like a dust storm blowing through the house.

There's no "Thanks for inviting me," or "How have you been?" or even, "Happy Birthday, Callan." That's not how Jenna works. She goes straight for the weakness that's consumed her life for twenty years.

"I do, Mom," Madison says, her sandals clicking against the tile as she moves closer. "It's on the counter."

I can smell Jenna's perfume before she approaches me from behind. It's patchouli oil. Quite possibly the worst smell in the world as far as I'm concerned.

"Oh, well hello, Ridley. Are you even going to say hello?"

No. I want you to leave.

I smile, despite my complete distaste for Madison's mother. "Jenna."

Her blue eyes stand out against her brown hair I know she dyes probably once a week. And then her stare moves to Callan, who's watching her. She hands him a present. "Happy Birthday."

Do you see how forced the "Happy Birthday" is? She once called him in July to wish him happy birthday. His birthday is February 27th. It certainly hasn't changed since his birth, which she was present and drunk at. We couldn't even let her hold him because she couldn't stand up straight.

She's part of the reason Madison has never touched a drop of alcohol in her life.

"Thanks, Jenna."

Ha. She gets first name basis too, but I've graduated to Dad! I fight the urge to stick my tongue out.

As Madison opens the wine, Jenna glances around the house, judging everything about it and Madison's decorating. They don't agree on much of anything.

"What happened in here?"

Madison shrugs. "Some mice and snakes got loose."

Jenna tenses. "Did you find them?"

"Yes." Madison laughs and hands her mother a glass of wine and then pours one for Nathalie who comes inside with Grady on her hip. He's thankfully asleep. "Ridley found them."

Jenna runs her fingers over a metal tray Madison has on the counter with oranges in it and then sips her wine. "I thought you had a new house? Why are you still living here?"

Ah, yes. I was wondering when this would be brought up again.

Drawing in a calming breath, I look to my wife, curious as to what her answer might be but she's watching me, waiting for my answer.

My eyes move to Callan as he opens the present in his hands. Play-Doh. She got a seven-year-old Play-Doh. I'm not even sure Noah even plays with it anymore. He might stick it up his nose or eat it, but he doesn't play with it much.

Callan glances up at me, then to his grandmother, if you can call her that. "Thanks." And then he tugs on my hand to whisper in my ear, "What's that smell?"

"It's the smell of a bitch," I tell him, only to have him laugh.

I know what you're thinking, why would you one, say that to your son, and two, say that in front of your son?

Just wait. You'll see why in about five minutes. The standard length of time it takes for Jenna to piss everyone off. I was there the second I heard her voice.

Callan spots Noah getting too close to one of his presents left outside on the patio and takes off outside. I'm thankful for him leaving the house because I know what's coming next.

Disaster.

Watch and you'll see.

"Ridley's still working on the house so we haven't moved yet," Madison says, putting the cork back on the wine and leaning into the counter with her hip. It's a moment later when our eyes meet and stay that way for a minute.

Is that another reason why she wants a divorce? Because I didn't finish the house?

I can see where that might upset her.

And here's the moment the disaster hits and my anger for her mother takes on its normal behavior.

"I don't understand you, Madison." Jenna pauses, eyeing me and then Madison. "You leave home to get an education, marry the first guy you meet and look at you now, two kids and a husband who can't deliver the promises he makes."

Please tell me you see why I called her a bitch?

Madison's too shocked to reply, blinking rapidly, looking from me to her mother and then Nathalie for inviting the whore.

"All right, that's enough," I say, my body trembling with anger. I remind myself this is Callan's birthday and I can't make a scene today. But he's outside, as are the other kids, and I have to say something. Jenna is constantly putting Madison down for making something of her life and it's not fair. "Don't put your bullshit on her. We didn't fuckin' ask you to come here."

"Stay out of this, Ridley," she says, regarding me directly for the first time. It's more than she does most of the time. At Christmas this year, she didn't say a fuckin' word to me in my own house for six hours. She's also the same woman who bought my wife a vibrator for our wedding with a note that said, "The only way you'll get off the rest of your life."

She's bitter. Her husband left when Madison was little. I'm not even sure Madison has ever seen him so it was just her mom raising her, if you can call it that. When she was six to the time she was fourteen, her grandmother raised her while her mother was out "finding herself."

Madison tries to maintain a relationship with her mostly because outside of me and the boys, she doesn't have any family since her grandparents passed away last spring.

But Jenna makes it really hard by acting like Madison will never be good enough, or I'm never good enough for her. And up until Tuesday, I thought I was. Now I'm beginning to wonder, and this isn't helping.

Here's where I lose my temper all together.

Nathalie clears her throat. "I'm going to put Grady down for a nap. Can I put him in Noah's room?"

Madison nods, her stare locked on mine.

"I was talking to my daughter, Ridley, and this has nothing to do with you," Jenna says, drinking her wine and watching Nathalie leave the room.

"Mom, come on. Don't act like this today," Madison begs, shoulders hunching and looking like she's about ready to burst into tears.

I can't imagine how Madison has dealt with this woman for as long as she has and I swore when we got married, I'd never standby and let her treat Madison badly.

I step toward Madison, though that might be a bad idea because I'm within distance of her smacking me now. "I won't stay out of it. This is my goddamn house, that wine you're drinking, I bought and Madison is…" I pause, my hesitation noticed by Madison. "My *wife*."

Do you notice the emphasis I put on wife?

Madison does.

"Yeah, and we'll see how much longer that lasts," Jenna has the nerve to say.

What happens when oxygen combines with a flammable vapor?

Well, nothing at first. But add a source of spark and you've got yourself a fire.

I feel like a fire right now. A raging fucking inferno.

"Get out." I slam my fist down on the counter. "Get the fuck out now before I throw you out." She doesn't move. "I mean it, get the fuck out!" I point toward the door in an aggravated jab.

"Ridley…." Madison sighs, she's not telling me to stop, but she's also not defending her mother.

Jenna looks offended. "Is that how you feel, Madison?"

Madison nods, swallowing hard. "I think you should leave. This is my son's birthday party and I won't have you treating me or Ridley like this."

Jenna sets down her glass of wine and walks away without another word, leaving behind a stench in the air.

That's when Madison starts crying.

I reach for her, kissing her forehead and she lets me, her head on my chest. "I'm sorry," I say, drawing her eyes to mine.

She sniffs, brushing away tears. "You don't have anything to be sorry about."

I nod, though I'm not convinced. I'm sure I have a lot to be sorry about.

My gaze moves from her mouth to her eyes. "I'm sorry because you don't deserve that. I know it was embarrassing for you."

She cries a little harder, the emotion of what just happened, and maybe what's happening between us, taking over.

I wrap both my arms around her. "Madison…." I let out a heavy sigh, wishing the worry would go with it, my lips pressing to her temple. I can be fifty feet tall and will still be brought to my knees anytime Madison needs me. "Don't let her win. Be stronger than her."

I can honestly say despite what's happening around us, Madison wants me holding her as she sinks into my arms. "Thank you."

"Did you tell your mom you filed for divorce?"

"No. I didn't," Madison says, moving around our bedroom in her nightgown. "I haven't really told anyone."

"Except for Nathalie," I point out, opening my laptop as I sit on the bed. Both Callan and Noah are asleep, leaving us alone for the first time tonight since Madison's mother left. We intended on making Callan's birthday special for him and I think we did that. He fell asleep at six thirty right after eating two pieces of his cake.

Sugar affects him differently than Noah, who basically acts like a spider monkey on crack when sugar hit his lips.

Madison sighs beside me. "Ridley, I don't want to fight with you tonight."

"Fine, I'm sleeping in the bed. The fucking couch is making me sore."

Madison doesn't say anything but moves to the bathroom to put on her anti-wrinkle cream she claims she needs. I don't see it. Madison can basically wear no make-up and not wash her hair for a week and I still see her natural beauty.

I pull up Google and type in: *Visiting Chernobyl.* A webpage pops up immediately and goes on to explain you can visit it.

There's a headline that catches my attention.

Is visiting Chernobyl dangerous? "*Yes, as much as visiting any other place in the world. The level of radiation is high only in some places.*"

Radiation? Jesus.

It goes on to say, "*Those places are avoided during the Chernobyl tour, or the group stays near these places only for a brief amount of time. During the two-day Chernobyl trip in the Chernobyl exclusion zone, the body receives a dose of radiation comparable to 0,001 dose by X-ray scan or to several hours spent in an airplane. In numbers, you will receive 5-7 microsieverts of gamma radiation – an absolutely non harmful dose of radiation. For comparison, most of the nuclear power plants around the world have a safety limit for their employees set at 50-100 microsieverts per day. During a one-day retro tour you will get even less: 2-3 microsieverts of gamma radiation. Most probably you will get more radiation during your flight to Kiev.*"

What in the actual fuck? He wants to go here? What if we turn into the Hulk after going there?

You have to admit, that might be kinda cool.

When Madison returns to the room, I'm itching my junk. Don't tell me you forgot about the waxing incident?

I didn't. It's like a good workout. You feel fine the next day; it's the second day that's hell and you can barely walk or lift your arms above your head. In the case of my balls, they itch to no end. I totally understand why dogs drag their asses on the ground sometimes. I know, gross but still, it itches.

"Can I just say, my balls are itching so bad? How long does this last?"

Madison rolls her eyes and gets into bed beside me. "Not long."

I raise an eyebrow. "Have you ever waxed your balls?"

"I've waxed before." She grabs the book she's been reading from the nightstand. "Stop being such a baby."

I stare at the book, and then her, my eyes moving over her features and the book. "Why did you tell Nathalie?"

"It just sorta of slipped out when she asked what you said about the divorce."

My throat tightens with the word divorce. "And you told her about the divorce?"

She doesn't say anything and stares at her book. "I told you, I don't want to fight tonight."

I can understand why. Today hasn't been easy on her with Jenna showing up, so I let it go for now.

"Ridley, why are you looking up plane tickets to Kiev, Ukraine?" she asks, peeking at my computer.

I shrug. "Callan wants to go there."

Her disapproving expression says it all. "I really don't think that's a good idea."

"Yeah, me either but I said I'd look into it." I look at the price. My God, it's $1300 to fly to Kiev.

"Is that country even safe?"

I laugh. "According to our seven-year-old, who I'm pretty sure is smarter than me, yes."

And then a look of confusion mares her features. "What's Chernobyl?

I raise an eyebrow thankful I'm not the only one. "You don't know?"

"No…."

Now I don't feel so bad. She didn't know either. "It's a nuclear power plant that blew up. Killed something like 200 people."

She's horrified, sitting up straighter in the bed, her book falling to her lap. "And he wants to visit this place?"

"Apparently they started doing tours a few years back."

"How is that safe?"

I point to my laptop. "Well, according to this website, you only receive *minor* doses of gamma radiation.

She rolls her eyes and picks her book up again. "Oh, well if it's minor, have a great time."

"Are you serious?"

I receive a "Have you lost your goddamn mind?" look. "No, Ridley, I'm *not* serious. You're not taking him there."

"Fine." I close my laptop and set it on the nightstand. "But you tell him. I'm not breaking his heart."

She laughs, shaking her head. "Pussy."

I waggle my eyebrows suggestively and place my hand on her inner thigh. "I'd like to see your pussy."

"And you're gross." She slaps my hand away. "Stop it."

There's a look on her face that tells me she's not in the mood and I let it go because I don't want to push her. Not after what her mother pulled today.

No matter how often I was trying to ignore what's happening, her filing for divorce… our problems I've apparently ignored, I can certainly see the darkness creeping in, like smoke spreading and smothering everything in its path the way a fire could.

Take a candle burning for example, and then put a lid on it. The fire goes out pretty quickly. Without oxygen, everything dies. We need it.

Without oxygen, you'll suffocate. Without oxygen, our communication, we were suffocating.

13

KIT THE KNIGHT RIDER

I'm not in the greatest mood Sunday morning. Mostly because nothing is going my way lately and my date with Madison is tonight. I'm scared. Honestly, I am. Do you know how long it's been since I've taken my wife on a date and had to make it perfect?

A while.

Not only that, Callan has a soccer game they moved from yesterday to today. A Sunday. A day I'm trying to get a house at least close to the primer stage before Tuesday afternoon when the compliance inspector will be back.

I go over everything Madison said the other night about me not being around and not helping. My mind is clearly elsewhere as I move outside to the backyard where we're installing an outdoor kitchen.

Pounding nails with a hammer into what will eventually be a pizza oven, my attention is elsewhere.

Brantley comes outside carrying a bag of nails and a caulking gun. "Hey, dude, what's—"

And I turn my head to look at him, but it would have been smart not to. I'm sure you can guess what I did. If not, think about it.

A man driving nails into drywall turns his head and is still hammering.

Finger. Nail. Not friends.

It takes me a minute, maybe from shock and the pure white look on Brantley's face before I understand, let alone feel what I've just done.

And when I do, it's quite possibly the worst pain imaginable as far as I'm concerned. Worse than having your ball skin ripped off.

To make matters worse, I try to move my left hand that has a nail in my index finger. I'm pretty much the dumbest motherfucker alive for doing that.

The next ten minutes are full of a lot of screaming, blood and more screaming as Brantley has to take the nail out of my finger because how else was I going to have it stitched up?

"Dude, it's turning black at the end," Brantley notes, handing me a towel to wrap around it.

Of course I'm in pain, but I'm more pissed than anything because I'm supposed to be at Callan's soccer game in two hours, and this is more than likely going to take more than two hours to fix. Kicking tools and shit out of my way, I mumble, "No fucking shit," to Brantley and nod to my truck. "Can you take me? I might pass out."

And I do, I think, because the next thing I remember I'm in the ER and there's a girl staring at me. "What did you do?"

"Nailed my hand to the wall."

"You're supposed to nail women, not your hand," she says, her cheeks warming with her words.

Is she for fucking real? Probably. I roll my eyes. Ordinarily I'd come back with something equally as snarky but I'm not in the mood today. "That's highly inappropriate."

"Oh stop," she teases, unwrapping the towel from my hand. "We need to get an X-ray to see if you broke the bone and then we'll clean it and get you stitched up."

The next two hours seem to go by so fucking slow. They X-ray it, tell me the bone splintered, but they don't think I'll need surgery. I'm not convinced because I don't trust these inappropriate flirty doctors. Then they clean it—which hurts about as bad as the waxing experience—and then stitch me up.

"Have you ever done stitches?" I ask the girl, the one who was flirting with me earlier, when she digs the needle in and practically hits the bone. "This isn't economics class. Pay attention."

"I've done stitches before." She flips her hand at me, as if to blow me off and then concentrates on my hand. "Stop complaining."

When I'm all stitched up, my hand is bandaged, and I'm given a prescription for antibiotics.

"You need to see an orthopedic surgeon next week to make sure the bone's healing." She hands me my discharge papers. "Try not to nail your hand to any more walls."

I slide down off the table. "Why didn't I think of that?"

Brantley laughs—who's stayed with me this entire time—gets the girl's phone number and then nods to my truck. "You good to drive home?" He gives a tip of his head toward the room I was just in. "I'm gonna see what that chick's doing for the next ten minutes."

I know what you're thinking. Is he for real? Sadly, he's serious. He'll probably bang her in a storage closet and have no shame about it.

Grunting, I practically drag myself out the ER doors. "Don't worry about me, I'll be fine. Try not to feel bad if I wreck my truck."

He shrugs and turns to walk away. "I won't."

He's telling the truth. I own 70 percent of Cooper Custom Homes, hence why my name's on it. If I die, my share goes to the boys but he gets to run the company. Some days I'm surprised he hasn't tried to kill me off yet.

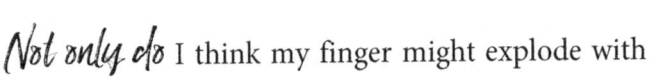

Not only do I think my finger might explode with pain, but I can't believe I'm running late to his first game. It's probably not even his first game and the fact that I don't know that only confirms the fact I'm a shitty dad these days.

Sure, I have a good excuse considering I nearly ripped my finger off, but for some reason, I don't think that's going to be good enough for Madison. It seems like nothing I do is good enough lately, but I'm not going to let that discourage me from my plan. As you know, I'm a pretty dedicated guy and I'm not about to let this stop me.

After parking my truck next to Madison's car, I head over to the fields I remember Callen practicing at but realize there are actually several games going on at the same time.

Shit. What color uniform does Callen wear? Shit. Shit. They all look alike.

Shaking my head at myself, because I really should have planned this better, I walk around looking for anyone I might recognize. It's the third field on the left when I spot Madison standing on the sidelines smiling and cheering the team on, Noah hanging onto her leg with what looks to be grass in his mouth.

I laugh, shaking my head. As crazy as that kid is, his personality will always bring a smile to my face.

As I approach, I'm annoyed at the dress she's wearing today. Do you see this shit Madison's wearing?

Right? Totally inappropriate. It looks like a fucking evening gown.

All right, all right, it's not an evening gown, but this is a kids' soccer game, not Berns Steak House. Cover your fucking tits.

And I'm about to tell her that as I approach, but then I can clearly see her cleavage, and my thoughts move to my hands on said tits and then my mouth and other nasty thoughts I shouldn't have in public because of the sudden tightening in my pants.

No wonder these douche heads were remarking about Madison's tits the other day.

"Why are you late?" is her first question to me.

"Stitches," I say, not expanding on my statement.

"What?"

I hold up my hand. "Stitches. Nearly cut a finger off. Do you care?"

She's just about to say something when the game ends. "Callan will be happy you at least made it."

Do you sense the sarcasm in her voice?

I do.

Madison makes her way over to the cooler where I assume she has the snack for the kids surrounding her. Callan comes over to me, smiling, his hair sticking up in odd directions from the sweat rolling down his temples. "Hey, bud, you looked great out there."

He gives me this blank stare like he's not sure what the fuck I'm talking about. "I didn't do anything, Dad. I just stood there."

"Yeah, but good effort standing there." I feel like a damn idiot now.

Noah hugs Callan, his tiny arms wrapped around his older brother's waist. "Cake."

"Cake?" I mouth at Madison who chuckles, shaking her head at our son.

"I think he's trying to say Callan, but I'm not sure."

Callan unwraps Noah's arms from around him and then hands him his shin guard he's taking off.

"Can you hold this?" Madison asks and then she looks at my hand. "Crap, you're probably not supposed to hold anything, are you?"

Is that concern I sense in her tone? Let's just go ahead and mark a point down for me here because I think it's necessary. She's actually concerned. Look at her! Her eyes are darting from the cooler to me and then to my hand.

Noah hits my hand right then with his, like he's high-fiving me—if punching someone in the hand was high-fiving them. I want to scream in pain, but I don't and smile at him. "Don't do that."

"Why?" He stares up at me.

"Because my hand hurts."

What does he do?

Hits it again.

It's illegal to hit your kids. I know this, but it doesn't stop me from wanting to.

Madison lets out a heavy sigh and picks Noah up so he can't hit me. "Noah, don't hit Daddy's hand. I can see if Kip will move it."

I glare, not intentionally, but it's my natural reaction whenever another man is mentioned. "I got it."

Madison shrugs. "Thanks." And bends down to close the lid before I pick it up.

Check out what happens when she bends down. Yeah, I didn't miss it either. The coach is staring at her tits again. At first I'm thinking, hey, that's okay. They're nice to look at. I get it but looking is as far as it goes. But I don't react that way at all. My blood begins to boil and my heart races. It's like I can't control any of my reactions these days.

Remember when Madison said, and I quote, "Kip warned be you'd react this way"? You didn't really think that little bit of information would slip by a man like me, did you?

Didn't think so.

I have a feeling this douche is Kip.

The guy must feel my burning stare of "you will die if you keep looking at her like that" because he straightens his posture and clears his throat. "Hey, Madison, what did you think of the game?" he asks her, smiling like he's waiting for her to glance his direction.

What did she think of the game? It's a bunch of seven-year-olds chasing a ball around a field until one of them by chance kicks it in the right direction and gets it into the net. What the hell could she think about the game?

To my surprise, Madison smiles and nods enthusiastically. "I thought it was great! The boys are really starting to come around out there. Your great coaching is really paying off."

My stomach twists and suddenly I have that acid reflux crap Brantley's always complaining about after we get tacos from Sonora Taco Shop. You know that feeling where the bile rises in your throat, and you're not sure if the contents of your stomach are coming up or not?

Only mine's not from Mexican food. It's from disgust.

What the fuck did she just say? I give Madison a blank stare, but she's staring at the coach. Did she not just watch the same game I did? I mean, don't get me wrong, the kids seemed to enjoy themselves, but I think they had more fun kicking each other than the ball.

Madison and coach continue to talk about the game, and I'm just standing like some loser sidekick holding a pink cooler full of whatever snack Madison deemed appropriate. Why isn't she introducing me? Does she not think it's important for Mr. Super Soccer Coach to know her incredibly handsome and physically fit husband is right behind her? I have half a mind to drop the cooler on his foot.

He's about my height, wearing shorts and a jersey that match the kids, fairly lean and looks to be about ten years older than me with his blondish-brown hair graying at his temples and the wrinkles around his eyes when he smiles at my wife.

Clearing my throat to bring the attention to myself, I drop the cooler, near his foot but not on it, and take a few steps forward to approach this asshole. Yes, asshole, and before you judge me for judging him before I've even spoken to him, let me remind you this man has been staring at my wife's tits and ass since I got here. I think I've earned the right to call him an asshole. The alternative would be me kicking his sorry ass in front of everyone. Believe me, it's crossed my mind already.

I'm not a complete asshole all the time. Watch. I'll show you just how nice I can be.

I reach out my hand to shake his and introduce myself. "Hey, I'm Ridley, you must be Callan's coach."

It takes a good amount of strength for him to do this, but he moves his eyes from my wife's tits and turns to face me. His eyes tell me to fuck off, but his fake smile attempts to be welcoming. "Ah, yeah, I'm Kip. Ridley, you say?" He shakes my hand and then buries his hands in the pockets of his shorts and smiles at Callan who's standing next to me now, watching our interaction closely. "Are you Callan's uncle?"

Ha. That's funny. Look at him trying to offend me. He knows I'm not Callan's fucking uncle. What a piece of shit. I should pull my son from the team right now. "No, actually I'm Callan's *dad*, you know Madison's husband?"

That's right asshole, I'm the husband.

I smile at my wife and wrap my arm around her, bringing her to my side. I point to Noah who's wearing Callan's shin guards on his forearms now. "He's mine too."

There's a brief moment when he glances at Madison, and then me. Do you see the way his eyes widen as he gives me a quick once-over? He's *judging* me. He's accessing whether I'm a threat to him and he honestly has no clue how miserable I could make his life if he touched my wife.

"Oh, sorry." *Oh, bullshit. You're not sorry.* "It's just… Madison and Callan haven't talked much about you… and when they did, I didn't get the impression you had time for things like your kids soccer game. Didn't mean to offend you, man." He motions to Callan and Madison with a flick of his wrist.

Bullshit he didn't mean to offend me. Look at him. He totally fucking meant it.

I squeeze Madison's shoulder with my hand, the hurt one. Burns like a son of a bitch, but I want her to know how bad that comment hurts.

This guy isn't messing around, is he? First punch and it's an uppercut straight to my jaw. Figuratively. No way in hell would he actually get a physical hit on me I can tell you that right now.

Can't really blame him. He had the opening and he took it. I shoot a look to Madison, whose face looks a bit flushed. She looks away quickly and at least has the decency to look embarrassed. This one is on her. If this guy is telling the truth, my own wife and son don't even feel the need to mention me other than my lack of involvement in the family. Not gonna lie, it stings. What sucks dick is this guy knows she's unhappy.

"I'm sorry but what did you say your name was? Kit?"

Kit Kat narrows his eyes at me and straightens his shoulders to stand a little taller.

You can try and stand tall all day, asshole, I'll still be taller and her husband.

He smiles at me as if to say touché. "Kip. I said my name is *Kip*." He pronounces the p as if I'm illiterate or something.

"Oh, Kip." I pop the P at the end of his name with a laugh. "Okay well, I guess that's okay too. Kit sounds cooler. I'd totally congratulate your parents taste in eighties TV shows."

Madison rolls her eyes and whispers, "Knock it off, Ridley," in my ear.

Kip blinks slowly. Of course he doesn't understand. "What do you mean? What does my name have to do with eighties TV shows?"

Is this guy serious? "Seriously?" I laugh, my arm dropping from around Madison's shoulder to protect my rib cage. I know after what I'm about to say, she's going to elbow me in the ribs. "Kit? *Knight Rider*? David Hasselhoff? Any of that ring a bell for ya?"

Nothing? You could hear grasshoppers mating with the silence I'm getting from this twat wad. Sure enough, Madison elbows me. In the ribs.

I clear my throat and step away from her about a foot. "Kit was the name of the car in the show *Knight Rider* starring David Hasselhoff. Don't tell me you don't know who The Hoff is?"

Still nothing. Honestly, I just feel bad for the guy. Who doesn't know about *Knight Rider*? Either way, Kip or Kit, asshole name, asshole guy. That's my assessment and you usually only get one with me.

First impressions are lasting impressions.

As if he's dismissing me, Kip turns back to Madison and resumes their conversation like I'm not even here. "So are you and the boys still up for pizza for lunch?"

Is this guy serious? Did he just ask my wife out on a date in front of me?

Madison must sense my anger starting to build because she pauses and looks over to me with sympathetic eyes. "Every Saturday after the game Kip and his son, Aldon… we all go out for lunch so the boys can play. It's kind of a tradition." And then she adds, after seeing the look on my face, "It's not just us. Sometimes other people go."

Uh huh. Do you believe her? I certainly don't.

Tradition? She has a tradition with another man? That feels like cheating. It screams cheating. It's not like I have a tradition with Kennedy to take her to lunch every Tuesday. I buy her lunch like once a month—Like as I buy it and she eats at her desk, and I eat in my office. We don't converse over a meal. We don't have actual fucking dates. Tradition means it's happened more than once and more than once is *way too many*.

Tradition huh?

Well, I hope you don't mind my joining in on your little *tradition.*

Kip glances my way, and I take this moment to really look at the guy. "It's no problem. You're welcome to join us."

I'm welcome? Did you hear that? I should feel all warm and fuzzy inside because Kitty invited me to pizza. What a fuck face. Why is it I get the feeling this jerk is trying to make me feel like the third wheel with my own family?

Callan taps me on the arm. "You're coming to pizza, right, Dad?" And then he notices my hand. "Why were you late? I was afraid you weren't coming to the game."

I look down into my son's eyes and see excitement, but also caution there. He really thought there was a chance I wouldn't show up at his game. Even after I told him I would and I'm not sure what makes me feel worse, the fact that some asshole is hitting on my wife right in front of me, or that my kid actually has reason to doubt my word.

I kneel. "Sorry I was late. I had a bit of an accident." I hold up my bandaged hand.

His eyes grow wide, and I can tell he's worried about what happened. "Are you okay? What happened? Maybe we should skip pizza?" His eyes dart from me to Madison, and then back and the expression on his face morphs from concern to what almost looks like hope. I'm getting the impression that Callen isn't as excited about the Saturday lunch tradition as Kipper is.

Noah takes that moment to jump on my back, his arms tight around my neck. "Daddy owie."

My proud stare moves to Kip. *That's right, my boys love me.*

Trying to loosen Noah's grip on my neck, I smile at Callan. "Don't worry, I'm okay. Just had to go to the ER and get some stitches. I'll be as good as new in no time." Standing, I keep Noah on my back and hold onto his legs. "We can go to pizza if you want."

"Um." Callan shrugs, making a face I know. It's pretty similar to the one he wears when he's playing soccer, but I can't tell what it is. Is he upset? "Okay. As long as you're sure because if you're in pain or anything, we can totally go home now."

Yup. There it is. My son wants nothing to do with this lunch, but unfortunately for him, his selfish father needs to ride this one out.

"Yeah, I'm sure. We'll just grab something quick and head home, sound good?"

"Sure." Callan looks behind him at who I can only guess is Kip's kid. I say this because he's got the same blond hair and same stupid look on his face as his father. I feel bad saying that about a child but hey, his dad is a prick. I'm sure the apple doesn't fall far from the tree. The only difference is that this kid is looking at my kid like he's some bug he wants to stomp on with his shoe.

"You guys ready to head out?" I turn back to Madison and plaster a big smile wrapping one arm around her but keeping Noah on my back, just to remind Knight Rider who Madison's husband is. "Why don't you lead the way, Kit?"

He shakes his head and leans down to pick up his bag and clipboard. "Kip. My name is Kip."

I grin. "Yeah, I know."

Madison shakes her head. "Cute, Ridley. Real cute."

I kiss her check only to have her smile. "I can't help it if he needs to know you still belong to me."

She takes Callan by the hand and whispers, "Why don't you just piss on my leg while you're at it to mark your territory."

"We'll save that for later." I wink. "Wouldn't want to offend him with the size of my—"

She immediately let's go of Callan's hand and slaps her hand across my mouth. "Don't you dare say that in front of him." She gives a nod to Noah. "Last time you said asshole in front of him, he went around saying it for two weeks to *everyone* we saw. Including my mother."

"Yeah, well, there's certainly some truth there." I laugh.

Do you see I'm the only one laughing at that remark? Even Callan's staring at me with a confused expression.

I almost forgot about Noah saying asshole for two weeks. It was as if he was that cat from Talking Tom and only knew one word. We'd ask him what he wanted for breakfast in the morning, and he'd scream, "Asshole," like he was so proud of himself.

Right then Noah remembers his favorite word and laughs, his head on my shoulder and screams. "Asshole!" in my ear.

Have you ever had your toddler yell in your ear? It fucking hurts. I think he ruptured my eardrum. Again.

Anyway, Noah screaming isn't the worst part. The real cake topper here is all the parents shuffling their kids through the parking lot staring at us.

"Great," Madison mumbles, walking faster to the car.

Callan shakes his head. "We can't take him anywhere."

I'm assuming he's talking about Noah, but there's a strong possibility he's throwing me in the mix too.

I leave my truck at the fields and ride over with Madison to the restaurant. As we pull up to the restaurant, I notice it's the same one as what's on the back of Callan's jersey. "Does this pizza place sponsor Callan's team?"

Madison reaches for her purse on the floor of the car. "Yeah, actually Kip owns it."

Oh well, isn't that convenient?

I make a mental note to start sponsoring all of Callan's extracurricular activities from now on. Two can play at that game.

Getting Noah out of his car seat is about as much fun as getting him in. I wish he'd make up his damn mind. He fights when you put him in, so much so that I've had to actually sit on him while Madison locks his belt, but then when you go to take him out, he tries to bite you when you go to unbuckle the damn belt. I swear this kid has to have more than one voice talking in his head.

"Can I get you out?" I ask, slowly reaching for buckle between his legs. "We're gonna eat lunch. You like pizza right?

Noah nods, but there's a look in his eye as I reach for his shoulder straps that tells me the little shit isn't going to let me off all that easy.

With my right hand, I move toward him, and he immediately tries to bite me.

"Dude! Seriously? What is your problem today?" I ask, expecting an answer.

I stand there waiting for an answer like it's really going to make any sense. All I'm given is, "Grr! I'm Wolverine!"

Oh Jesus, not this again.

"All right, buddy, you're Wolverine but let me give you a little hint, Wolverine doesn't bite people he has claws in his hands, and he stabs them."

Noah's eyes grow wide like I just shared with him the most amazing fact known to man.

"Ridley!" Madison scolds me from behind, slapping my back. "What the hell? Do you really think it's a good idea to tell him it's not okay to bite but stabbing is just fine?"

My first instinct is to defend myself. I want to tell her if she thinks it was such a bad idea then why doesn't she come over here and try to get Cujo out of his damn car seat. But when I give it a minute and look back down at Noah who's staring at his hands like he's contemplating how to attach knives to them, I can see her point.

I take a stance of authority. You know the one where you stand tall and cross your arms over your chest like that's going to make any toddler listen to you more attentively. "Listen, bud, bottom line, we don't bite and we don't stab or run over them with our big wheels." I had to throw that one in there. "And while we're at it, we don't hit Daddy's bad hand."

For a second I think I've got him but then my moment of triumph is smashed by his loud giggles. "Daddy funny!"

Callan crawls over to Noah and unlatches the belt while I have his attention. I throw him an appreciative grin. "Thanks, big man."

The smile that crosses his face makes my heart burst. "No problem, Dad. We make a good team."

Reaching forward, I ruffle his hair and return the smile sticking my hand out for a high-five. "Yeah, we do. Now let's get inside. We wouldn't want to keep Kit waiting."

Callan laughs, but Madison throws me a glare. It's a warning, but she should know better. There's no way I'm gonna back off this guy until it's made perfectly clear this is my family.

When we walk in the door, I realize while the front gives the impression the restaurant is small, once you enter, it's actually pretty impressive for a pizza place.

Kips calls us over to a larger section of tables that's ready and waiting for us. "Hey, I thought maybe you guys got lost."

"No, sorry. Noah can be a handful sometimes," Madison says, sitting down in the chair I pull out.

I glare at Kip. That's right asswipe, I'm a gentleman. She wants to divorce me but still, I can treat her like a fucking lady.

Sitting down next to Madison and Noah, Callan sits across from us next to Kip's son.

Watching Kip talk to my wife, I need a minute to decide my course of action. On the one hand, I can lunge across this table and beat the living shit out of him while taking notes from Noah and yelling, "I am Wolverine."

Or I could take the mature route and *verbally* beat the shit out of the pussy-named bastard.

Normally option one would be the most appealing, but because of the stitches currently residing in my hand, I can't imagine it would feel all that appealing in the aftermath.

Option two it is.

"So, Kit," I begin.

"It's Kip. With a p on the end. Not Kit."

"Yeah, right. I'm not good with names. I was wondering is there a Mrs. Kip?"

I'm thinking the question is innocent enough, but it earns me a narrowed-eye glare from Kip and a pretty forceful elbow from Madison.

Ah, I've touch on a sore subject. Score one for me.

"Sara and I are newly divorced."

Divorced? I mentally laugh and can't help but wonder if maybe his ex-wife left his ass so she could find a man with a manly name like Stone or Colt or even better… Ridley.

"So, Ridley, why is it this is the first game we've seen you at?"

God, he's a dick.

You know what thought keeps crossing my mind? Not only is he a dick, but I'd like to pull my dick out right now and slap it right on his forehead. Maybe then he'd shut the fuck up.

"I own a custom home building business, and it keeps me really busy. Seven days a week is my usual work week."

Kip stares at me like I'm crazy. "Yeah, but I can't imagine you couldn't get a little time away once a week to come and watch your son play? Right? I mean if it was important to you, wouldn't you just make the time?"

I want to jab his eyeballs out.

I sit there for what seems like forever but is probably just a few seconds completely stunned by what this asshole just said. Is he really calling me out right here in front of my wife and kids? Of course he is. He knows this is a competition and he's decided to play to win.

I cross my arms over my chest and shake my head in disbelief. Did this tool talk my wife into a divorce?

Madison won't even look at me. "Yeah well, I can see how someone like yourself would think that," I say with a good amount of sarcasm laced in my voice, "but when I say I *own* a custom home building company, I mean I build custom homes myself. From the ground up. The entire process. I don't have a bunch of guys working for me doing all the work. It's me and my partner putting out a product we take a lot of pride in. I love what I do, but yeah, sometimes it takes me away from my family whether I want that or not." I stare at Madison as she looks over at me finally. "There's nothing more important to me than my family and because of that, I will do anything to make sure they're taken care of even if it means sacrificing my time."

Take that, fuck face.

Kip shakes his head and stares at me with a smirk on his face. "Yeah, but it's not just your time you're sacrificing, is it? I mean sure, you're putting in a lot of hours but in the end, isn't the family you say you're working so hard for the ones you're actually sacrificing?"

"Kip," Madison growls, shocked by what he's saying. "That's enough!"

Can I knock his teeth in yet? Come on, you're thinking it too, aren't you?

"Listen, you piece of—" I go to stand because option one just came back into play when Madison grabs my forearm and squeezes to get my attention. I glance over and see her pleading eyes locked on mine. She's silently begging me not to do something that will cause a scene. And then her eyes dart to the kids, and Callan's stare locked on me. I relax beside her.

She's right. I can't make a scene in front of him despite me desperately wanting to.

Just then two young girls show up at our table carrying two large pizzas and breadsticks. I never understood the need for breadsticks when you order pizza. Isn't the crust basically a bread stick? Just seems like overkill to me. Anyway, I decide to let this shit go for the moment and try to enjoy the free food because if asshole thinks I'm paying for this shit, he's fucking delusional.

Glancing around the restaurant, I notice it's nice. As much as I don't want to admit it, Kip has a pretty good thing going here. All the tables are filled and the customers look happy.

Well, all but one. When I look over to Callan, he's just staring down at his pizza picking at it like it's some sort of science experiment. This wouldn't bother me so much if one, pizza wasn't one of his favorite foods and two, I can see Kip's son beside him elbowing him like he's trying to get him to do something he doesn't want to do. This is also the friend of the kid who kicked his magazine out of his hand on Tuesday. He probably thinks I don't remember that, but I do.

"Hey, bud." I tap my knuckles to the table to get Callan's attention. "Is everything okay with your pizza?"

"Um, yeah." He pushes his plate away from him. "I'm not hungry."

Madison turns to face Callan. "Are you feeling okay, honey? Pizza is usually your favorite."

Callan turns a little red with embarrassment from his mom babying him and nods. "I'm fine. Can I go play the video games?"

I reach inside my pocket for quarters. "Yeah, here's some money."

Callan takes off, and the kid jumps up to go with him when my leg has a cramp. I straighten it out and send Kip Jr. straight to the floor.

"Easy there, buddy," I say, helping him up. See? Nice guy sometimes. "You gotta watch where you're walking."

The kid glares a look similar to his father because he knows I tripped him, but nobody else in this place does.

Madison jumps up from her chair and starts looking around frantically.

Grabbing her hand to get her attention, I look up at her, "What's the matter?

"Noah. He's gone. He was right here and now he's gone."

I know what you're thinking. We're in a restaurant; there's only one entrance, and he's only three so he couldn't get too far, but that's where you're wrong.

Noah's a fucking ninja.

I'm not even kidding. It's like he's an escape savant.

Ten minutes later we find him with another family eating pizza with them.

"We weren't sure what to do, so we gave him a slice of pizza," they say, handing Wolverine and his pizza back to us.

I look at him, and then the nice couple and back to Noah in my arms. "You're so weird."

I'm not sure what's weirder, them feeding him or Noah being completely comfortable with another family.

"I like them," he says as I take him back to our table and hand him to Madison.

"Where was he?" she asks, checking him out and looking for scratches.

"With another family. Turns out, he wants a new family too."

Okay, not my best line but damn it, Kit pissed me off.

"God, you can be such an asshole sometimes!" Madison says when we're outside, keeping her voice down so the boys can't hear us.

I hit a nerve, didn't I?

"I'm just curious here." I lean back against her car, my arms crossed over my chest. "When you said, and quote me here because I remember the words exactly, Kip said you'd react this way… what exactly were you referring to?"

"I just talked to him about it briefly," she admits, her words shaking when she sees how pissed off I am about this.

Have you ever seen those movies where they stick an unsuspecting person in with a bull, and they have to try and escape with their lives?

That's what today felt like. Gang up on Ridley because he works all the time. Well, fuck that. "So what, you complain to him about me and how fucking awful your life is? Does he let you cry on his shoulder so you'll spread your legs for him?"

"Screw you, Ridley." And then she starts to walk away from me.

I grab her by the arm. "No, really, I'm curious. Is that what this is? He's your shoulder to cry on when I'm not around which evidently is never?"

"No, it's not like that. But if we're being honest, he does listen to me, which is more than I can say for you. All you do is work and sleep."

"Not true," I say, wanting to kick the side of her car like a child trying to get his point across. "This week I've watched a toddler kill a cat, had my balls skinned, chased four mice, put a goddamn nail through my hand because I wasn't paying attention and this just in, chastised in front of my family for trying to provide for them. Pretty sure I've done more than work and sleep. In fact, not much work has been done because I'm constantly trying to make you love me."

When I glance up, her face hardens, a flood of anger flushing her cheeks. I want to take back what I said, but then again, I spoke the truth. Maybe a little harsher than I needed.

I've heard people say divorce is ugly. I've heard them say it gets really bad before you come to an agreement. Is this the ugly? Us blaming and accusing and avoiding the real issues to place the blame on anyone but ourselves. Squeezing her eyes shut, she manages to keep her voice even when she says, "Just because you suddenly decided you care, doesn't mean shit. I'm not going to apologize for him looking out for me. You're the one who's never around, and I'm forced to go to these games and do all of this myself."

"You keep saying that, but you're forgetting why I've done all this. I work this hard for you and the boys, so you can have nice things and drive around town in an eighty-thousand-dollar SUV," I spit out through gritted teeth, moving away from her.

I know what you're thinking. I'm an asshole. Please for the love of God see that it's not just me here though.

There is a pang of guilt that hits me because I don't want to say these things to her. I don't. But I am, and part of me doesn't know why.

Am I finally seeing what I've been missing all along?

14

ONE STEP BACK

Two weeks go by. Two fucking weeks and Madison still won't talk to me after our lunch with Kip. Which I think is completely fucking ridiculous because I was only defending myself.

Put yourself in my position here. Did I act like an asshole?

If you said yes, piss off.

I can't say Madison and I don't talk because there's discussion about the kids, but nothing about us. And I'm sleeping on the couch again.

It's awful, the sleeping on the couch, and while I can see where I *may* have overreacted the other day, I'm down to something like forty days before this nightmare is final and it's game time.

"Hey, you never told me what happened on your date?"

"What date? After meeting Kip, she told me she didn't want to go on a date with me."

Brantley snorts. "What kind of name is Kip?" This is why we're friends. And then he adds, confirming why he's my best friend, "It'd be cooler if his name was Kit."

"I'm dying here, man," I tell Brantley as we look through paperwork on Friday morning in the office. We're searching for a permit Kennedy had in here and guess what? She's late. You know my feelings about people being late. "I need some ideas, fast."

"You have plenty of time."

"No, I don't. I have like four weeks left. This calls for drastic measures."

Brantley's deep in thought for about five minutes and then grins. I'm not sure I like this grin. Look at him. He looks like the Joker. "Couples therapy."

"What?"

"You know… they have that hotel up in Sedona? The resort that specializes in couple's therapy. Haven't you seen their commercials on TV?"

"Apparently we watch different shows."

"The resort looks fucking amazing if you ask me, but they do like couples counseling or some shit like that where they help you remember why you fell in love. Maybe take her there."

He has a point. A good one. Since my date night didn't work, maybe this would? If I could get her away from everything and everyone, there's a chance.

The door to our office opens, and Kennedy finally walks in around nine that morning when she starts at eight. I'm just about to demand she tell me why she's late when I notice her appearance.

Remember when you were little and you'd ride your bike with no shoes and your toes looked like you grated them?

Well, if you didn't do that, good for you, but picture doing that and your toes would look similar to Kennedy's chin, elbows, and knees. Or my balls after having them waxed. I assure you it's similar. Just believe me.

I focus on Kennedy and what she's wearing. Why she wore a dress looking like this is beyond me.

"Jesus, what happened to you?"

She whines and gingerly sits done as if moving around hurts. "Well, you know that boyfriend I have?"

I raise an eyebrow. "Jason?"

"No. His name is Jacob."

Clearly you know by now, I'm not good with names. Anyway, focus, Kennedy is telling us something.

"That piece of shit." Digging inside her purse, she pulls out an Elsa Band-Aid and sticks it to her knee. "Well apparently, he has a drug problem, which if we're being honest, I knew about." Both Brantley and I nod because we met this dude once and if you've ever seen someone high on meth, it's easy to spot. "Anyhow"—Kennedy shakes her head and sits down, staring at her skinned elbows—"we were out on a date last night, right? And he gets pulled over. So what does he do? He pushes me out of the car while it's moving and then leads the police on a car chase down I-10. I'm surprised you didn't hear about it."

Brantley laughs, shaking his head. "Oh, I heard about it. It was on the news this morning. I just didn't realize it was *you* who tuck and rolled off the interstate."

"Yes, it was me. And I clearly didn't tuck. I rolled, but tucking escaped me."

I blink, trying to process what she said. And here Madison thinks she has it bad. At least I didn't throw her from a moving car. I thought about it a time or two, but I wouldn't actually do it. "What an asshole," I say, trying to be a compassionate boss. It's really hard, but I do care that she's still alive. Finding good office staff is a lot harder than you think.

Kennedy reaches for an ice pack she brought with her, propping her legs up on her desk. Did I mention she's wearing a dress? I turn my head but Brantley, he doesn't. Are you surprised?

Me either.

"In his defense, it was actually pretty nice of him to throw me out of the car," Kennedy says, "when you think about it. If I had stayed, I would have been an accessory or some shit like that."

I'm more focused on the fact that she was fifty minutes late. I don't do late, remember? "Is that why you were late?"

"Well no, I slept in, but I was up a little late."

This kind of pisses me off and she knows it. "Oh, stop, I'm kidding. I didn't oversleep. I had to stop by the police station and they weren't open until eight." She motions to my phone. "I sent you a text message."

She did? I hadn't even realized my phone was in my office, plus I hadn't checked it since leaving the house.

"What were you guys talking about when I came in?" Kennedy asks, motioning between us.

"Nothing." I push a stack of paper toward her. "Can you find the permits for the Peterson house? You lost them."

"I did not. They're on your desk," she grumbles, standing up and limping toward the coffee pot. "They're probably next to your cell phone you don't check."

I still might look for a new office manager. This one's getting lippy.

"Ridley's taking his wife to couples counseling," Brantley says, ratting me out.

What a fuck face. So much for him keeping secrets. I guess they only apply to his life.

Up until now, I hadn't told Kennedy about Madison filing for divorce, though I'm sure she's come to some assumptions lately.

"That's sweet. At least you try. I just want to date a guy who has a job and doesn't use my rent money to buy crack."

I look back at her over my shoulder as I head to my office. "You really need to break up with that guy."

I find the permits on my desk where she said they were next to my phone. No missed calls from Madison, like I was hoping there would be, but Kennedy's right. She sent me a message saying she'd be late.

I guess I'll let her lateness slide this one time.

"Why are you wearing a dress today when you look like that?" I ask, handing the permits to Brantley so we can place the order for the flooring.

"Going to my sister's wedding tonight." And then she holds up two lipsticks. "What shade of lipstick clearly states, I'm only attending this wedding for the drugs and the best man?"

I laugh and point to the hot pink lipstick. "I take it you're not close with your sister?"

"Fuck no. She's a whore."

Brantley perks up. "Like *really* a whore?"

"No, not really, B." She points in his face. "Stay away from her. She's getting married. Pretty sure she's only sucked one cock her entire life. And that's just sad. But anyway, you stay far away from her wedding." And then she looks at me. "I just don't like her. She used to steal my Barbies."

I know why I hired Kennedy. We're a lot alike.

Since Madison hasn't kicked me out entirely—just to the couch—when I get home from work that night, I don't bother telling her I've already booked our trip for tonight and arranged for Brantley to watch the boys. He'll be here in an hour.

I know what you're thinking. One, how could you book it without talking to her, and two, why in the fuck would you have Brantley watch your kids?

He's actually great with kids as long as women aren't around.

"You look amazing today," I say when I see Madison in the kitchen cutting up chicken nuggets for the boys.

Gag me. Just fucking wrap a noose around my neck at this point. Who is this guy? I'd like to punch myself and ask if I'm getting my balls back for Christmas.

"Shut up," she mumbles, looking out to the backyard where the boys are playing with each other. Noah's on the swings while Callan has a book in one hand and he's pushing him with the other. At least they're playing together.

"How about we go away for the weekend?" I push the brochure toward her, sliding it across the granite countertop between us.

Madison glances down at the brochure and then back to me. "What's this?"

"A resort. We can get away and remember why we fell in love."

She rolls her eyes and throws it in the garbage. "No."

Do you see my heart in there with it? It's buried at the bottom where she keeps kicking it aside.

Where's that noose again? Listen to me! I sound pathetic.

"Come on." I grab her hand and pull her toward me, trapping her against the counter and my body. "I told you I was sorry about the other day. I *am*." Her eyes search mine and I'm confident all she sees is honesty from me. "I was just caught off guard and didn't know how to react. And I'm man enough to admit I reacted horribly."

"You think?"

"You have to admit Kip was an asshole."

She nods. "He was. You didn't deserve that."

I lean in a little more, but I don't kiss her despite desperately wanting to. "If you have any ounce of love left for me, you'll come with me, and we'll try."

"I don't know...."

She didn't say she didn't have an ounce of love left, so there's some hope, right?

And then she draws in a weighted breath and lets it out with a sigh. "When?"

Score! Finally, a fucking break.

"We leave in an hour."

Her eyes widen. "We can't. Callan has soccer tomorrow."

"I can skip it," he says from behind us. "I want you guys to stay married."

A constricting weight hits my chest, my shoulders feeling about the same. Madison and I stare at one another. We should have known he'd notice what was happening between us at some point. The argument beside the car was most certainly heard by him.

Noah appears at the door and hits Callan's hand. "Push me!"

He rolls his eyes. "I'll be right there. Hold on." And then he glances back at us. "Please go. I don't want you to get a divorce."

I picture myself at his age, begging my dad to stay, only he didn't. He untied my hands from the grip I had on his arm and walked out of my life when I was six. We have a relationship now, but that's a lasting memory I will never forget.

Madison kneels and pushes Callan's hair from his face, her hands cradling his cheeks. "Oh honey, we will. We're making every effort to fix this."

I want to snort and say, "Really, are you, Madison?" But I don't because I'm a step ahead and that will only make things worse.

"Uncle B will be here any minute," I tell him, my hands buried in my pocket.

Madison shoots me a glare and stands up when Callan smiles. "Yay!" Then he takes off, running to the backyard to push Wolverine.

"You can't be serious? You're having Brantley watch them?"

"What? It can't be any worse than the Queen of Hearts lady."

"You're unbelievable." And then she pushes past me. "I'm going to pack."

"Pack less underwear. You won't need them."

She snorts, but there's some amusement to it. "Uh-huh."

15

DISTRACTIONS

"It's beautiful out here," Madison says, staring up at the sky through the sunroof in my truck.

The night's fallen around us. The sky that was once painted with hues of red, orange, and pink around the canyons has faded leaving a matte-black canvas and tiny specs of light.

The burnt-orange canyons still visible in the distance from where we're parked, a reminder of how absolutely breathtaking this state is when you get outside the city.

I stare at her, memories flashing in my eyes of a time when this was easy. Her thoughts soften her hardened expression and she smiles, just a little bit, but I can't ignore it. It's in the darkness we exist, here, alone.

"*Please*, don't ignore me anymore." My hand rests on her knee, gripping it enough for her to know what kind of want I'm implying here. "I don't care about anything else right now. Just give me something." My hungry lips seek hers, desperate, needing, giving in.

I'm not sure, but I think she's taken back by my sudden need. And for a moment, I lose myself in the desire to have her, right now, right this second in my truck.

And then she's kissing me back, and I feel like I've fucking won the lottery, her warm hands move over my shoulders as she fights to get her seat belt loose.

In the heat of the moment I assume, I grab her hand and drag her onto my lap. It's not easy, but I do it and then reach for the door handle.

"What are you doing?" she asks, excitement in her voice and eyes.

"What I should have done weeks ago."

Once I have the door open, I carry her around to the back of my truck and open the tailgate to set her on it.

She breathes in heavily, but she's still smiling as I rip my shirt over my head and onto the ground. It's right now in this second I see her moment of weakness, and I know her desire's controlling her next movements.

I can't take it any longer, the violent rise and fall of my chest drawing her stare lower. She sees how desperate I am.

"What are you doing? We're in the middle of nowhere." Her hands that were once beside her move to my chest, pushing back.

I draw back, eyes wild and reckless, everything she's making me feel lately. "Don't think. Just be here."

I reach for her hips and slide her to the edge of the tailgate, my hands moving up her dress to the edge of her panties. "Stop backing away from me," I growl, coming forward again, a soft rumble in my chest as it presses into hers. My head hits her shoulder. "I don't like being denied something for so long," I tell her, turning my head, my lips at her ear, breath cool compared to the heat around us. "It only makes me want you more."

"Ridley." She pushes back against my chest again, her palms flat, but she's not pushing me away.

"Don't tell me to stop." My hand raises to touch the side of her face, my weight pressing forward in an attempt to make contact with her again. My right thumb slides over her lips. "You know you want me too."

"I just don't think we should be doing this out here. We don't even know where we are."

I shake my head, refusing to acknowledge her denial. "Who cares? Be in the moment."

"Stop." She pushes back away from me, sliding further back in my truck bed. "Not right now."

"You're saying no?" I raise an eyebrow, and she nods. "Should I remind you how good it is with me before you say no? Remind you of how good it always is between us?"

My eyes fall to her legs, watching my tentative touch move higher. Climbing in the bed of the truck with her, I remove my hands from her to my shorts. Lazy lidded, I undo them. I'll stop if she really wants me to. I'm certainly not that guy, but look at her right now. Those beautiful begging blue eyes are telling me another story. She's pleading for me to take her in the bed of my truck, in the middle of nowhere because I can't fucking stand it anymore.

She blinks and it's as if memories of us are flashing in her eyes.

Do you see the way she's giving in? It's in the way she's watching me. At least I see it.

"Please...," I beg. "I can't stop thinking about how much I want you and this dress...." I shake my head, drawing a whistled breath between my teeth. "I *need* you."

I know this doesn't fix anything, and it's just sex, but you can't blame me for trying because when you think about it, before the whole Kip drama, sex got her at least talking to me.

I don't give her a chance to utter her denial. Instead I lean in, kissing her with hungry lips, seeking her warm ones. My tongue strokes her lips before pulling it inside my mouth harshly.

Sighing, I draw back, mouth lingering over the top of hers. "Why do you torture me? Why is this so fucking hard?"

Her body trembles as my fingers weave into her hair, grasping a handful and pulling as her mouth covers mine. Pressing forward, I lie on top of her.

"I don't mean to torture you," she answers breathlessly, watchful of my reaction.

She kisses me back right then. Gripping my neck, her hands fist in my hair tighter.

I moan quietly as our tongues meet and pin her to the bed of the truck with my hips, so strong and forceful she'll know just how much I want her to fulfill this burning ache I have deep within to have her this way.

Shaking with a subtle tremor, her body curves, bending around mine as she spreads her legs wider. My mouth moves hastily from her ear to her neck and down her collarbone, before returning to her mouth.

With lust-stricken eyes, I move back far enough to get my shorts undone and her panties removed.

Madison's hands slide from my hair to my shoulders, brushing up over my arms and grabbing my biceps, feeling them flex and tighten beneath her grasp as I move forward and press my weight into her again.

"Tell me you don't want this, and I'll stop."

I know she's not going to deny me. I see it written on her face, but I'm curious what she's going to do.

"I don't want you to stop," she breathes. "I *want you*, Ridley."

Did you see the emphasis she put on those words?

I certainly did.

Without breaking the kiss, my mouth is back to her neck when my hips move against hers. There's no denying what's going on when my hips drag over hers.

And then she angles her hips, making more direct, persistent contact with mine.

I make some kind of noise close to her ear, somewhere between a gasp and a groan, as my body answers her reactions. "I can't wait any longer," I tell her, moving my hips once more.

Supporting my weight against the bed by propping myself up on the one hand, my left-hand moves to her breasts, massaging them with need and desire. My hips push against hers again, savoring the feeling. The sensation, a reminder, jolts through my body like a spark.

Pressing my lips to hers, I stare down at her and wink, but say nothing as I reach between us to position myself at her wet entrance.

Her cheeks flush in the night as I push forward, words rushing from my lips. "Oh God, baby… fuck, that's so good."

Madison tosses her head back against the bed, her hands still firmly on my shoulders as I pound into her with need.

I know what you're thinking. You're having sex right now? Isn't that just covering your problems with sex?

Yes, it is, and as you can see, Madison and I are good at that.

Women? Here's the thing. Men can be pissed at you, screaming at the top of their lungs mad, but if you drop to your knees and give us head, we're gonna let you. And then when you swallow, we'll go back to arguing with you. See how I added the swallow part? I'm just being honest.

Does it matter if you swallow?

Let me put it to you this way. Let's say you're having sex with your man and he finds just the right spot to get you off but then just before you come, he moves. What would you do?

Madison would straight up punch me in the face and tell me to get back to work.

My point is, if you're going to go through all the work to give your man a blow job, finish the job. Don't be a quitter or a spitter.

Anyway, my point is we don't think of sex in the same way you do. We just want it whenever you're willing to give it up.

"Faster," Madison moans, drawing me from my thoughts.

"You're not going to be able to walk tomorrow," I growl against her skin.

"Oh God," she whispers, a slow shake of her head like she can't believe we're doing this, but she also doesn't have the strength to stop me because she wants it just as bad. I'll take anything I can get at this point, so I don't stop, and I'm intent on showing her just how badly she needs me by knowing I'm the only one who can make her feel like this.

"Say it, Madison," I beg, my breathing heavy as my hands wrap tightly around her hair, tugging so her head angles toward me, eyes locking when I press all of my weight into her. "Tell me you want me too. Tell me you're mine." I pause, swallowing with a regretful shake of my head. I'm not sure what I'll do if she says she's not.

Sometimes you have to ask for something you want, and I'm fixated on making her do just that because if she does, there's hope. This isn't all a waste of time. Madison never says what she really means but if I can see her eyes, I know when she's telling the truth.

She stares back at me, blues glowing in the night. "I'm yours...."

And there's the truth. Look at her. Do you see it? There's not a chance in hell she's lying to me. She may not be willing to make it work, but there's no denying this woman is mine.

"Oh God, Madison...." Her name is my weakness, spoken like a prayer against her lips as if I'm giving everything I have for her to love me enough to stay.

Her eyes snap shut when I slam into her again, filling her, over and over again. I want to slow it down, but I know we can't, and I won't. Her moans of pleasure mix with my grunts of need.

It's quick—give me a break—it's been weeks, and my body shakes as I let go, strangled words falling from my lips, my head thrown back.

When my body stops shaking, I wonder what she's going to say to me next. It could be anything.

She stares at me, her hand drifting up to run her fingertips along the edge of my jaw. I'm dying to see warmth and connection in her face, and I do, but fear and sadness are there too. She's so beautiful in this light, the moon shining down on her face outlining her perfectly defined cheek bones and that cute nose I love to kiss.

Her lids fall shut, tears rolling down her temples but she brings our lips together.

I kiss her back, trying to understand the tears and sadness because I thought she enjoyed that. Didn't she? Normally you don't cry after sex unless you're a virgin.

Did it hurt?

I stare down at her, trying to figure out what she's thinking. Under that sadness—the vulnerability and the emotion—there's something in the way she looks at me, like I'm all she's ever wanted, ever.

Her breathing falters when I slide out, her tears slowing.

She watches me with almost a confused look on her face.

I'm not sure what her reaction will be next, but I kiss her, once, and then move back, my knees sliding against the truck bed. My hand moves to my hair as I try to slow my breathing.

Madison sits up, brushing tears away and reaching for her panties beside her. There's a moment when our eyes meet, and our situation is clear. This was just a Band-Aid for an underlying issue, but still, she felt something in the last five minutes she hasn't felt in a while.

The air changes and I feel it. It's in the confused expression as her brows pull together, silently asking me what that was.

"We should probably get going," I say, reaching for her hand to help her out of the back of the truck. When she's standing in front of me smoothing out her dress, I cup her cheeks in my hands, forcing her to look at me. "Don't over think this. The purpose of this weekend is to try and recapture the love I know we still have. This is part of that process. I'm just trying to make this work," I state, feeling the need to clarify what this is, even though I don't really need to. If I want to fuck my wife on the side of the road, I should be able to, right?

Something flickers in her eyes, though, and I don't know what it is.

Giving me a fleeting look, she turns and gets inside the truck, slamming the door without another word.

16

LOST IN MORE THAN ONE WAY

"We're lost. Just pull over."

"Why? Do you see anyone I can ask for directions? No. You don't."

Before you say, "wow, stop being a jerk," I don't "do" being lost. I like to know where I'm going at all times and if I don't know, I become Wolverine, like Noah when you wake him up in the morning.

"If we pull over, we can at least look at a map."

She's purposely trying to drive me off the deep end. I know it. She's probably hoping I'll drive off one of these cliffs so I don't have to hear this bullshit and you know, I'd fucking do it at this point if I knew it wouldn't kill me. I'd gladly take a broken arm, even a leg than subject myself to this.

My finger's still healing from the nail incident, so what's one more broken bone?

"What map?" I laugh, but there's not a lot of amusement in my tone. "Do you have one hidden up your ass?"

She cocks an eyebrow smugly. "Funny." She snorts. "Real fucking funny. I meant our cell phones."

I stare at her in disbelief. Is she for real? "Do you honestly think we have service out here? Even the navigation is at a loss." I point to the screen that's been stuck on recalculating for an hour.

"You know for a man who hates to be lost, or late to anything, you'd think you would have programmed the address in and stuck to it," she says to me bitterly.

Do you hear that?

Do you fucking believe she has the nerve to be bitter right now?

Do you want to know *why* we're lost?

Madison wanted to see the stars. That being said, she had me pull over onto a road I didn't know, drive down said road until we came to a canyon.

And that's not the worst part. The stars were beautiful, and the sex was amazing.

But now I don't know how to get back to the main road.

Want to test a marriage?

Well… you could start by one of you filing for divorce and not telling the spouse and then serve them with divorce papers. That's one way.

The other?

Take a wrong turn. Guaranteed argument.

"I think you turn right here?" Madison points to her right, staring off into the darkness as we drive through the canyons, bouncing around in the truck with the uneven road.

"Really? You think that? Well, guess what, if I turn right, we die."

"What are you talking about?"

"Look out your window." I jerk the wheel to the right to give her a scare but not enough we actually go over the side but then I say, "It's a fucking cliff."

She doesn't appreciate my humor one bit. Her arm jets out and smacks me in the chest. "Damn you, don't scare me like that."

Scare her? I bet now isn't the time to tell her I ran over what looked to be a dog when I swerved. It was probably a coyote though. I once tried to feed one a cheeseburger when I was a kid. He looked hungry. Just in case you're wondering, don't attempt to approach a coyote, or feed one. It's a horrible idea but that's a story for another day.

Glancing in the mirror, I see it limping away but can't make out what it was. No way I'm saying anything.

After another ten minutes, Madison sighs heavily. "Do you really think this is going to work?"

"I'll find the road eventually."

Her lips press together in a tight line, and her expression turns serious. "I'm not talking about the road, Ridley. I'm talking about *us*."

Of course she is. I might not have explained this until now, but there's things Madison and I are good at. Annoying each other is one of them. We're good at sex and laughing at each other's jokes.

What we're not good at is communication. Surprising huh? Probably not. You've been with this train wreck a while now to see we're a straight-up soap opera shit show.

I don't talk. Never have. I'll keep my thoughts to myself as long as possible until one day I explode. I think

I might explode now as she's nitpicking me to death about being lost and trying to start arguments. But I hold back.

Madison, she's emotional and believe it or not, insecure in some ways. She also can't make a decision to save her ass, and when she does, she's never confident with it and questions herself. I'm mostly talking about ordering off menus, but I think you see it since she filed for divorce. She wasn't 100 percent sure of the decision. No fucking way.

So because of those two personalities crashing into one another, we have this fucking void between us that neither of us wants to cross. Is that our problem? Is that the underlying issue here?

If so, we don't need this couples retreat, but I know as well as you do, it's not just that.

Every marriage has its problems. You're fucking smoking crack if you can actually sit here and tell me it's perfect all the time.

And trying to make her see what's right in front of us and worth fighting for is becoming exhausting if she's not willing to at least work with me.

"I think"—I turn down another road and see the hotel lights in the distance—"this is our best chance to find out if we can make it work."

One would think we were okay, right? Everything will go smoothly once we get to the hotel.

One would be wrong.

One needs to be punched in the face.

As we enter the hotel, the Sahara Resort and Spa, I have our bags in hand, and Madison is following behind me. There's a sign above the counter that says "Check-in" so I step forward.

That's when I hear, "Madison, is that you?" from behind.

I turn to see who's talking to her, as does my wife and I groan, out loud. "You have to be fucking kidding me."

Madison elbows me. "Oh, hey, Thomas."

Fuck me.

Great. Just fucking great. Have I mentioned Thomas yet?

I haven't, have I? Probably because the ex-boyfriend *never* matters. I'm the better guy. Believe me on this one.

Well, until now when my wife is you know, contemplating divorce.

Is God trying to tell me something here? Is he saying, *"Fuck off, Ridley. Just let her go!"*

I'm beginning to think that way.

Madison laughs casually, but there's a good amount of hesitation in the laugh. Her eyes dart from mine to Thomas. I watch her face closely, every single emotion that dances behind her eyes.

Do you see me there? Muscles and jaw tensed like I'm about to lose it? I feel like a can of soda that's been shaken constantly, and I'm about ready to explode. You know that feeling right before you vomit where you break out into a cold sweat and your heart starts pounding?

That's me right now.

"Are you checking in?" a voice behind me asks.

Go to hell.

I catch a man's stare behind me. "Oh, yeah." I reach for my wallet, and I want to toss it behind me and tell him to take care of everything because I don't want to miss anything Thomas has to say to Madison or vice versa.

Thomas is smiling like he's been given a gift, a second chance. No fucking way.

"Mr. Cooper?"

Goddamn it.

With a heavy sigh, I turn around to hand the hotel clerk my credit card and attempt to hear what they're saying behind me.

They chat. Simple things like, how are you? Got any kids? What are you doing here?

I'm okay with that part.

It's when he says, "So what made you guys come to Sahara? Are you having troubles?"

Say no. For the love of God, SAY NO, MADISON!

Sahara Resort is advertised as a couples retreat. A place where you can come to get away and fall in love again. If we're here, it's clear we're having some sort of martial issue, right?

And I hate, absolutely *hate*, that her ex-boyfriend is asking this. You never ever want the ex to know there are problems.

"Well," she looks at me, probably waiting for me to say something, "we just needed to get away for the weekend." She pauses, my heart evens out, but then she crushes my soul with, "Remember why we're together."

Ordinarily, this wouldn't be a big deal. There's nothing wrong with needing to remember, right?

Wrong. This is a jab at me that I'm not doing my job. I know this and guess what? Thomas knows now.

He nods as though he's agreeing, but inside he's grinning like a fool.

Have you ever heard of cape buffalo? They're in Africa. Anyway, the male bulls have to fight their way high enough up the dominance hierarchy to secure his opportunity to mate. Do you hear that? Eight years. We've been married for eight years. I'd be damned if this guy or any other guy for that matter would take my place in the hierarchy.

I grab my wife's hand. "All checked in. Let's go." And I practically drag her to our room and slam the door behind us before she, or Thomas, can say anything.

As we stand in the room staring at one another, romance all around us from the wine to the flowers… it's like a honeymoon suite. But I stand there silent because for once, I've got nothing to say.

Are you surprised?

Maybe don't answer that.

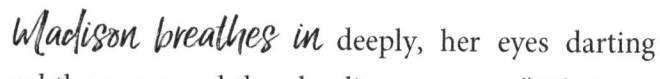

Madison breathes in deeply, her eyes darting around the room and then landing on mine. "What was that about down there?" she asks.

Reaching for the wine bottle on the dresser, I wink and flop myself back on the bed. "I don't know what you're talking about."

Glancing around the room, Madison sighs. "I'm hungry."

I sit up with the bottle of wine. "Let's drink then."

She frowns. "You know I don't drink."

"Yeah, I know." Swinging my legs around, I stand up from the bed and set the wine on the nightstand. "Let's go downstairs and get something to eat. There's a restaurant down there."

She heads for the door without looking at me. "Okay."

The restaurant is nice, elegant I suppose and we're probably under dressed. Well, I am, wearing gray shorts and a black polo shirt but Madison, she's always perfect in anything she has on. Tonight she's wearing a simple white sundress with black and yellow flowers that moves with her body as she walks ahead of me to our table.

There's music playing and a small yet convenient dance floor to our right. Before we get to the table, I grab Madison by the wrist when I notice the song playing. "Dance with me."

"Why?" she asks, pressed to my chest now.

I wink at the waiter holding our menu's and then lead Madison to the dance floor with my hand on the small of her back. "Because there's music playing."

Her hands slip gently over my shoulders, lashes fluttering with thoughts. "So?"

"Come on." I wrap my arms around her waist pulling her closer, no amount of space between our bodies. "You know you want to."

"Fine." And then she glares at me, though I can see she's amused at something. "Since you asked so nicely."

"When have you ever needed a please when it comes to demands," I murmur against the shell of her ear, our bodies swaying to "Let It Be Me" by Ray LaMontagne's. "You're a dirty girl and you like to be told what to do."

Madison snorts, slapping the back of my head. "Stop that. Be a gentleman."

I laugh. "I don't know how."

Another snort. "That's for sure."

"Hey now, this is me being a gentleman." I pull back, smiling. "Be nice."

We're quiet, moving effortlessly around the dance floor when I notice we're the only ones dancing in this restaurant. Everyone else is at a table, across from their significant other, candles creating a romantic atmosphere while the lost souls make sense of what they're actually doing here. I don't know this for sure but they all seem to have the same weary looks on their faces. Do they even want to be here? They look like they're being forced into detention, or worse, the ballet.

Some stare at the televisions on the wall in the bar, others at their phones but the thing is, nobody is actually *talking* to one another. It's sad. Really fucking sad.

My stare moves to Madison. "Look at these people, Mad." She does, her tender eyes darting around the room, saddened by what she sees. "They're not us. There's love here…." I raise my right hand from her waist, my fingertips brushing over her left breast. "I know I've made some mistakes and made you feel alone but I'm asking you not to give up."

She nods. "I'm here for us to try, Ridley."

My mouth lowers to her collarbone whispering the words, "Thank you."

Once we're seated at a table, I scan the room and see Thomas sitting with two other guys at the bar about thirty feet away. Ordinarily you'd think I would ignore him and look away, right?

The answer would be no. I probably wouldn't because this is the guy Madison left for me. In my mind, I have to convince him there was a reason as to *why* she did that. May seem like stupid guy logic to you, but it's my logic. For right now anyways.

Just watch what happens next.

So there we are after our dance, seated in a booth looking over menu's and I have a clear view of Thomas. Madison's view is blocked by a plant. I'll thank this plant later because if you don't know what I'm about to do, you don't know me at all.

Madison doesn't need a lot of romance and likes to live on the edge a little. Don't believe me? Well for starters, that first night we met at a Halloween party, I fucked her in a bathroom of the house with two people passed out in the shower. She didn't care and neither did I.

And here's one more example for you. At our wedding, our first dance was to Michael Jackson's "Thriller" which I'd like to add I rocked the shit out of.

Anyways, back to my point. Madison doesn't need a lot of romance and likes adventure. So I have something in mind.

Leaning into her, my left arm wraps around her shoulder, squeezing lightly.

She looks up from her menu at my hand on her shoulder and then my face knowing damn well I'm up to something. "What are you doing?"

I shrug and nod south as I move my right hand on her thigh pushing her dress up. "What does it look like? Take them off."

"What?" she gasps setting her water down on the table and then begins fidgeting with the edge of her dress trying to pull it back down.

"Your panties." I draw my voice out, the words slowly slipping through my lips in a mumble. "Take them off."

"No."

I hold her stare with a serious look, my hand inching higher, the heat of her center noticeable now. “Are you telling me no?”

She stares at me, playfully, yet frightened and then her eyes dart around the restaurant. “Ridley, what if someone sees us?”

I press my lips to her ear. “I think that’s part of the fun here, isn’t it?”

My hand is up her thigh, my dick straining against my shorts, begging for some sort of friction. Drawing back, I meet her stare calmly and smile. Judging by the heat between her legs, she’s *not* going to tell me no.

My hand moves further up her thigh until I reach the edge of her panties. “You should have taken these off.” I breath slowly into the side of her neck letting my eyes drift to the bar. “I want all these people to see that you’re *mine*.” Mostly Thomas. “And I’m not going to stop until you come all over my fingers.”

Moving her panties aside, my middle and forefingers glide into her and my thumb presses against her clit. She jerks slightly in her seat, inhaling sharply at my touch. “That’s it, honey. Let me take care of you....”

Circling and swirling my fingers, Madison shifts her legs and spreads them apart giving me more room to work. My fingers press deeper and I’m rewarded with heat and wetness of her pussy on my fingers and palm. Madison’s eyes flutter shut and she inhales sharply, her breathing hitching with my movements between her thighs.

When she does open her eyes, she’s frantically searching the room for who can see. And no one can, but Thomas and his friends. His friends aren’t looking but Thomas, his eyes are locked on us with a glare.

Other than tonight, I’ve only met Thomas one other time.

Guess what?

It ended in a fight. In my defense, he started it and threw the first swing. I just finished it.

Judging by the set scowl and the white-knuckled grip on his glass, I'd say there's a 50/50 chance he wants to hit me again.

"Relax," I whisper. "Just enjoy what I'm giving you."

Madison makes a noise, a gentle sigh and I lean forward a couple inches sliding my middle finger deeper, rubbing across her clit with the pad of my thumb, circling it gently.

Moving my lips along her jaw to her mouth, she faces me and kisses me deeply while grabbing my wrist with her left hand coaxing me along.

Fuck yeah, she's into it now.

She moans into my mouth as I inhale her breath, my thumb teasing her swollen clit as I begin moving faster and harder. Believe me when I tell you I know how to get my wife off. This isn't me being overly cocky. This is me knowing what I'm doing for the last eight years.

Breaking the kiss, Madison's eyes remained closed, her head now buried between my neck and shoulder like she's telling me a secret. A very dirty secret I desperately want to hear.

I can't see her face, but judging by the sounds of pure pleasure falling from her lips, I'd say I'm doing a pretty good fucking job here and wearing a look of smug satisfaction. If anyone, such as Thomas, was to look over here, it's fairly obvious what's happening but I'm not about to let Madison know that. She's losing herself in the passion and it's the most beautiful thing I've seen in a while.

"You're so wet," I whisper brushing her hair from her neck with my left hand that's still wrapped around her shoulder. Knowing she loves this shit, I grip the back of her neck a little harder than I usually would. "I want you to come all over the seat and my hand." My fingers speed up, my voice chanting in her ear.

My voice, my movements, it's too much for her and she lets out a short burst of air, her legs convulsively widening a fraction then clamping together on my hand and wrist. "Oh God…." She breaths out, her body shaking as she does in fact come on my fingers. Her left hand pushes mine deeper, rocking her hips slightly as she rides out the last of her orgasm, panting into the side of my neck.

When her thighs relax, I lean into her ear, my stare on Thomas. He's captivated by what I'm doing, his eyes darting around the room but always returning to us.

Turning my head, I stare at her, lips slightly parted, still panting. Her tongue darts out, wetting her bottom lip as she says, "I can't believe you just did that."

Oh yeah? Watch carefully as to what I do next.

Raising my hand from between her legs, I place my index and middle finger in my mouth and suck her sweet juices from them. Leaning in closer so our faces are almost touching, she turns to face me and then kisses me, her soft lips yielding to my own.

I break the kiss before she wants me to and whisper, "Are you sure you want a divorce? Nobody can get you off like I do." She knows this is true and I'm confident enough to say it.

Madison sits up a little straighter and reaches for her menu as if nothing happened. She also doesn't answer my question because she knows I'm right.

I discreetly adjust myself—wishing Madison would lay her mouth in my lap—and then I wink at Thomas.

You didn't think he'd turn away from this, did you? Nope. He's still fixated on us.

When I wink, his head snaps the other direction, quickly, his eyes on the television to his right but there's no way he's forgetting what he just witnessed. I certainly wouldn't.

Before you go judging me, think about what I'm attempting to do here.

Everywhere I turn there's another obstacle in my way. I have to use my advantages where I can, even if that means finger fucking my wife while her ex-boyfriend watches to let him know there's absolutely no fucking way he has a chance with her again.

The waiter approaches, glances at me and then Madison. "Are you ready to order, Mrs.?"

Do you see the way her posture stiffens and the pink on her cheeks? It's an indication she's still trying to calm herself down.

"She'll need a minute… to decide," I tell the waiter, proudly.

He nods and darts his eyes to mine. "Take your time."

Madison's mouth presses into a firm line. "Ridley?"

"Yes?"

"Did you do that because Thomas is sitting in the bar and can see us?"

I shrug, reaching for my water. I look a little closer at what I thought was a plant. It wasn't. It was some woman's hat and she moved. I can't lie to her. A smile pulls at the edges of my mouth when I say, "Maybe."

"Well…." Her right hand glides up my thigh and then stops at the bulge in my pants. "I was going to repay the favor, in front of everyone… but now I think I'll make you wait a little while, *husband*."

On the bright side, she called me her husband for the first time in months. There's that.

Not so bright side?

My smooth balls are blue.

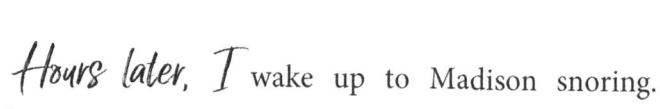

Hours later, I wake up to Madison snoring. Madison swears she doesn't snore. She'd be wrong. I think she's trying to annoy me with it. Ordinarily her snoring doesn't bother me but tonight, I'm about ready to smother her because I'm sexually frustrated and have no tolerance for her snoring or her need to constantly be moving while sleeping.

And look at her all nice and cozy and sexually satisfied. Me on the other hand, she didn't return the favor once we got upstairs. Mostly because she found out I was putting on a show for her ex, but that's not the point here.

The point is I'm *horny* and can't sleep and I know if I wake her up for sex she'll straight up punch me in the face or the dick.

So there I lay, staring at the ceiling wide awake with Madison's legs on mine. I've never understood the movies where couples sleep right on top of each other in loving embraces. It's not accurate. Stop lying, Hollywood. I need my space, and I hate noises at night. And movement. Madison does both all night long and sleeps like a fucking chicken wing.

"Just stop moving around," I tell her, kicking her leg off me.

"What?" She startles awake as if she's doing nothing wrong. "What's your problem?"

"You. You're my problem with your overactive feet."

"You're impossible. You want me to sleep in the bed with you, but you can't stop complaining." She pulls the blankets toward her.

"I'm impossible?" I take a handful of blankets and rip them my way. "Why can't you just lie here and sleep? You're the impossible one and annoying."

"I am not."

My grandparents slept in separate rooms, and I always thought that was odd. Not so much anymore. I totally understand why people have separate bedrooms.

Ten minutes later, Madison is back to snoring.

I kick her in the shin, hoping she'll wake up and stop those horrid noises coming from her mouth. I mean, who makes noises like that? She sounds like a pissed off Donald Duck. Was she suffocating? My God.

"What was that?" she yelps, grabbing her calf.

I smile. I can't help myself. "Maybe you have a Charlie horse."

Rolling over, she faces me. My attempts to get her to move away from me backfire because now she's facing me and breathing, no, snoring on my neck. How can she sleep with those noises emanating from her?

Lying there awake, I stare at the ceiling trying to think of all the ways to make her stop snoring just so I can get some sleep. Nothing comes to mind, short of suffocation. That's permanent. Tossing and turning, violently I might add, I think if I move as much as she does, maybe she'll wake up.

All my rolling around gets me a trip to the floor when I roll right off the bed to the hardwood floor.

Too bad it didn't knock me out.

That's when I decide to throw a pillow at her. At that point, I wish it'd knock her out. "Shut up!" I yell.

"What?" she asks, rubbing her head. "What happened?"

By now I'm so annoyed I go to sleep on the couch in the living room.

As I lie here awake, a faint glow of lights from the courtyard streaming through the curtains, I think about why we're here and what I'm trying to mend. I can't pinpoint any day specifically when I started working so much and ignoring everything else. It was a gradual progression as the business grew.

When you get married, you never assume you're going to drift apart. I didn't. I swore it wouldn't happen. So when did it happen? When did we become this couple making decisions together but two people living separate lives linked by the two children we've created?

We used to be one person, one heart, and one soul fighting together. Now we're struggling to find our way, lost in clouds of smoke with no visibility.

I need to make her see she still loves me regardless of anything around us. She needs to know it's not just our boys tying us together. When you get married, something brought you together. Something made you say I do. So just because you're having problems, or the rope between the two of you is fraying, it doesn't mean the love is gone. You just have to remember what it was that tied the two of you together in the first place.

But how will I do that?

Let's hope this couple counsoler knows what the fuck they're doing because I sure as shit don't.

17

WHAT THE SHIT?

You're probably wondering what happens when you're at a resort that specializes in couple's therapy, right?

Me too.

I don't actually know yet, but the brochure indicates you have skill building sessions, which is a fancy name for supervised arguing if you ask me. It's like we're being sent to the principal's office to discuss our problems.

Saturday morning after getting very little sleep, thanks to Madison and her snoring, I'm not exactly in the best of moods. Making our way through the hotel lobby in search of coffee, Madison stops at the customer service desk. "Do you care if I get a massage? My lower back is hurting today."

It's probably because you wouldn't stop moving last night.

I shrug. "Sure. Go ahead. I think our session's at noon."

Madison smiles and schedules herself for a massage in a half hour. I'm thinking in that half hour, after I get coffee, a blow job would be nice and put me in a *way* better mood, but Madison doesn't see it that way and drags me inside the restaurant to the left of the hotel lobby for food.

"I'm starving!" she announces, eyeing their buffet spread. I have to admit it looks good, but buffets have never been appealing to me. Mostly because anybody could have touched the food you're about to eat, or worse, sneezed on it.

As we stand there, those same couples I saw in the bar, now silently eating breakfast with one another, I can't wrap my mind around anything aside from *why* we're here.

How'd it get this bad?

Maybe I'm just now coming to the realization that my marriage has the potential to be over, but it's just like me to be obsessing over it. You probably know this by now.

Madison and I grab a table near the windows overlooking the vast burnt-orange canyons surrounding Sedona, Arizona. It's beautiful here. Absolutely gorgeous and reminds me of the area around our new house in Cave Creek.

"I don't know what to get," Madison notes as we're in the buffet line, trying to decide between oatmeal and a bagel.

Decisions aren't her specialty.

"Get both and I'll eat the bagel." I chose the bagel because it's in an enclosed bin, less likely to have been sneezed on, and the cream cheese is in a fridge to my right. "Then if you decide you want the bagel, you can have it."

She nods, and reaches for the oatmeal.

We're quiet as we eat, my gaze drifting around the restaurant, hers on her oatmeal. I'd give anything to know what she's thinking right now. I think back to everything she's said over the last month, and what led us here. Me working all the time, my lack of presence in a life we created together, the house I didn't finish....

My eyes raise to hers, lost in her beauty as she moves her hair off her shoulders. "I'm going to finish the house when I get back," I tell her, picking apart the bagel on my plate.

She doesn't look up from oatmeal but her lashes flutter. "Why now?"

"Because it needs to be finished. And if you decide this"—I wave my hand around, barely able to say the word—"divorce is what you want, you can have it."

She stiffens, her eyes raising to mine, then dropping just as suddenly. She takes another spoonful of her oatmeal and then raises her fork to her mouth. "You don't have to finish for me."

I blow out a breath. My voice is soft and strained, begging her to understand it was never my intention to forget about the house. "I know, but I saw your face when your mom asked about it. You're mad I didn't finish it. Besides, I started it for you, I'll finish it *for you.*"

Thoughtfully, she leans back in her chair. "I know you didn't mean to put it aside." Her voice is soft, and I know she believes me.

I don't believe in regret. I think it's a dumb word because if you live your life and do the things you want, you shouldn't have regret, right?

I'm not sure, but I think this is what regret feels like. That aching pit in my stomach wishing I could go back and change the last year, stop this before it happened. Stop this look I'm receiving, the one where she's staring at me like she knows I'm trying to fix this and it might not be worth saving to her.

And then she makes a face, swallowing hard. "I'll be right back. I'm not feeling so good."

She disappears and I don't think anything of it. Believe me, this comes back to bite me in the ass too. Just wait.

Returning from the bathroom, she glances down at her phone. "You okay?"

She nods. "Yeah, I'm fine. I get shitty reception here. What time is the counseling session?"

"Noon."

She looks at her phone. "I should be done just in time."

"Okay." I nod outside. "I'm going to go for a run." Believe me, it's needed. I'm so wound up over all of this, my muscles have literally been on lock down for a month.

Leaning in, Madison kisses me. On the lips. "Sounds good. See you in a couple hours."

And then I watch her ass as she walks away. Madison has the best ass and I'm immediately thinking of my dick pressed between her ass cheeks.

Don't look at me like that. Every man thinks that. If they tell you they don't, divorce him. He's lying.

I'm totally kidding. Don't divorce him. It's a disaster and he's probably a good guy. Maybe. I don't like anyone so you shouldn't listen to me.

I go for a run but let's just fast forward to about noon. You remember what happens at noon, right?

Principal's office. Controlled arguments.

Guess who's sitting in the neutral-colored room with the cracked mosaic tiles, alone?

Me. By myself.

You know how I feel about tardiness and my wife's being late is no exception. If she tells me she's going to be somewhere at a certain time, I believe her. I've never had any reason to. Until now. Patience is a virtue but it's certainly not mine.

"She knows about the appointment, right?" The lady across from me asks. She's the therapist apparently. Doesn't she look like Judge Judy?

I thought so too.

"Yeah, she had a massage this morning, but it was over an hour ago." I clench my jaw shut, the muscles in my body annoyed and protesting from tensing for so long.

"Are you happy, Mr. Cooper?"

You can't punch this chick. I actually tell myself that. "What are you talking about?"

"Are you happy?"

"No." I snort. "I'm pissed off my wife isn't here and she's not answering her phone. Again."

The lady taps her pen against a note pad on her lap. "What brought the two of you here?"

I look out the window. "She wants a divorce."

"And you don't?"

"No, I don't. I love my wife." I can't sit here anymore and not know where Madison is.

I'm just about to leave when she glances down at her watch. "You're going to have to re-schedule for tomorrow."

Standing, I level Judge Judy a glare. "Fine."

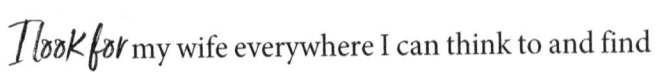

I look for my wife everywhere I can think to and find her at the last place I would have expected. The bar.

I'm pissed by the time I finally spot her, and that's when I see Madison sitting at a table with guess who.

Thomas.

Her fucking ex. Remember? The guy she cheated on with me?

Oh, well maybe I didn't tell you that. But she did. That night at the Halloween party she had been dating Thomas Dean. And let's just be honest here, what kind of name is Thomas Dean?

Sounds like Harvard law students name. Ridley Cooper, that's a fucking man's name.

Do you see them sitting there? She's leaned in, listening intently to his words and he's acting like he's what, pouring his heart out to her?

Let's just focus on the fact they look pretty fucking cozy, don't they? Aren't they cute?

If you say yes right now, I'll punch you.

Thomas Dean spots me first and gives me a head nod like we're old friends. We would *never* be friends. Most of the time I'd never give much thought to an ex because let's face it, he's gone from the picture and in this instance, she left him for me. Win for me, right?

Now I'm not so sure because of the impending doom of the D word.

As soon as Madison spots me standing near the door, she literally jumps up from the table rattling the glasses of water. "I was just going to find you."

Sure she was. Doesn't look like it to me judging by the drink in front of her. And the two empty ones beside them. Madison doesn't drink. Ever. Her dad was a raging piece-of-shit alcoholic who used to beat the crap out of her mom. And you met her mother. In fear she may have a drinking problem, she never touches alcohol.

Stepping forward, I make my way over to them. I want to say something funny and not let on how pissed I am, but I don't. I've got nothing. My sense of humor and smart-ass remarks desert me like a cabby when you don't have the fare. "Did you forget we have a counseling session? Looks like you did, huh?" I motion to the drinks on the table.

"Oh my God." Her hand flies to her mouth. "I'm so sorry, Ridley. I ran into Thomas after my massage and we got to chatting, and I lost track of time. Will they let us reschedule?"

"No." Do you sense the sarcasm in my tone?

So does Madison when her eyelashes flicker like she can't believe I'm being this harsh with her in front of someone else. "So you're drinking now?"

"It's water. Thomas was having a beer."

Of all the fucking times to see this Thomas dude, it's now, and I want to knock his goddamn teeth in. Usually I'd say, this guy doesn't matter. But he does. He fucking does and I know it.

I nod, shaking my head with a patronizing smirk plastered on my face. "Uh-huh."

The waitress approaches me. "Can I get you something?"

"No, honey." I wink at her, my eyes drifting back to Madison. *That's right, I called another woman honey.*

How does it feel? "I'm good." And then I smile at Thomas. "Hope you had a nice time with my wife."

Yeah, I throw in my wife because it's a title I'm sure as shit confident he'll never hold with her. But then again, am I?

Thomas clears his throat. "Ridley, honestly, it's my fault. I was just telling—"

I shoot him a murderous glare and cut him off. "Was I talking to you?"

His jaw tightens, working back and forth as he keeps one hand on his beer. "I think you're overreacting."

I slam both my hands down on the table in front of them, leaning in. "Am I?" I look at Madison. "Am I?"

Madison's head jerks back in disgust, completely appalled at my behavior. "Ridley, stop it. You don't have to be such a jerk. I was just catching up with him."

Standing up straight, my eyes drift to her wedding ring, and then to her eyes again. "So spending time with him is better than trying to make our marriage work? I waited *thirty* minutes before the counselor, who I might add is a bitch, told me we had to reschedule tomorrow." The thought that I'm not good enough for her to remember *why* we're here in the first place punches my heart, gives my blood a rush as it pumps through my veins.

Madison doesn't say anything. She just stares at me with these wide glassy eyes that scream she's sorry only I'm so pissed I don't see the apology in them. I see her choosing him over me.

I'm pretty good at digging the knife in and twisting. Just watch. It gets worse.

I hold her weary stare for a long beat. "What? Nothing to say now?" I nod once, and then shrug, but my shoulders feel so heavy it's hard to do. My whole body is rigid and stuck in a moment I can't escape, one where I'm not even sure about the words coming out of my mouth except that they are and I can't stop them. "You know, *never mind.* I'm not even sure why I came looking for you because it's clear you never had any intention of making this work."

I can't tell you why Thomas is my breaking point, he just is. Or maybe it's the fact that I keep trying to fix this and she's not doing a goddamn thing to help me out.

Turning around, I draw in a heavy breath and then begin walking back to the hotel. I'm not sticking around for this crap. Why am I the only one trying? If she's not going to make an effort at all, why am I continuing to put myself through this bullshit?

Here's another buffalo fun fact for you. When hunted by humans, cape buffalo have a reputation for circling back on the hunter and attacking them. They attack with their heads up and at the last minute, lower their head to deliver a bone-crunching crash.

Where's a fucking buffalo when you need one.

"Goddamn it, Ridley, slow down!"

I don't.

I can't.

I won't anymore.

The sky is restless above us, thick black clouds dragged down by heavy rain. I feel exactly like those clouds, sick of trying, wanting to let go. I stare at the sky hoping maybe by some chance a bolt of lightning will hit me in the fucking heart and put me out of my goddamn misery.

It's then the sky opens and dumps two inches of rain in a matter of minutes as we're crossing the courtyard to the hotel lobby. Maybe not two inches but with the amount of water coming down, I can barely make out the hotel doors.

"Ridley," Madison yells from behind me, her footsteps splashing in the puddles against the stone courtyard. She reaches out to grab my arm to whirl me to face her, but I resist and keep walking. "Will you please stop?"

I turn around once we're in the lobby, both of us soaking wet, water dripping from every part of our body. People around us gasp, some stare, but they haven't seen anything yet.

Look at us, both of us drenched, clothes clinging to our bodies, hair matted to our heads, but it's the look in our eyes that should shock most. Mine one of confusion and anger, hers of desperation, finally. It's a look I haven't seen in a while.

She steps in front of me, but I look past her, through her, like she's not even there. She opens her mouth to try to say something, but I ask, "Why? *Why* do you want me to stop and listen? I mean seriously, what the fuck? You missed the appointment to have drinks with your ex?"

"It wasn't like that. I was coming back from my spa appointment and ran into him. He asked if I wanted to have a drink and catch up, so I did, thinking I had some extra time. I didn't mean anything by it."

I laugh. Not because what she's saying is funny. I laugh mostly because I can't believe what I'm hearing. "Are you fucking him?" Maybe I shouldn't have asked that. The look on her face tells me I shouldn't have, but to be honest, I'm so far gone at this point there could be a neon sign blinking in my face telling me TURN BACK and WRONG WAY yet I wouldn't have noticed. "Did you tell *Thomas Dean* the reason you dumped his ass in the first place was because you were fucking me? Does he know that?"

Her cheeks flush and maybe, and this is a strong maybe, she wants to kill me for asking that. “Go to hell, Ridley.”

I laugh, again. But it’s more like a hard chuckle, and I fight the urge to clap slowly. “You filed for divorce. Pretty sure I’m already there.”

She stiffens. “Just because I forget one appointment doesn’t give you the right to treat me like this when you’ve basically been absent these last five years working and forgetting you had a family at home who loves and needs you.”

The words hit me straight in the chest. How could she ever think I’ve forgotten about them? Everything I do is for her and the boys. “Unbelievable.”

“There’s a lot you refuse to believe.”

“Why did you come here, Madison? Were you actually going to give us a chance or was this just another ploy to appease me until it’s final?”

She says nothing.

“We built a life together, and you’re just throwing it away. There’s some things worth fighting for, and I’m asking if you’re going to *fight for me*.”

She blinks, tears welling up and she looks like she wants to vomit. “Ridley, I just don’t know anymore.”

“You don’t know? You don’t fucking know?

“It just sucks. It fucking sucks that for years you were gone and never making an effort.”

“Don’t you dare stand here and tell me I haven’t been trying! I am. I was. I had my fucking nut sack waxed to make you see I cared and wanted your attention!” By the way, the entire lobby heard that, and I guarantee most of them are eyeing my junk right now. “You were just to blind to notice.”

“I’ve been busting my ass for the last month trying to make you fall back in love with me. All I’ve done is try and be there for you and the boys, and *this* is how you act now? I'm doing my best here, Madison. It's not like I ever had a good example of the model husband or father. I'm literally learning as I go here and trying like hell to keep you happy. I didn't want you and the boys to go through what my mother and I did. I never want Callan and Noah to have the feelings I did growing up, wondering why I was never good enough for my father. But you know what, what I finally realize today… it takes two people. I can't be the one trying constantly to make this better."

"Well, now you know how I've felt."

Pay close attention to this next part. Or look away, whatever you prefer, because I'm pretty sure this is where I'm about to fuck everything up. Are you surprised?

Might as well go down in a blaze of glory, right?

"You know what, I'm done having this same argument with you. I'm done."

She grabs my arm, panic flooding her eyes. "What do you mean you're done?"

"It's what I mean. I'm done. You win." I throw my arms up in the air and let them fall to my sides. "If you want a divorce, I'll give it to you. I'm tired of fighting for someone who doesn't want to be married to me."

Tears roll down her cheeks. "This is what you're good at, isn't it… walking away?"

What the fuck is she talking about?

"I'm just taking lessons from *you*."

Let's just skip to the part where she tells me to fuck off because it's coming and all this arguing is making my brain hurt.

Guess what? This isn't the first time a woman's tried to slap me. You're not surprised by that, are you?

But, like a man, I catch her arm by the wrist before she makes contact with my cheek. "Don't you dare."

And then as my luck would have it, she tries to hit me with the other hand. So there I am holding both of them. I'm apparently in asshole "I don't give a flying fuck about anything" mode because I smile. "Is that all you got?"

Never ever say that to a woman because I'm holding both her hands and if she really wants to bring me to my knees where do you think she's going to go next?

But she surprises me and doesn't knee me in the junk. Instead, she practically spits in my face as she yells, "Fuck you!"

"Fuck you more!" I shout back.

All right, we're being childish, but it's the best I could do. I want to fuck her, sorry, but I do. Mostly I want to kiss her and take away this pain we're feeling and lashing out at. I want to kiss the Madison from our wedding night. The girl with the smiles and the one who couldn't wait to marry me, so much so her hands shook the entire time we said our vows.

I want to kiss that girl because she remembers why she married me. This Madison, she's forgotten.

I edge closer, my body against hers so she can feel the warmth of mine scorch her skin. "I'm fucking obsessed with this, and you're teasing me. Admit it, you made up your mind when you filed for divorce, and I was never going to change it, was I?"

Come on, give me something. You've taken so much from me lately. At least give me your eyes.

And when those beautiful blue eyes do find mine, it wrecks me.

I hear the sniff, the gasp, the moment reality hits her, and I meet her eyes despite not wanting to. I don't want to look at her, but I have to. My heart drops when I see her tears, and I try to ignore them, I do, but I can't.

Just let her go.

My eyes squeeze shut, and I know she sees the pain in them before I deny her the sight. My head hangs, my body wanting to give out, fall before her and beg her to put me out of my misery already.

Madison's a strong woman, maybe even stronger than I've given her credit for all these years but she couldn't, wouldn't fight for us.

In a huffed breath, she lets out a sarcastic laugh, shaking her head. Madison turns to leave. And I don't follow her, but as she's walking away, she mumbles, "Thomas's wife was killed in a car accident two years ago with their two-year-old son. He became a therapist here because when she died, he realized they'd grown apart and he had no idea who she was anymore."

That was ugly.

Fuck me. No really, just fucking stab me in the heart already. Better yet, rip it out. I don't need the useless organ anymore.

18

SIGN HERE

Here's the thing. Life is a train wreck for most people. Sure, they smile and tell you their blessed and hashtag everything is perfect in their lives in an Instagram post, but it's not.

They're fucking liars.

Madison and I don't talk the entire drive back home Sunday afternoon. I know Callan's going to be at the house with Brantley, waiting for us, and what am I going to say to him?

That I gave up?

My mind replays everything on repeat. My attempts to win her back, the nut sac waxing, hammering my hand to a wall… it's not only taken a toll on me physically but emotionally, this fucking hurts. I'm not going to lie.

Especially when you know deep down, you don't want it. But the thing is, I shouldn't have to convince my wife she wants to be with me, should I?

When someone you've promised your heart to, vowed to love and cherish till death do you part wants out, it feels like the world's closing in on you and nothing will ever be the same again.

In our case, it won't.

I've done some research on Chernobyl. After the nuclear meltdown, nothing about that city was the same. Have you seen what it looks like? It's like the day after a carnival leaves town with empty streets and trash all over the place.

That's essentially how I feel. Empty. Abandoned.

When we pull up to the house, the lump in my throat gets so big I can barely swallow.

I can't help the emotion swelling up, and I look over at her. I memorize the details of her face like it's the first time I'm seeing her, only I know it's the last. "We need to tell the boys."

She nods, but I can tell she doesn't want to. I don't want to either. It's the last thing I want to do.

I'll be honest with you, I thought if we went away, we could fix it that weekend and she would see she still loved me, but it didn't happen that way. I knew it was a long shot, but I've never been the kind of guy to back down from a challenge. Deep down, I never thought I deserved a woman like Madison. Maybe this was fate finally delivering its fast "fuck you" ball.

I take the bags inside while Madison goes upstairs without saying a word. I can hear laughter outside and smile, the first one today. Running upstairs, I fill a bag of clothes. She's up there in our bedroom on the bed, her face in her hands crying.

I'm not as much of an asshole as you'd think so I sit next to her and wrap my arm around her. She doesn't drop her hands and continues to cry.

"I'm sorry," I tell her, though I don't know exactly what I'm sorry for. Maybe for everything, but mostly for what I said in anger.

"Me too," she mumbles, pulling away and escaping to the bathroom.

Heading back downstairs, I think about everything I need to get done this week. I've neglected so much I'm behind at the office and the Wellington house. In the kitchen, I grab my laptop and charger and toss it in my bag along with some files I had in my office.

Brantley rushes inside, a water gun in his hand, Noah attached to his foot. "Come on, Wolverine, wingman. I need my wingman. We're going down!" Dropping to his knees, he grabs Noah by the waist and holds him to the ground.

"Grr!" Noah growls at him, attempting to bite his nose.

Just then Callan runs inside after them, cackling with his super soaker in his hand and sprays Brantley's back.

Someday, Brantley's going to make a great dad. "Daddy!" Callan yells when he sees me and drops his gun on the kitchen floor running over to me. And then he sees my bag on the floor, and his stare holds mine. "Where are you going?"

I don't want to tell him, but he's here and questioning. He's too smart for his own good.

I look at Brantley, who gives me a sympathetic smile. I swallow, my voice cracking when I say, "Come in here, buddy." I move into the family room off the kitchen and then pat the spot next to me on the couch. "I need to talk to you."

He shakes his head, knowing what I'm going to say. "I wanted you guys to fix your issues."

I brush his hair from his face. "I tried, buddy, but sometimes you can't fix it."

"You didn't try hard enough. It's what you tell me. You do what you have to do to make it work, no matter what."

I want to tell him he's right, because he is. I should have tried harder but so should she.

Tears roll down his innocent face. "I don't want you to move away."

Jesus Christ, it's like a goddamn sledgehammer has hit my chest. "I'll still be around," I tell him, my chin shaking as I lean in to kiss his forehead. "I'm never going to leave you. I just won't be living here with you, and I'll be at your game on Saturday."

Callan stands, tears coming stronger now and I try to stop him, but he pushes past me and runs upstairs.

Goddamn it.

I look at Brantley who's holding Noah. He sets him down, a frown set on his lips.

Standing, I take Noah from him. He slaps my cheek. "Hi, Daddy."

"Hey, bud." I kiss his cheek, and he frowns.

He pushes my face away and wiggles out of my arms. "No kisses."

Noah's young enough he won't understand most of this, but there will be a time when he does.

He runs upstairs.

"Need a place to stay?" Brantley asks.

I nod. I've got nothing to say.

You can't believe that, right?

Well, it's true.

The next few days pass in a blur, and before I know it, it's Saturday morning.

Do you see that guy standing twenty feet from his soon-to-be ex-wife?

He's fucking miserable. He's barely slept, barely ate and this just in, homeless. Well, I'm sleeping on Brantley's couch, but it sucks. I've always known he's a bit strange, but the dude eats his cereal separate from his milk. Like he takes a bite of dry cereal and then takes a drink of milk.

He claims it keeps the cereal in the bottom of the bowl from getting stale.

Callan's team is well into the second inning, I mean, quarter, or period… I don't fucking know what it is, just that there are a bunch of kids kicking around a ball.

I'm not paying much attention to my surroundings, other than watching one of my son's play soccer and the other one trying to befriend a lizard next to him.

That's when I notice Nathalie standing next to me watching Brantley play with her little devil child.

Call me an asshole, but I say with a chuckle, "So you're pretty excited to have a new girl in your club, aren't you, Natalie."

Without looking at me, she wipes what looks to be a tear from her face. Girls like Nathalie don't cry though. It's probably sweat. "What are you talking about, Ridge?"

Ha. That's funny. Look at her purposely fucking up my name like I do hers.

"Your single mommies club. I'm sure she told you we're getting a divorce." The words burn my throat. "Now you have a partner in crime, and you can do everything single moms do, like talk shit about the ex and how useless he is."

That's when she turns to me, and I see she's crying. Actual fucking tears. "I never wanted that for her. This isn't a life I'd wish upon anyone." She motions over her shoulder to her son. "Raising a child, raising a son by yourself isn't ideal. It's fucking hard, and there's times where I hate myself for doing it alone. Mostly because if anyone is hurting, it's Grady because when he finds out his father didn't want him, I can't imagine how that's going to feel for him."

I can. It's a shitty fucking feeling, believe me.

And then I feel bad for being mean to her. For a half a second. This is Nathalie we're talking about.

That's when Kip walks up to me. "Where's Madison?"

The last person I want to see today is this dick tip. I don't look at him. "How should I know?"

"Well,"—he pushes his sunglasses up over his head—"she's your wife."

I notice his right eye is bruised. Probably from another one of these dad's. I bet he made a move on their wife. I'd deck the fucker too. I shrug and walk away from him to wait for Callan. I'm sure as shit not telling him we're getting a divorce.

About fifteen feet away I can see Noah playing in the park where Grady is, and out of nowhere, another little boy about two feet taller than my son pushes him down. I don't do anything because I'm half expecting Noah to stand up and bite him. Wouldn't be the first time he bit someone.

But he doesn't. He sits there staring at the kid.

What a fuck face. The kid, not Noah. I'm just about to walk over there when Grady picks up a handful of rocks and chucks them at the kid's face.

Nathalie gasps from behind me. "Oh my God, Grady don't throw rocks!" And then she takes off running toward them.

Madison reappears from the bathroom, and Noah runs toward her like nothing happened. She smiles when she notices me standing on the sideline. "Oh, hey."

I smile too, but it's forced and painful because I don't think I have a reason to smile. "Hey."

She's quiet for a moment and then carefully looks at me, her voice just above a whisper. "Do you want to come by after the game and have dinner?"

"I thought you and Kip have pizza after every game. It's like a tradition, right?"

Madison frowns. "We'd rather have dinner with *you*."

Did you catch the *we*? I did. What the fuck is that supposed to mean?

I don't say anything, and she panics a little, her cheeks flushing. "If you already have plans... I understand."

"It's not that I have plans. It's just I left a jobsite to come here, and I need to get back."

And here I am choosing work over my family again. Isn't that why she wanted a divorce in the first place?

"I'll come over around five, is that okay?"

Her eyes brighten. "Yes, that works perfect."

We have dinner that night and it's as if nothing's changed when you look at us from the outside. A family of four, eating, talking, laughing, but something has changed. It hurts to think this won't be happening anymore and I won't be sharing a home with them.

When dinner's finished, Madison stands to clean up the table and Noah since most of his food went on the floor or himself. I grab the plate from her hand. "I can do this."

"The dishwasher isn't working." She turns her head for a moment to look at Noah who's now crawling on the floor in the kitchen under the table eating what he threw down there.

"I'll do these for you."

Callan stands up from his place beside me. "I'll help, Dad."

I'm not wild about him helping and you'll see why in a minute, but I'm more caught up in the fact that he's calling me Dad all the time now and not ignoring me after the other night.

Callan's idea of doing the dishes is washing one dish, drying it, putting it away and then starting on the next. It goes to show you how different our personalities are in that aspect. I usually always break at least one dish while I'm doing them.

I laugh when he reaches for a bowl.

He looks at me. "What?"

I nudge his shoulder with mine. "I love your thought process."

He glances behind us when we hear a noise in the living room. It's Noah, naked from his bath Madison must have given him. He's also peeing on a plant next to the window.

"Should we tell Mom?"

"Nah. I think that plant likes urine because he's been doing it for the last six months and it hasn't died yet."

Callan smiles, reaching for another plate.

We finish the dishes and Callan goes upstairs to get ready for bed. That's when Madison finds me in the Kitchen. "Thanks for coming tonight. I know the boys enjoyed having you here."

I nod and lean into the counter. "Have you talked to Callan about the other school?"

Madison shakes her head. "I didn't, but I've given it a lot of thought and I don't think we should put him in a different school. He's already upset he's different from the other kids his age. I just think uprooting him to a new school will make it harder on him." She motions with a flick of her wrist between us. "All this is going to be hard enough."

When my parents divorced, my mom and I moved to Phoenix where her sister lived. My dad moved to Vegas. I remember being so upset with both my parents for making me change schools during the middle of the year and not only that, forcing me to start a whole new life somewhere else because they couldn't get their shit together.

I didn't talk to my dad for two years after that.

I couldn't let that happen to Callan and Noah. I wouldn't.

I stand there and wait for Madison to look at me, devastation in both our eyes. "I want to be able to see them whenever I want. You can have the house, cars, whatever you want from me, but don't take them away too."

She nods. "I wouldn't do that to you, Ridley."

Wouldn't she? I never thought she'd file for a divorce without coming and talking to me first, but she did that.

I give a tip of my head upstairs. “I’m gonna say goodnight to the boys.”

Noah’s already asleep. You can literally put him in bed and he’s asleep in two minutes. And if he doesn’t fall asleep right away, sing gangster rap.

Callan’s another story. He likes to read before bed so I know he’ll be up. Knocking lightly on his door, I enter quietly. “Hey, bud, I’m gonna head out. Just wanted to tuck you in.”

He smiles and sets his book aside when I sit on the edge of his bed. “I’ve been thinking….” And the look on his face tells me he has. “Since you won’t be around, will you take me to Ukraine? It'd make me feel better about all this.”

I can’t believe what I’m hearing. He’s playing me and you know what, I’m kinda proud he’s pulling this card out. I laugh. “Are you trying to bribe me?

He shrugs. “Maybe a little.”

I pull his blankets up. “How about this, how about I check into it?” I have checked into it a little. Remember? Gamma radiation and $1300 air fare.

He lies back on his bed. “Good enough for me.”

I glance at the book I got him for his birthday, the one he’s been reading. “What's with you and nuclear bombs?”

“You mean power plants? Because that's what Chernobyl was.”

“Yes, sorry.”

His eyes brighten. Probably because I’m taking interest. “It's not the power plant itself, it’s the fact that those power plants were originally made so they could enrich uranium to be used as fuel for a nuclear bomb.”

“So bombs fascinate you?”

“Yeah, they’re cool. You can level an entire city with one!”

I raise an eyebrow. “Should I be scared?”

“Well no.” He waves me off. “I’m not going to set one off, but I’d love to build one.”

Oh dear God. Really?

We laugh together and he grabs my left hand and sees I’m still wearing my ring. “I think you’re going to work it out.”

My brow pulls together, my stomach dipping. “Why do you say that?”

He sets my hand down. “Mommy cries a lot more. She misses you. We miss you.”

Tears sting my eyes, emotion surfacing for what I can’t change and desperately want to. “You know I love you, right? This doesn’t change anything between us and never will.”

His eyes move around his room and then land on mine. “I know. I love you, too, Dad.”

There’s one thing I can appreciate about my nuclear bomb obsessed seven-year-old. He may be into science and bombs and way smarter than me, but it doesn’t change the fact that he’s still seven and forgiveness comes easy for him. Life hasn’t taught him the harsh lessons of trust and betrayal. No one important in his life has lied to him or broken promises made only to diffuse a moment.

I wasn’t going to be the first. I wouldn’t, I *couldn’t* go back on this one. Whatever happened between Madison and me, it wouldn’t come between me and my boys.

Downstairs, Madison's in the living room picking up toys off the floor and I can see what Callan's referring to. She's sad.

I clear my throat when I'm standing near the front door and she looks up. "I'm gonna head out."

Her glassy eyes move around the room and then land on mine, uneasiness masking her features. There's something else about her I can't place, an emotion. "Okay."

I study her thoughtfully for a moment, desperately wanting the uneasy look she carries to disappear.

I shouldn't leave, should I? You're thinking it, I know you are. In your head, or maybe out-loud, you're screaming at me to walk over to her, apologize and carry her upstairs where I do something romantic.

And I want to, I do, but my pride holds me back.

Madison reaches up and tugs at her hair, letting down her ponytail. Her dark hair spills around her should as she stands, a firetruck in her other hand at her hip. "Thanks for spending time with them."

My heart lurches thinking of everything Callan said upstairs. With a sigh, my shoulders hunch. "It's no problem. I'll come by tomorrow night and say goodnight to them, if that's okay?"

She nods, breathing out even breaths. "You can come by anytime you want."

Despite everything that happened between us, I'm thankful for this right here. Our ability to put our own differences aside and see what matters most. The kids and their wellbeing.

As I'm leaving, I sneak a glance over my shoulder at her, hating the sorrow lingering in her every feature.

19

MY FATHER THE BACHELOR

For the next three weeks, I work.

Nonstop.

Isn't that what Madison said drove her away?

Well this time, I work on our house, the new one and with Brantley's help, we finish it. I still make sure to see the boys. I show up every night to tuck them into bed and read with Callan.

I can honestly say despite this being a really fucking shitty situation, it's brought me closer to the boys.

I look around the house I've finally finished. Knowing they'll be moving into it soon, without me, my chest constricts and my heart begins to pound. How could I have let this happen?

"This place is beautiful, man," Brantley says beside me when the inspector leaves after the final walk through.

I lean into the kitchen island, my arms crossed over my chest and stare at the keys in front of me. "Thanks for your help with it. I owe you big time."

"Yes, you do." He chuckles and nods to the keys. "Are you giving them to her today?"

"Yeah, I signed the divorce papers and I need to give them to her. We're approaching the sixty days here soon." I shrug and put the keys in my pocket. "I guess I'll just give them to her with the keys to the house."

When I think about those divorce papers, and the finality they'll soon have, I want to get away from everything. It may not be the most responsible time to leave, but I need to.

"Can you take care of things for a few days?" I ask Brantley.

He knows what I'm going through and nods. "Yeah, I got it." And then he shakes his head, clasping his hand on my shoulder. "I'm really sorry things didn't work out with you and Madison."

"Yeah, me too." And he has no idea just how badly I am sorry.

"Where are you going?"

I shrug. "Thinking about going to see my dad for a few days since we can't start the Murphy project until next week."

Brantley's eyes light up remembering the last time we visited my dad in Vegas. "I'm coming with you."

"No, you're *not*."

It's a Tuesday morning when I leave for my dad's house in Nevada. I hate Tuesdays. I left the keys to the new house and the signed divorce papers on the counter in an envelope this morning. I wasn't sure what she'd think when she got them and I didn't leave a note. I was hoping she'd notice the keys and go look at the house but I wasn't sure. Maybe she'd throw them away at this point.

Madison promised me I could have the boys this weekend, but the last place I want to take them is to my dad's. Last time I took them there, Callan wanted to move to Vegas and Noah pretty much attached himself to my father like he was the greatest thing in the world.

Didn't do a lot for my own ego, but this is Mike Cooper we're talking about. Surely if they spent enough time around him, they'd see he's not much but a sixty-two-year-old eternal bachelor, who in my opinion, should be in a nursing home.

Staring at the road ahead of me, I can't help but think about how different my life will be. I'm the weekend dad. And forget about getting regular pussy. I don't have time to go out and look for it. Not that I want it. I don't want it. I want one pussy. Madison's.

When I'm driving, I like to sing sometimes, and lately it seems country music is always on and every song fits my life as far as I'm concerned. Especially Blackhawk's song "Goodbye Says it All."

"Blackhawk didn't sing about your life," Brantley says beside me, staring at his phone. "Will you stop it?"

Remember when I said no to him coming with me? He clearly didn't listen to me, or I didn't hold my ground. Either way, he's coming with me.

"Yes, they did. Think about it." I jab my finger at the radio. "This is my life. My wife left me."

He rolls his eyes but doesn't look over at me. "You're being dramatic."

I raise an eyebrow. "Am I?"

He finally looks at me. "Yes!"

"Am not." I'm sure you can imagine, but I'm pouting.

"Listen." Brantley sets his phone down in the cup holder. "Nathalie said—"

"Shut up," I interrupt him. "I hate her."

"You hate everyone. Just listen...."

"Do I have to?"

"Yes." He smacks my shoulder and I jerk the wheel slightly at the impact. "You do."

"No, I don't," I point out. "I could open the door and jump out."

He laughs and shakes his head. "Well then, make sure you tuck and roll better than Kennedy did."

"I will." And then I remember I'm driving and that really wouldn't work very well. My luck I'd run over myself with my own truck.

I sigh dramatically after two minutes. I want to know what Nathalie said, damn it.

"What did she say?"

He sighs, too. "She said Madison's crying all the time."

I saw Madison yesterday when I stopped by to tuck the boys into bed. I try to recall her face and the expression on it. At the time I thought maybe she was frustrated I kept showing up every night, but it wasn't that. It was one of sadness. And then I thought, okay, well, I'm sad, so she's probably sad too. You don't spend eight years of your life with someone and just stop caring. I knew that much.

"Did she say anything else?"

"That Madison is probably going to come talk to you about it." He gives me a sincere look. "I don't think she wants it to be over."

His words make my stomach dip and my heart pound in my ears. Part of me is angry by what he's saying because if she didn't want it, why'd she file for divorce? Why was nothing I did good enough these last two months?

The drive to my dad's house in Boulder City takes us about five hours. He owns a hotel in Vegas. Not one of the nice casinos. Think like the Pink Flamingo with trashy women and disease-infested pools. That's not really the case, but whatever. He has a big-ass mansion in the hills, and I intend on crashing it for a couple days to clear my head.

I'm assuming by now you know my father and I don't have the greatest relationship. And your assessment would be spot on. Now, before you meet my father, his interpretation of our relationship and mine are completely different. Like Dr. Jekyll and Mr. Hyde. Only I'm not entirely sure who's who because we change roles a lot.

Do you see the man who looks like he's spent the last twenty years tanning every day? Not the woman with the leather skin beside him hacking up a lung, look to the left, around her, though their skin is fairly similar. He's the one with a white button-down shirt with his thick chest hair sticking out. He's also smoking a cigar and wearing board shorts. Classy huh?

That's Mike Cooper. My father. Looks can be deceiving but in this case, what you're thinking about him is probably pretty spot on. A man who's spent too much time beside the pool might possibly have an STD and thinks highly of himself. If you're thinking that, then you'd be correct.

Did you ever see the movie *Weekend at Bernies*? My dad is exactly like Bernie Lomax.

The woman beside him disappears inside the house and he smiles when Brantley and I make it to the door, my bag on my shoulder. "I'm glad you came. Why didn't you bring Madison and the boys?"

"They're at home. Callan has school." *And Madison and I are getting a divorce.*

Notice how that last parts not said out loud?

He does too.

Brantley snorts beside me. "Uh, hello? What about me?"

"I saw you last month."

I turn to look at Brantley. "You saw him last month?"

He shrugs, appearing guilty. "I was in town?"

"Bullshit."

"Well, I'm glad you decided to come see your old man," my dad says, attempting to change the subject. I'm really not surprised Brantley comes to see my dad. He's like his hero and I'll never understand why. Probably because they both think they're Hugh Heffner. "It's been too long since we've had guy time."

His idea and my idea of "guy time" are completely different. Believe me.

When we're inside, he grabs his gun from the safe. "Come on, boys. Let's go hunt some pigs."

See what I mean? We just got here after driving five hours, and he wants us to go hunt pigs.

"Who's that woman?" I point to Leather Lady in the kitchen.

Dad shrugs. "My housekeeper."

More like maid he fucks on the side. My dad has never ever been faithful to one woman. I think it's impossible for him to remain monogamous.

Setting my bag inside, Brantley and I follow him out the door when he hands the both of us a rifle. I'll never pull the trigger, but I won't tell him that. "How're the boys and Madison?"

"They're good." I get inside his truck and close the door while Brantley gets in the back. "Callan's playing soccer and doing great in school. Noah runs around the house with a cape screaming he's Wolverine. Typical shit."

Did you notice I didn't say anything about Madison?

My dad does too and quirks an eyebrow at me but lets it go.

"So what about you and what's her name?" I say what's her name because I honestly don't know who his ex-wife was or is or if he has a new one or not. Hell, knowing him he might marry Leather Lady next week and I wouldn't know about it until he tells me they're getting a divorce.

"Laura?"

I stare out the window. "Sure."

"Well let's see, she took about twenty-five thousand in the divorce and got my house in Palm Springs."

"You have a house in Palm Springs?"

"*Had*. Past tense." He pulls down a gravel road I'm sure we shouldn't be on. Mostly because it said no trespassing, but my dad thinks those kind of rules don't apply to him. I'm serious. Speed limits, traffic laws, property boundaries, he pays no mind to any of them ever. I doubt he even has a valid driver's license anymore.

You're surprised he owns a hotel and lives in a mansion, aren't you?

Well when I say he doesn't abide by certain rules, he's incredibly business savvy, and I'm thankful I inherited that from him.

"Dad, it says no trespassing back there."

He looks over his shoulder. "I didn't see it." And then he punches my shoulder. "I noticed you avoided my question about Madison. What's going on?"

Brantley goes to say something in the backseat but I take the butt end of the rifle and smack him lightly in the head, hoping he shuts the fuck up.

Sighing, I stare out ahead of me at the barren desert "no trespassing" land. "She filed for divorce. For two months I tried to get her to fall back in love with me and get her to see it was a mistake, but she didn't see it that way. I really thought I'd be able to fix it. I never wanted the boys to go through what I did… the weekend dad." I laugh sarcastically. "Though you weren't around much."

Dad shrugs. "I know I wasn't. I did a pretty shitty job as a father."

We agree on that much. "You did." It may sound like I'm being a total shit to my dad, but things were pretty bad between us for a number of years, but since then we've gotten closer.

"I'm sorry you're going through this. It's tough. I should know since I've been through it four times."

I know he's trying to make me feel better about it, but the comment only pisses me off. "Why did you get married that many times? I don't get it. Why'd you always have to be in a relationship?" I ask this, but what I really mean is why wasn't I good enough.

I'm my dad's only child. That he knows about. I'm sure there are others, but he's not aware of any that I know of.

But here's the thing. In *all* those marriages, he went from one to the next and I was never part of their lives together until I was fifteen and I had to be when my mother died and I had nowhere else to go. I lived with him in Boulder City from fifteen to eighteen and moved out the day I graduated. In all that time, four years, he had two different wives and six different girlfriends. It's amazing I turned out so damn good because the example set by him was horrible.

"I know you think it was something you did, but it wasn't," he finally says. "It was never about you, or your mom. I'll never love another woman the way I loved Evelyn." By the way, Evelyn is my mother. "I fucked up. Plain and simple, and I never planned on being married that many times. Truth is, I don't like being alone."

"You weren't alone. You had me."

"I made a lot of mistakes," he admits. "Don't be like me. Be there for your boys. Put them before everything else because you never know when you're going to need them. I was a horrible father. Don't be like me."

I'm not a hugger. I've never been one. My father? He likes to hug, and I'm not sure why that is. So he pulls me into a one-armed hug and jerks the steering wheel in the process. "Let's go hunt some pigs."

That's if we make it there alive because when he jerks the steering wheel we end up in a ditch and then catapult over it into the desert where he announces, "Perfect spot."

Crazy bastard.

I said I'd explain my distaste for cats later, right?

It's later.

Here's a story for you. I've never been into hunting. I once shot my neighbor's cat with a BB gun in the back.

Not my best decision but I was six, and it seemed like a good idea because the fucking cat was an asshole. And I was six, who gives a six-year-old a BB gun? Mike Cooper does.

Anyway, it didn't kill him. Instead, it broke his back, and I had to listen to it moan outside my window for an hour because it couldn't move. Well, it could, but it was pathetic. Its front legs worked but the back legs wouldn't. Think of a sit and spin. You know those things you sit on and spin you around? That's what this cat looked like because it just kept crawling in a circle.

Anyway, the damn thing was loud, and my dad found out and made me go outside and put it out of its misery. So with a shovel in hand, I attempted to kill it. I've never felt so horrible in my life. I honestly thought I was going to hell for that. When it was dead, I threw up and vowed to never harm an animal again.

Little hard when your dad's an avid hunter and drags you with him for his father-son time. In reality, it's a time when he says, "Hold my gun, I gotta take a piss and if you see a deer, shoot the fucker."

He one, has a weak bladder and two, doesn't realize how many bucks I turned my head on.

So there he is, staring down a javelina with his rifle pointed right between its eyes.

"I'm not gonna lie, Dad. If you end up shooting that, I'm gonna have to cover my eyes."

"You pussy. No wonder Madison wants a divorce."

He's real supportive, isn't he?

The answer to that would be no.

I'm not even paying attention to the pigs, I can't. It makes me sick to my stomach.

"Noah killed a cat last month," Brantley tells my dad.

"No shit?" He chuckles, still focused on the pig in his sight. "I knew he was my grandkid."

A loud boom rattles through the valley we're in and the pig drops to the ground. I hope he doesn't think I'm eating pork tonight.

Brantley elbows me. "Your dad is awesome."

"Ugh!" I say, sounding like Callan when he's annoyed. I should draw a picture with stick figures and pigs to display my distaste for what we're doing like Callan does. But I don't. Instead I'm researching again.

"What are you doing?" Brantley asks, slapping my phone out of my hand when my dad goes to get the pig he murdered.

I grab my phone from the dirt and blow it off refusing to watch the pig get slaughtered. "I'm checking on a vacation to Ukraine."

He makes a face of disgust, his rifle on his shoulder like he's some kind of sniper. Which he's not. Brantley's never shot anything, that I know of. But then again, he tells me nothing so I really wouldn't know. "Why?"

"Callan wants to go see Chernobyl."

"What the hell is Chernobyl."

"Only the biggest nuclear disaster in the world," I say proudly, like I know what the fuck I'm talking about.

My dad and Brantley shoot three pigs, toss them in the back of his truck and we head back to dad's house where he cleans them and I nearly vomit three times.

That's when they say, "We're going out," like I should be excited about this.

"I don't want to go out." Though I'm thankful to not be eating those pigs they shot, I don't want to go out to dinner with them because I know where that will lead. They'll get me drunk, convince me to go to a strip club and I'll end the night with another tattoo of Tinkerbell on my ankle. It took me a year to have that one removed and I can still see her wings if I look closely.

"You're coming with us," Brantley says, setting a shot of Midleton whiskey down in front of me. "Drink this and you'll forget about your problems."

"I don't want to because if we go out, the next thing I know you'll drag me to another strip club."

My dad rolls his eyes as he's fixing his shirt to make his chest hair visible. At this point, he might as well just unbutton it all the way because he literally has only three buttons fastened and I can see his bellybutton.

I stare at his chest like I'm offended by his choice of attire, because I am. It's gross. "This isn't *Miami Vice*. Why are you dressed like that?"

He blows me off by waving his hand in my face. "I look good. And no, we won't drag you to a strip club because the last time we went you yelled, 'You bitches gonna let me titty fuck you later?' in a blonde's face."

"That was one time and I was in college. You can't blame me."

Brantley chuckles and downs his own shot. "Well, it left a lasting impression on said titty bar because you're not allowed back there… for life."

I wave my hand at them but I take the shot anyway. "They didn't say life."

"I was there. They did."

I roll my eyes and flop my head down on the table I'm sitting at. And no, I won't explain that night because I don't remember it. If it wasn't for Tinkerbell, I'd swear they were making it all up.

"What's wrong with you? Where's your balls?" my dad asks, and my head shoots up from the table because I know exactly what's coming out of Brantley's mouth next.

And it does. "Madison skinned them. He let her wax his nut sac."

I glare at him. "I told you that in confidence," I seethe.

"No, you didn't. Nathalie told me."

"Ugh!" I groan again.

My dad groans too. "Get off your ass, you pussy. I'm hungry."

I end up going out to dinner with my dad and Brantley and we *don't* go to the strip club. Well, they do *after* dinner, but I don't go with them. I stay at the house where they drop me off and FaceTime Callan and Noah while trying to read Madison's every expression as the boys sit on her lap. This, her, them, it's all a reminder as to why I have no business being at a strip club. I'm still in love with my wife.

The day Brantley and I leave, my dad offers me some advice I take to heart.

"Are you willing to be there for your boys no matter what comes their way?"

I nod. "Yes."

Why do I feel like I'm on trial here?

"Are you willing to raise them to be young men and not pussies?"

Is he referring to me? What a dick. He probably is. But I answer with, "Yes."

"Are you willing to push them to become men and treat women with respect?"

Again, is he fucking talking about me here? He certainly isn't talking about himself. This man doesn't know respect around women.

When I nod, he shoves my shoulder, once and pushes me into the side of my truck. "Then don't give up on them. Don't make the same mistakes I did."

I'm not at all sure how to process his words of wisdom or bullshit, but it makes me think on the drive home. I will never be like Mike Cooper.

That's sad to say, but my mom once told me my father may not be an example of what to be like, but at least he was an example of what not to be.

So as I head home, my intention is to never make my boys feel like any of this is their fault and set a good example for them. Not a sixty-two-year-old bachelor who's been married four times and shoots pigs for fun.

20

THE TROJAN HORSE DECEPTION

It's been fifty-two days since Madison filed the paperwork and every day closer to that sixty-day deadline is about as painful as stabbing myself in the heart repeatedly.

I wake up every morning and think to myself, this can't be real, can it? It's a joke, right?

I wish it was.

I don't know why I go by the new house when I make it back to town Friday morning. Maybe because I built the place and I want to see it one last time. I'm not sure.

When I started building this house, Madison, Callan—Noah didn't really give a shit—and I were so excited to have something of our own that I built and I took pride in that. I took pride in the fact I was creating our home we'd share for years to come, and my craftsmanship would welcome them. Everywhere they'd look, they'd see me in this house, even when I wasn't there to be with them.

I wondered even now with me not living here if Madison wouldn't think of me when she was here. Would Callan proudly tell his friends, "My dad built this house himself."

How did it fall apart right before my eyes? Part of me knows I only have myself to blame for all this. If I would have paid attention, saw what was happening, maybe I could have changed before it all went to shit.

As I stand there staring out the house from the backyard, I get the feeling I'm not alone.

You know when someone's standing behind you. I also don't need to turn around to know who it is because whenever she's around me, I *feel* it. I *feel* her. "I see you got the key so you must have the signed divorce papers I left for you too. I just want you to know I'm willing to walk away, give you what you want, but I'm not giving up custody of the boys. You will let me see my sons whenever I want. Joint custody is the only option, so don't even think about trying for anything less."

When I do face her, she's crying, and though I'm not surprised she's in tears because she has been the last three times I've seen her, there's something different about her I can't place.

"What's wrong? Isn't the house what you thought it would be? If there is something you don't like, just tell me and we'll change it. I want you and the boys to be happy here." What the fuck am I saying? I want her to be happy? Is that even true?

Of course it is. She's the mother of my sons. I absolutely want her to be happy because right now I see my mother standing there, crying, asking my father why we weren't good enough for him. I don't remember that many of their fights, but I remember that one.

I've never been one to comfort people. I always feel awkward doing it so I just stand there with my hands in my pockets wondering what I should do. She wanted a divorce, yet she's constantly in tears. Isn't that the opposite reaction if it's something you want?

"The house is perfect. I haven't seen the inside yet, but it's just like we dreamed."

My stare drops from hers as a pang of sadness hits me. This house is exactly what we dreamed of. Everything we ever wanted, I gave them. "I'm glad you like it. Maybe it will give you that fresh start you're looking for." Look at me not being bitter. See. And you thought I was only an asshole. Admit it, you thought it a time or two.

I certainly did.

"I love it, but I want to live in it as a family, not just Callan, Noah, and me."

I'm confused. Did she just say that? Reaching up, I scratch the side of my head. "What do you mean as a family?"

"I never wanted the divorce," she whispers.

"Excuse me?"

"Do you remember the day you got the papers, that morning in the shower?" she asks, afraid to look at me. I'm not sure why she's asking. Or maybe I do.

"I do." I stare at my hands instead of her face, trying desperately to shut down and not care about anything she's about to say to me in fear it will only hurt.

Our eyes catch then, despite me not wanting to look at her. She tilts her head, a wince to her features.

"That morning, I told myself I wasn't going to do it," she admits, but there's more she isn't saying.

I shift my stance and shove my shaking hands in the pockets of my shorts. "What are you talking about?"

"Me filing for divorce...."

I groan. I don't want to keep talking about this anymore. "Mad, I signed the papers. We don't have to keep hashing this out. I get it, you want a divorce, and I'm giving it to you."

"I don't know…." Look at her face, she really doesn't and she's talking in circles. She's lost in thought and then says, "This past month has been hell without you. I hate it."

There's part of me that doesn't want to stand here and listen to her say anything else. And then I do, because I deserve that much, right? The diligent side of me wants some fucking answers. I want the bloody, gory details that led up to my slaying.

Might be a bad example considering, but still, it's true.

As we stare at one another, it's as if the air around us stills, my focus entirely on her.

"I miss you, Ridley," she says, opening herself up, showing me herself, leading into something. What, I don't know.

"Why, Mad?" I whisper into the night, the setting sun around us lighting up the side of her face. "Why did you use me that morning only to rip my heart out hours later?"

We're both silent, but I can tell by the tension in her body she's working herself up to say something, finally.

Her eyes are puffy, wearing these last two months on her face. "Can you listen to me?" she begs desperately, hopeful I might.

"Only if you tell me the truth," I say smugly.

She nods, blowing out a huge breath like she's completely ridding her body of oxygen. "Can you just please listen to me and hear me out?"

My mouth goes dry looking at her. Waiting for my answer, she's taking large even breaths, warming herself up for something, or maybe settling her nerves.

I throw my hands up in the air. "*Jesus Christ*, just tell me already!"

Frowning, her frustration takes over. I can tell after our argument at the hotel that night, it's still affecting her and she's struggling to express herself to me now. Dropping her head forward, it's like she's giving up.

"I get it. You did what you needed to do," I finish for her, ready to walk away.

That's when her eyes lift to meet mine. "It's not like that, Ridley."

I nod, my voice hitching when I say, "Then what was it like? Because the way I see it, you wanted a divorce and you put me through hell for it."

She tips her head to the side. "You believe that, don't you?"

My heart jumps, my eyes tearing up, filling with the sadness I know too well these days. "How can I not believe it?"

"That's not everything," she says, regret thick as her glossy eyes return to mine. "You don't know everything."

"What are you talking about?"

I don't like the way she says I don't know everything. It makes me feel like she's hiding something from me and I immediately wonder if she's cheated on me. Is that why she wanted a divorce? She said it wasn't that at the hotel, but maybe she just couldn't tell me at the time, and now it's eating at her, and she has to tell me the truth. My face contorts with the thoughts, my heartbeat increasing with every breath it hurts to take.

"About me asking for a divorce…."

The way her voice trails off has my heart in my throat again and my skin prickling with anticipation of her lies.

"I filed for divorce to get your attention," she whispers. "I was trying to think of ways to get your attention, make you see our problems were more than either of us realized, and Nathalie suggested I file for divorce knowing it wouldn't be final for a while and would give us time to work things out." Her eyes drop with the admittance, unable to hold mine anymore. "And right before we left for Sedona, I found out I was pregnant, and it confused me even more. I lied," she says, stepping toward me with a good amount of hesitation. "I never wanted a divorce. I was so frustrated with you and your lack of being present in our lives that I wanted to shake you up. I just… I *wanted* you to be around more, and I didn't know how to come and talk to you."

I stare at her in disbelief. For a long fucking time. I'm talking like solid minutes here, not seconds.

Did she really just say that to me?

Am I getting this right?

The last two months have been a joke?

She played me to get my attention?

Madison starts to fidget and breaks the silence. "Ridley say something."

Say something? She wants me to say something. I don't think she wants to hear what I'm thinking. I'm almost certain she doesn't. Does she even understand the deceit I'm experiencing in this moment? It's like I'm the Greeks in the Trojan war.

Have you ever heard of the story of the Trojan horse? If you haven't, it goes something like this. When the Trojan Paris ran away with Helen, the Spartan king's wife, everything went to shit and war broke out. Think about it. His wife ran away with another man. I'd be pissed too. Anyway, this fucking war went on for something like ten years when the Trojan's thought they'd overtook the Greeks.

But that wasn't the case at all. Now comes for the curve ball, the lie. The deception.

Thinking they were being sneaky, or just plain assholes, the Greeks built an enormous wooden horse with a hollow belly where they would hide men. So after the Greeks convinced these poor ignorant bastards this fucking horse was a peace offering, the Trojan's accepted the horse and brought it into Troy. Cool right? All's fair in love and war?

Not exactly. We all know that's bullshit by now. Look at me. Anyway, that night as the Trojan's slept peacefully, the Greeks snuck outside the horse's ass and proceeded to slaughter their enemy. It's pretty fucked up when you think about it, huh? Or genius depending on what side you're on.

But in this case, I'm positive I now know how the people of Troy felt. Gutted.

Do you see that guy? The one barely breathing and blood pressure through the roof? If you don't, he's the one who looks like he's going to kill the woman in front of him. He won't, believe me. As we've discussed, he doesn't have murder in him but he's really upset.

Shaking my head, I close my eyes against the adrenaline hitting me straight to the heart. I didn't want to know this truth, and I'm beyond the limits of furious; I'm gone. I can't process this truth.

She lied.

She did it to get my attention and what, now she's fucking pregnant? That's probably the only goddamn reason she's telling me this shit. She knows she has three kids now and no husband. Maybe she's only telling me this because she needs my fucking money.

Is the baby even mine?

You have to admit after everything, it's a valid thought.

Needing a breath, I breathe in, the sound sharp and sudden as if I've finally come up for air. When she says those words, when those lies became a reality, my feet and hands tingle, my whole life changing in front of me, out of reach because what I know is a lie, an illusion she led me to believe was a lie. A fucking lie.

"Ridley…." Madison's voice draws me from my thoughts, and my anger hits me.

"Are you fucking serious? I've spent the last two months busting my ass trying to become the man you told me you needed me to be. I've neglected my business and for what?" I throw my hands up in the air. "So you and Nathalie could play me like a puppet and get a good laugh? Is that what you fucking wanted?"

Madison reaches out to touch my arm, only I jerk it away from her. I can't have her touching me. "No, Ridley, that's not it at all. Everything I told you was true. The loneliness I felt, the void you were putting between us, the constant neglect of your family, that was all true. I just wanted you to be around more, to care more."

I pause, swallowing over the words, attempting to process what she's saying, but I fail. The anger, the resentment, all roll through me and shake my bones. I can't fucking believe this.

My thought process to those words is something like shock, then denial and ultimately, anger. She has to notice the widening of my eyes, the shake of my head and then the clenching of my fists. The words hit me like a ton of bricks.

"To care more? Please tell me you just didn't say that."

Can you believe this shit?

"To care more? Jesus Christ, all I do is *care*! Why do you think I work those long hours Madison? Do you honestly believe I'm happy working seven days a week, twelve hours a day? Fuck no, I'm not! I do *all* of it for you. I've spent my whole adult life working my ass off so we would never have to struggle like my mom and I did when I was growing up. You, Callan, Noah… everything I do is to show you how much I care. I've never wanted you to worry. I wanted you to have the freedom to live a life with luxuries and conveniences. I wanted your working to be a choice and not a necessity. Don't you get it?" My voice is pleading, a man breaking apart at the very thought of losing his family over this shit. "Everything I've done for the past eight years has been for you!"

Her chin quivers, but she straightens her posture like she's refusing to let herself cry yet. "I'm not your mom, and you're not your dad, Ridley. I never asked for any of that. Never once have I complained I didn't have enough things! No, the only thing I've ever complained about is that I didn't have enough of you. I don't give a damn about material objects! What good is having 'everything' when all it does is make you feel like you've got nothing?"

"It's easy to say that now, Madison, but I never heard one complaint when I would buy you a new car, or we were able to afford the furniture you loved." I know it's a dick move to be bringing up all this, but can you honestly fucking blame me at this point? "All I've ever done since the day I've met you is try and be someone who deserves you and yet again I'm being reminded that I'm failing miserably."

"I have never asked you to be someone you're not." She moves closer to me, but I can't take the heat of her body near me. I step back. "The night we met at the Halloween party, the cocky, handsome son of a bitch I met that night, that's who I fell for, not some workaholic who is so disconnected from his family he didn't know his son played soccer. Seriously, Ridley, is that who you want to be?"

Goddamn it. She has a point. A good one. Still, I'm not budging yet. Do you see me? I cross my arms over my chest defiantly.

And then she continues with, "You can't tell me that over the last two months you haven't enjoyed actually getting to know your son? Callan has never been happier than he's been these last two months. He's always been content, but it seemed he was constantly trying to find a way to fit into a mold that he thought you would want him to fit into. I think he thought if he were more normal, then maybe you would be around more. You asked me why he played soccer? Well, why do you think? It's not just to fit with the other kids. It's because he thought that maybe if he was playing a sport, you would take more notice."

Fuck, I know what she's saying is true, but shit, it just proves I'm more of a fuck up than I thought. I'm doing exactly what I always feared, what I suffered through growing up and swore I would *never* allow to happen to my kids—struggling for their father's attention. Throwing themselves into activities and behavior to please their parents. I did that for years with my own father.

"I'm listening to everything you're saying, Madison, but you know what the problem is? All I hear is that you lied to me. That you filed for divorce to fuck with me! Jesus, I don't even know what to say to you! Do you even understand how fucked up that sounds?"

"I know how fucked up it sounds." She nods. "I do, and I'm sorry."

"Why?" I shout, my voice breaking around the blistering words ringing through the yard. "Why couldn't you have just fucking talked to me instead of making me believe you wanted out?"

Madison takes a deep breath before continuing, and even though her voice is soft, I can hear the embarrassment in her words. "I never meant to hurt you. I thought if I got your attention, you would see the life we're living, the one where we were nothing more than roommates, and it wouldn't be the life you wanted anymore."

"Oh, well hell, you're forgiven then." I try to swallow, but I can't swallow over the dryness. It's impossible.

"Really?" She's watching me again as if she will sacrifice the beat in her chest for the break she's caused in mine. She's completely freaking out but trying really hard not to let it show. I have to give her credit, she's doing a good job controlling herself at the moment.

"No. Go fuck yourself."

Is that harsh? Maybe so, but look at the shit she put me through by filing for divorce to get my attention? Whatever happened to saying, hey, dude, I'm feeling neglected?

The sky around us, once cloudless, rumbles and growls, turning gray, and I know the steady sprinkle is about to turn to a wall of rain, much like the night in Sedona when this all fell apart the first time.

Does it just rain every time we fight?

"I don't blame you if you hate me," Madison murmurs. "I expect it. No… I *deserve* it."

"Really?" I shake my head. After everything, she has no idea how much she deserves it. I look back at her, so furiously hurt I'm scared my voice is going to break, and I won't get out what I need to say. "You expected it? Deserved it? Fucking right you do. Goddamn it, Mad, I love you. And not just any love. It's the kind of love where I can't even think straight. I nearly lost my fucking business trying to make you see that. It's the kind of fucking love where I was half myself for sixty days because by filing those papers, you ripped out my goddamn heart!" I nearly faint after getting all that out, but the look on her face is what sends me to my knees. Nearly. But instead, I walk away from her because I don't care what she's going to say to me next.

In her mind, the conversation is far from over, and she continues to chase after me as I walk around the front of the house, intending to leave. "Just talk to me, please," she begs, sounding like she's ready to drop to her knees at my feet. "Don't leave, please, Ridley!"

I fucking hope she falls to her goddamn knees because then she'll finally be where I've been these past two months. Maybe then she'll finally feel an ounce of pain I've endured.

But then again, I don't want her to trip and hurt herself.

Fuck me for caring.

Turning to leave, Madison reaches to grab my arm, but I sidestep her. "No. No, I need to get out of here. I need to think."

I can't even think of facing her. She's a stranger to me, and I can't look in her eyes and face the reality that the woman I love, the woman I vowed to win back and have busted my ass to remind why we fell in love in the first place, isn't the person I thought she was.

"Ridley, please stop. I get you need time to think, but please don't run. Stay here. I'll give you all the space you need but *please,* don't leave."

I stop. The quiver in her voice when she asks me not to leave is enough to force me to stay where I am. It only takes me a minute to realize that I don't *want* to leave.

"Why?" I shout. "Give me one good reason as to why I should stay."

"Because there are some things I need to say to you," she says, like it's that easy. She's caught up with me at the truck as a flash through the sky and a loud crack of thunder silences the two of us.

The sound stops me, and I look at her, throwing my hands in the air. Racing through thoughts, trying to wrap my mind around my own hurt, I ask, "Why? Wanna make me feel like shit some more? Or wait, maybe you could tell me that baby's not mine." I motion to her stomach. "Is that what you want to explain?"

"Damn it, Ridley, please." She breaths out deeply, frustration clear on her face. "Don't walk away. I just want to talk to you calmly."

Can you believe her? This is just crazy shit, right?

"You can't stand here and tell me you fucking filed for divorce to get my attention. Who fucking does that, Madison? That's some serious bullshit. You're not a kid anymore. That's not how married people communicate. It doesn't work that way, Madison."

"Why can't I explain?" She sounds confused, and I want to laugh in her face. Unbelievable.

My stomach lurches and I feel like we're back in that hotel lobby, my confusion and sadness twisting into more anger and resentment.

"You know what, fuck you!" I reach for the handle of my truck, hoping she will finally leave me alone and give up just like I did.

Of course she doesn't and puts her hand over mine, and I'm pissed to no end. I face her, my eyes fixated on hers. "When did you find out you were pregnant? Was that part of your plan too? Get pregnant so you could take more of my money in the divorce?"

Madison groans as if hearing my words makes her sick to her stomach. "It wasn't like that. I didn't intend on getting pregnant but apparently that morning in the shower, well, that's when it happened," she says, looking like she's really going to vomit. "I found out a few days before we left for Sedona. That's why I agreed to go with you despite not wanting to. I knew we needed to work on things."

Agreed to go with me?

I certainly don't remember it going down like that. It was more along the lines of me begging and her agreeing because Callan was standing next to us, but whatever.

By the look on her face, which is pale, she really looks like she's going to vomit now. I hope she throws up. I hoped all of this has made her physically sick because maybe it's a fraction of what I've been going through these last few days knowing my marriage to a woman I loved more than life itself was over.

Looking up at her, I have to ask, "Then why didn't you *try* in Sedona? Why did you go to lunch with Thomas and blow me off if you're pregnant with my baby and wanting to make it work? Do you have any idea how *I* feel right now?"

She starts crying, slow tears at first but I know what's coming. "I don't know—"

"Shut up." I'm so frustrated with the same bullshit answers. "Just stop talking."

21

FORGIVENESS WORKS BOTH WAYS

We stand there staring at one another. She's afraid to speak, probably since I just told her to shut up and I'm terrified to say anything else.

Truth is, I don't want to hurt her. Drawing in a heavy breath, I let it out slowly and shake my head. Madison attempts to reach for my hand, her footing off somehow and slips on the wet concrete.

I catch her, my hands supporting under her elbows as she studies her footing knowing damn well we shouldn't be standing outside in a thunderstorm. "Go inside the house, I'll follow you."

Jesus, don't look at me like that. No, I'm not going to murder her. I don't have murder in me and despite this anger and pain taking over, I still love Madison. Unfortunately, that will never ever go away. I say unfortunately because if you haven't noticed by now, these past couple months have fucking sucked balls.

Literally.

Once we're inside the house, our shoes squeaking against the tile entry way, I'm reminded of why I built this house and how beautiful it turned out. Everything from the imported wood floors in the family room, the black cabinets she said she always wanted to the granite countertops with the black and gold streaks.

I think it's also the first time Madison has seen the inside despite the fact I gave her the keys a week ago. She gasps, her hand over her mouth and turns to look at me. "Oh my God, Ridley, it's beautiful."

I don't say anything. A thank-you doesn't seem appropriate.

Twisting around, I want to tell her how much it hurts to be in this house and have this reaction from her. I almost want her to hate the house, as crazy as that sounds.

It hurts because inside, it feels like nothing is ever going to be the same again. I don't say anything as her eyes roam around the house from the exotic hardwood floors we ordered from South Africa, the ones with my DNA on them from where they ripped my thumbnail off, to the kitchen with her commercial appliances she asked for to the French doors leading out to the outdoor kitchen. A place where we intended to make memories as a family.

Bowing her head, Madison's hands rise to cover her face, as if in those moments, she's realizing we might not ever be a family again.

Do you see my face? That's a man who would give anything to take away her pain despite what's going on between us.

Bringing in an unsteady breath, I let it out with a whoosh. "Looks like the rain's letting up. I'm going to go now."

"Please *don't* leave." She steps toward me, her hand on my forearm. "I want to talk about things."

My eyes drop to her hand on me, and then to her eyes. "I can't do that." As my luck would have it, the rain picks up again.

Fuck you Mother Nature. You're really pissing me off.

"Please stay."

I shake my head, barely able to stand here without feeling like my body will give out. "I can't."

"You can't or won't?"

"Won't."

"Well…" She hangs her head, hand falling away. "That changes things then."

I stare her down, making sure she knows exactly what I mean. "As it should, Mad."

"I thought by doing it, you'd see what was happening to us, and you did. Our problems lay a lot deeper than either of us wanted to admit, but you have to admit by me doing it, you finally saw what I was talking about," she says, shaking her head and throwing her arms up, as if she's completely lost all hope. "I'm so unbelievably sorry for the way I went about it, but I'm not sorry for you finally seeing our marriage wasn't perfect like you thought it was."

Remember when I said Madison can't make a decision to save her life and is constantly changing her mind? Exactly my goddamn point. She made the decision to file for divorce and then she didn't know what to do because she wasn't sure about it.

"I feel like I don't even know who you are… like I never knew," I mumble, hoping she heard me. "If I didn't know how bad things were, I obviously didn't know you."

"You do know me." Her voice comes out shattered. Her appearance isn't any better as she pushes herself against the wall in the entryway and slides to the floor.

"No, I don't." Shaking my head, I repeat, "I *don't know* you because the Madison I knew would have come and talked to me before it got so bad to the point where she felt it was necessary to lie to me to get my attention. And then when she did have my attention, she wouldn't have given me the cold shoulder."

This girl at my feet, the one who filed for divorce and then lied to me about it for sixty days, I don't know her. I don't.

Madison stares up at me, and for a moment, she lets me see just how truly tired she is of this. How completely beat down she had become by this one secret, the one thing she knew would destroy us if she admitted the truth.

The man still in love with her, he wants to help her, ease the burden, letting her know she didn't have to deal with it alone, even though I'm the one hurting here. But the thing is, I wouldn't be me if I let her deal with this alone because I'd be doing the same thing I hated about my own father.

Madison frowns, as if she can see I'm trying to make sense of this and I wait for her to say something, tell me this is all a sick joke, but she doesn't.

Something flickers behind her eyes, but she blinks, and it's gone, a thought she'll never put words to. And then, as I let go and lean against the wall, sliding down to sit across from her, she asks, "Can you hear me out?"

In just those few words, something in her tone—something buried deep inside that makes me curious as to what she might say to me to make this all right, to make her lies warranted.

I tell myself I will listen, calmly, carefully, and consider why she did it. I tell myself I'm not going to be an asshole and get angry.

Knowing me, I probably won't listen to myself.

There's a strong possibility the moment she starts talking, I won't hear anything she's going to say. It's also completely possible that by her telling the truth, I might just say fuck it and walk away.

But, for Callan, for Noah, for this baby she says is mine, I'm going to sit right here and attempt to listen. I'll do that because deep down, I know this is our last chance—our final opportunity to salvage some good from the train wreck that's been our relationship these last two months.

"I'm sorry," is what she says first.

"You *should* be sorry, Mad," is what I tell her, because fucking right she should be. So much for listening to her. "None of this is okay. I worked my ass off to make you see I cared before you threw our family away and it was all a joke?" She flinches at my harsh words. "Do you honestly realize what I went through these last two months, or last three weeks? Do you realize what we put the boys through?" And I know I've said this all before and I'm starting to sound like her and her apologies, but I can't understand what the hell her thought process would have been here.

"You're right!" she shouts back at me, her voice louder than I've ever heard before. Standing, she throws her hands up. "I'm so fucking sorry, Ridley. I never meant for it to go this far. I don't know what I can say except that I was tired of living the way we were, but in these last two months, I finally saw the man I married. The one willing to do anything to save his family and remind me I was in love with him."

At least she's got that right, huh? But she forgot to mention the time she ripped my ball skin off. I really wished she'd at least acknowledge that part.

I stand up, intending to give her a piece of my mind too.

"So you telling me you didn't love me and the way you kept saying you weren't sure it would work out, was that a lie too?"

She blinks, slowly. "I will always love you, but I wasn't sure at that point because of how bad things had gotten, and I was honest when I said I didn't know if things would work out. I didn't. Just because I did it to get your attention, didn't mean my feelings weren't warranted. They're real."

"How come you couldn't have just talked to me and said, hey, dude, help me out? You're being a bad husband." I shrug, completely defeated. "But you didn't do that."

"I don't know what else you want me to say," Madison mumbles, just as defeated. "I didn't know how else to do it. It felt like every time I tried to talk to you my words fell on deaf ears. When Nathalie suggested it, I thought it was a good idea. I *clearly* didn't think it through."

"Clearly," I slur, sitting back down.

"Can you honestly tell me that you were happy before this? You didn't even know where Callan went to school, let alone what he was into, and now you do. You two are closer than ever before. Not that I'm defending what I did, but I think in some ways, it was a wake-up call for all of us."

I nod because sadly, there's a hell of a lot of truth to what she's saying to me. I didn't know my son before this and had she not filed for divorce, I'm not sure I would have seen it. Sure, she could have come and talked to me, but would I have listened?

No really, I'm asking myself.

What the shit? She's right. I wouldn't have. I would have nodded, promised to do better and weeks later would have been caught back up in working and life.

"I'm not saying any of this to defend what I did. I'm saying this because I didn't do it completely out of spite, Ridley. I love you, and I wanted so badly to make it work too. And then I started to see how bad it really was and then Sedona happened and I panicked, thinking I'd lost you for good." Her emotions and words are raw. And in the depth of her eyes and the tears clouding them, she means everything she's saying. She's staring at me again, longing for a redemption she knows someone like me doesn't give easily. When my dad walked out, I didn't talk to him for two years because he lied to me about having an affair on my mom. I hold grudges.

"Ridley?"

"Yeah?"

"I rehearsed what I wanted to say in my mind on the way here," she says, obviously embarrassed, "and it sounded put together and reasonable, but the truth is, you're intimidating, and I find myself afraid to tell you how I really feel most of the time." *I'm intimidating? No way.* "It's probably why I never came out and told you what was the matter and how I was feeling before this. I wanted to. I'd lay awake at night and tell myself, I'm going to tell him tomorrow. And then morning would come and you would leave for work and I'd tell myself, when he gets home, I'm going to do it. Weeks would go by and I didn't. I was afraid you'd either react badly or blow off my concerns as a crazy housewife who needs a life. Or, you'd tell me I was trying to pick a fight with you." *Oh God, she's right. I've said that before.* "But the thing is, they were *real* issues to me, and when I filed those papers, I honestly believed it was the only way to get you to take me seriously. I'm so sorry for the way I went about it."

"I just can't believe you felt I wouldn't listen," I say, finally feeling a little weight lift. She's being honest. *You need to be honest too. You wouldn't have listened.*

Her eyes trail over my face, watchful of my every reaction. "Do you think if I would have come to you and said we had problems, you would have listened to me?"

I shake my head trying to fight the emotion I feel creeping on. "I'm not sure."

When did this happen? When did it get to this that we went from being newlyweds and in love, to these people? When did I become a man obsessed with work and her, a woman afraid to tell her husband how she really felt?

"So everything that happened the last two months, you telling me you didn't love me, Kip, all that crap, it was all to get me to see that I wasn't giving you and our sons enough attention?"

"No. It wasn't like that. I never meant for anything to get out of hand, and I fully admit Kip is creepy, and yes, he tried to make a move, but remember when he had that black eye at the last game? That was me. I punched him."

Damn. I hope she didn't hurt herself. And fuck that guy. Next time I see him I'll knock his teeth in.

For a second, I let myself look at her without the distorting haze of anger and resentment I've been feeling, and I see her as I used to—beautiful and special, remarkable, and the woman I fell madly in love with eight years ago, despite the unexpected. Her eyes catch mine, and suddenly I'm back to the day we first met. The day I first saw those eyes looking at me like no one else ever had. Me in my vampire costume, her dressed as Catwoman.

You start off a relationship pure, and somewhere along the way, you lose track of what brought you together in the first place. And then you get a glimpse, like right now, and you think, there. It's right there. That's why I fell.

I think Madison knew the power she had over me all along and part of me hated that from the beginning. I loved her that much and hated she could harness that much control over me. One kiss with her demolished the protective defense I had in place since my mother died, and I swore I wouldn't depend on anyone.

The Madison who stole my heart that night at the Halloween party, she never gave it back and wouldn't now. The Madison who's beautiful and damaged to the point where in reality, I'm the only man she's ever loved who hasn't left her. Until now. Until I did. And I guess, I didn't even realize I had, because even though I hadn't left on a physical sense, there's a reality here that she truly felt alone in our marriage.

"Why did you come here, Madison?" I finally ask. "Why are you telling me all of this now? Is it because you found out you were pregnant and just need the money, or you actually want to make this work?"

"I came because I don't want a divorce," she admits, wiping away tears. "These last three weeks since Sedona have been hell, because I finally saw what life would be like without you and it's miserable. I'm unhappy, Callan's depressed. I just… I hadn't realized what I was missing. It's awful to say, but it's exactly like what they say, you don't miss something until it's gone, and there's so much truth to it. I thought it was bad before I attempted to do something about it, but *this*, it's so much worse."

I blow out a breath, shaking my head because I felt the same way. "You never planned on telling me it was all to get my attention, did you?" I ask. "Had everything went okay in Sedona, and I begged you to not go through with it, would you have honestly told me the truth?"

"I don't know," she admits, her chin shaking as a new round of tears hit her. "I never meant to hurt you, Ridley." She keeps apologizing and repeating herself, but still, I don't have the answer I'm looking for.

For about ten minutes she lets me be and finally stops apologizing—probably because I tell her I'm going to walk out the door and never look back if she says it one more time.

And then, after a few drinks from the whiskey I left in the cupboard, I need some answers.

Leaning against the counter in the kitchen now, I sigh, again. "No more bullshit. Be completely honest with me. You *wouldn't* have told me, would you?"

Standing five feet from me near the kitchen island, Madison draws in another deep breath and turns her head to look at me. "I think I would have eventually told you because there's no way I could have lived with that hanging over my head."

As shocked as I am, I know she's not lying to me. The Madison I know, the one I fell in love with, she couldn't live with a lie. It's probably half the reason she filed in the first place. Despite wanting my attention, she couldn't live with feeling like we weren't giving our relationship everything it deserved.

"I wanted to tell you." Her voice is timid, seeming far away and lonely much like she's felt over the years. I can't believe I let it get that bad. "So many times I wanted to, but I couldn't say it to you. And then I found out I was pregnant and I didn't know what to do." Her hand is on her chest now, staring at me with regret.

Sighing, I nod, accepting her truth.

She's staring at me, wide-eyed and confused, giving way to guilt and sorrow for the damage we've done. "I understand if you can't forgive me." Her sadness moves through her, shaking her body. "Just know that I didn't mean to hurt you."

Part of me thought I should have picked up on this after the first couple days, shouldn't I have?

"I can't even tell you how hard it was to see you doing so much and not acknowledging it. Especially you waxing your balls to prove it."

I smile, sensing a small victory. Finally, she acknowledged my efforts. Still, why'd she drag me along? Why was nothing I did ever good enough in those two months?

"So you did it to get my attention, but how come nothing I did was good enough? I kept making the effort and you constantly blew me off. If you really wanted to make things work, how come you weren't trying?"

Tears slowly found their way down her cheeks. "I don't know why. I guess I thought if I acknowledged anything you were doing, things would go back to normal in a week or so and nothing would have changed." She breaths in, slow and deep, as if she's calming herself down. "I love you, Ridley. I know I said I didn't, but I do. I also can't tell you how it felt to have you look at me the way you did in Sedona"—her chin shakes again—"and now, so full of hate and resentment for me."

"I don't hate you, Mad. I never could, but why was lying to me about it was easier?"

Women?

Men are inherently ignorant. If you don't tell us, we don't know. Plain and simple.

"You think it was easy to lie to you?" Her gaze falters, and I see it. There's no way it was *easy* on her. "You don't think it would have been worse if I had told you right away, that I just did it to get your attention? After a while, I didn't know *how* to tell you. You were finally making an effort to be a part of our lives, and I didn't want you to think it was for nothing." She stares at me, and the honesty in her face knocks me sideways. There's no more apologizing or begging. There's only this. Her regrets and my lack of attention to what really mattered. "That night in the car when we were lost…." Her voice trails off, but of course, I remember what she's talking about. The sex in the back of my truck. "I had every intention of telling you what I'd done, but I didn't want to ruin the moment. I thought once we got to the resort, we could talk about it. But I was scared of what you'd say."

She's looking at me again. I can't deal with the vulnerable side of her; it makes me feel vulnerable, too, so I drop my eyes to the floor.

"Tell me what you want, Ridley. Do you want a divorce?" she asks, stepping forward to close the space between us. Reaching out, her fingers lightly touch my hand. Bending down, I lower my lips to her forehead, pressing lightly, warm and soft. Her reaction is anything but gentle.

And then neither is mine. I inhale loudly, my breath in my lungs exhaling just as harshly. "The way I feel about you hasn't changed. It *never* will."

She draws back and stares at me with pleading eyes, her breathing heavy. "Does that mean… you still want me?"

I hate the way the words send a sharp pain to my chest. Like there was ever a question if I wanted her. There wasn't. But I still don't know how to process all this.

I sigh. "I think I need some time to think about all this and process everything."

She steps back so she can see my face clearly, her hand gently running over my jaw. "Ridley, I—"

"I want to be with you," I interrupt her. "Always. I just want *you.* Now. A week from now. A year from now. Whenever you're ready. What I want is never going to change. It's you. Just you. Always has been. Always will be." Callan's face flashes in my mind, my eyes stinging with tears. "The worst part was leaving that day and the look on Callan's face… the realization I had failed my family in making it work. And then I went to see my dad, for God knows what reason. Brantley and him tried to get me to go out to a strip club and I *couldn't* do it. I *couldn't* even think of looking at another woman. So I sat on FaceTime with you and boys, hating that I was going to be a weekend dad." She's crying again, slow steady tears that feel like drops of acid hitting my heart. "I can admit, the papers woke me up, but then when you didn't give me any effort back, I gave up." I swallow, heavily, and then shake my head. "I just… need some time to process this."

She turns her back on me, and it isn't out of hate or regret or whatever other reasons she might have resorted to lying to me. She's trying to give me some space, I suppose.

But I also know if she walks out that door tonight, we'll only be hurting ourselves.

I know what my heart wants. I also know Madison is worth it. I've always known that. I knew it before she did. Real love is taking two hearts, two bodies, two souls and creating one that can laugh and have fun together despite what's going on around us. If these last two months taught me anything, it was that we could still laugh together despite us trying to one over the other. I guess my dad was right. That's when you know it's pure and worth fighting for.

This is what matters. The experience. The forgiveness and how it makes you feel.

My eyes drift to hers and a familiar ache weaves around my heart, threatening to suffocate my words.

"I want you to stay. That's what I want you to do, but right now, I can't make this decision. I need to think."

"Okay," she says, nodding. "Do you want me to leave? What do you want me to do, Ridley? I'll do anything but please just don't shut me out."

"I'm not shutting you out. Just give me a minute."

Sitting and staring. I've been doing that a lot lately. It's funny, I don't think I've taken this much time to just consider life, since well, ever. I've always been on the go. I've always believed I think better on my feet so to speak. But sitting here looking out into the night and truly going through my thoughts and feelings, I'm a bit overwhelmed.

Everything that's happened over the past two months comes crashing in on me. The confusion I experienced when I was served the divorce papers, the moment in the bedroom when Madison told me she didn't love me anymore, the nights I've spent watching Callan at soccer practice and his games, realizing from the beginning my son was unhappy but not knowing exactly what to do about it. All of my attempts to win back the one woman, besides my mother, I've ever truly loved. All these thoughts and moments come rushing back and fuck if it doesn't make my stomach turn.

The storm passed through, the rain all but gone, left puddles on the stone porch outside. We step outside, searching for the soul cleansing rain can offer, our shoulders touching as we sit on the edge of the built-in benches surrounding the outdoor kitchen. The sun's setting to the west, lighting up the sky in purple and pink streaks.

Madison gave me close to twenty minutes outside by myself as she called Nathalie to tell her she wouldn't be home tonight and to put Callan and Noah to bed for her. I certainly wasn't wild about Nathalie watching the boys after she filled my wife's head full of bullshit, but I guess I'll cross that bridge when we get there. Like tomorrow. I'll definitely be talking to her tomorrow and letting her know she's to keep her "single mommy" thoughts to herself next time.

As we sit there in complete silence, both our thoughts scrambling to make sense of where we go from here, I know we won't be perfect because both of us have faults deeper than we care to admit, but I like my faults with her.

"I'm not asking for forgiveness here, Ridley," she finally says, breaking the silence. "I'm asking for a chance, I guess." Her hands fidget in her lap. "Maybe we could go on a date one night and remember why we fell in love."

I can't help my laugh, but this time it's not bitter. "We tried that, remember?"

She knows what I'm referring to. Sedona and the shit show that was.

She nods, trying to remain calm, despite me being a jerk. "I know, but I want us to try again."

Her face is etched in regret as she watches me, waiting for the denial she thinks is coming. When she closes her eyes, I want to pry them open again just so she can see what she put me through. But in some ways, she already sees it. It's why she's here, asking for me not to give up.

Her voice wavers when she says, "I mean it. If this isn't what you want, I'll give you the divorce, and we can work out a parenting plan," she admits in that slow, drawn-out voice she has when she doesn't like what she's saying. I'm still hung up on the pretense of what she did, filing for divorce to get my attention when it really doesn't mean anything. Regardless of the contents of the papers or what Madison wanted to prove, it's still just a circumstance, one that opened my eyes to a lot of things.

I can't be that angry with her. In a sense, and I don't even like saying this, but I feel guilty she felt the need to resort to this, as if somehow I had something to do with it, and sadly I did. I'm her husband. She should have felt comfortable coming and talking to me.

I understood just like everyone else when you make a mistake, you're usually harder on yourself than anyone else. And I know Madison. She probably spent every night these past few weeks trying to tell me what really happened.

"If you did this to get my attention, why did you say you didn't love me?"

The color drains from her face. Maybe she knew I'd ask this eventually because even now those words remain in my head. I'll never forget the way they punched my chest that night. Silence looms between us for a moment, my stomach churning with fear and anxiety.

"I didn't mean it." She bites her lip, her eyes dropping to the floor. "I just… I wasn't sure what to do at that point. I panicked and said what I thought would get your attention."

My face clouds with uneasiness. "Do you want this? Do you want there to be an *us*?" I ask, my stomach dipping for the unknown.

"Yes. I do." The words are said with such affection I don't doubt her.

I can feel my heart in my throat, much like the day she served me with the papers. "Then we try."

Madison and I sleep on the floor in the new house that night. Well, I don't know how much sleep is achieved, but we lie there and talk.

Sitting on the floor beside her, I wait for her to wake up and watch her sleep a little while. The sun is up, the morning sunlight warming me. I haven't turned on the air conditioning yet, but damn, I need to soon.

When Madison finally does wake, she looks at me warily. Sitting up, her eyes shift from mine to my body and hands, searching my face for answers. I do the same, only hers don't offer anything but the evidence of a rough night.

Now here we are. Two hearts, two souls, one outcome.

"I want to be married to you," I say, leaning into her slightly, my hand on her cheek again. "I never wanted the divorce. I want you and Callan and Wolverine." Madison lets out a laugh, her body shaking in the process. My hand moves to her stomach. "And this baby."

Tilting my head and kissing the side of her neck and then her lips, I'm showing her exactly what I mean, the way I know how. Sex.

Don't look at me like that. I'm just being honest here. It's been like a fucking month.

"I'd say I'd like to knock you up again, but I already did that, so let's just fuck on the floor and christen the house."

She laughs, her hands on my shoulders pulling me into her. "You haven't changed, have you?"

"No, not in that sense. I still want to fuck you, but I'll give you some romance too." And then I kiss her tenderly, with meaning and well, romance.

And then we have sex.

It's not gentle, or slow; it's actually pretty fucking passionate and rough, and everything Madison and I are. My eyes are fire, hands gripping her waist tightly.

It's then I know our intentions, no longer deceitful, are pure, caught up with what our bodies and heart crave.

As I taste her lips, her tongue, we're alive with temptation we can't resist.

When we part, she doesn't move for the longest time.

Her arms wrap around me, and I bury my head into her neck, letting out a shuddering sigh. I want more than just kissing, and I think she knows it.

"I'm sorry for so many things."

"Me too," I tell her, laying her down on the floor.

Forehead to forehead, hot breath mixing together, my lips slowly teasing hers, both of us refuse to let go. "We're different, Ridley. What if we grew apart too much?"

"We didn't."

"I think we're different." Madison stares at me, her lashes fluttering with tears.

I take in an uneven breath as her eyes move over my face. “Then we love the people we’ve become.”

My dad once said to me when your life changes, it either happens suddenly or over time, or because you changed it. I tend to think my dad is full of shit, but on this, maybe he’s right.

“Are you sure you’re okay with this?” she asks, smiling at me.

Lacing my fingers with hers as we lie on the floor, I kiss her knuckles. Everything inside of me knows that to have her, I’ll do anything, go through anything. “I’ll go along with whatever you want… as long as I have *you* in return.”

“You will.” Her hand moves to her stomach. “You have us.” And then she rolls to face me. “I’m going to be really clingy and needy for the next couple of months.”

“Don’t worry, I’ll be insecure and jealous and want a lot of sex to make up for not having any. We should be perfect for each other.”

I know what you’re thinking, you forgave her pretty easily?

Or maybe it’s just me thinking I had, but look at it this way. Madison’s the mother of my boys and we have another baby on the way. What kind of man would I be if I just said fuck it, you lied to me, it’s over?

What’s that teaching my boys?

That’s not being a very good person if you ask me.

I had to look at it for what it was: she didn’t know how to talk to me. That was just as much my fault as it was hers for going about it wrong. She did it because she loves me.

I wasn’t happy about it, and it would certainly take some time for the pain to go away, but it would, eventually.

Madison knew what she did wasn't right but neither was me making her feel like she was in our marriage without a partner. Sure, I worked my ass off to provide a life for her and the boys, but I forgot the reason I was doing it and Madison reminded me of it. Them. If I wasn't around, the money, the life I gave them, it wasn't worth it to them, or me.

22

MAKING TIME

Women, and most people, like some men who don't have their balls anymore, assume after you have kids, your sex life goes to shit.

Why do they think that?

It's bullshit if you ask me.

I think, and let's not put too much weight into *my* thoughts, but maybe it's lack of time, or maybe those same kids you had are in the way?

But you know what, eventually those kids fall asleep. That's when you should make time.

"How long has it been?" I ask Madison, looking over at the clock to see it's six in the morning and I have to be at a jobsite by eight today. Technically I should be up already and helping get Callan ready for school, Noah eating breakfast and Evie at least changed for Madison, but sex, what man would pass up that opportunity?

Not me.

I'm sure you're thinking to yourself at this point, who's Evie?

The baby. Our six-month-old daughter. And the cutest most adorable little thing I've ever seen, but you'll see her later.

Focus. We're trying to seduce Madison at the moment.

"I don't know, probably at least two weeks," Mad tells me, rolling toward me. I catch her in my arms, breathing out against her neck.

Do you see us there? Those two naked people under the covers getting closer.

It's a good thing you can't because, underneath those cover, I'm naked. So maybe that's not a bad thing, right?

Right.

"It's been *too* fucking long," I groan, palming my dick under the blankets between us.

"Actually…" Madison's close enough now she's kissing my neck, my shoulder, any place bare skin is found. And it's then I wonder if I pushed her head lower, will she kiss something else. "We had sex in the shower last week. Remember?"

"No, I don't remember," I mumble, my hand finding its way between her legs to see if she's wet. "That was last week."

With my eyes on hers, I dip my head, snuggling between her shoulder and her neck and then scoot toward her, bringing our bodies in line, our chests touching. My left hand moves to her hip as she hitches it around my waist and I squeeze a little, loving that she hasn't lost all the baby weight because it gives me something to hang onto.

Women? Listen up. Men like a little something to grab, so don't be too concerned with being stick thin. We don't want to fuck a bag of bones. We like curves. And more importantly, we like to put our hands on said curves so when we reach out and give you a little squeeze, don't push us away.

Madison interrupts my thoughts when she grabs a fistful of my hair and forces me look at her. "If you're going to fuck me, stop messing around. We don't have a lot of time before the baby's up."

She's right. I need to get to work.

"Jesus," I draw out, moving between her legs, her knees created an opening for me. Hovering above her, my lips move to hers, my hands beside her head, holding myself up.

Immediately, she's breathing heavily, cheeks and neck flushed. She's easy to read.

So we came to the conclusion it's been a week, so naturally, it's one of those times when we find ourselves fumbling around, and the only sounds are grunts and groans because we need it that bad.

"Fuck," I whisper, suddenly the one rushing now, a gasping breath against her cheek as my mouth moves along her jaw and to her neck. "Hurry up, baby." My hips press forward, my patience gone. "They'll be up soon."

"Then get a condom on and stop fucking around."

She has a very good point. And we certainly don't need another baby just yet. You'll see why soon.

In record speed, I jump out of bed, lock the dog in the bathroom and grab a condom from the nightstand. I love my kids, but no, I don't want another one. After getting it on, I'm back between her legs, bringing my left hand to her cheek as I enter her. It's my attempt to be romantic.

Our lips meet at the same time. Licking the seam of her lips, she opens her mouth for me, my tongue meeting hers. I damn near moan at the sensation, but I don't, and she does, her hands moving across my back and to the nape of my neck before they take up residence in my hair.

This image of us right now, the one you have of two people frantically trying to get in the few moments of privacy they are allowed as parents, is one you'll see in most bedrooms where children are raised. Alone time is something that's never scheduled but stolen when the crazy little bundles of energy are asleep.

"Stop thinking," I whisper, knowing her mind is elsewhere, despite her kisses never faltering. "That's it. No more thinking."

I know when she finally stops thinking and melts into me. But it's hard when our overly curious and insane black lab begins scratching and barking at the bathroom door where I've barricaded him so we could have sex. If he isn't locked in another room, he stares at us the entire time. Believe me, it's unnerving having a dog stare at you as you fuck your wife. I don't even like dogs.

Gripping my neck, Madison looks over my right shoulder at the door to the bathroom to make sure that asshole of a dog stays put. Just when we think maybe we might make it before he starts in with the barking, he begins to howl.

Little bastard has the worst timing and I know any minute he's going to wake the baby in the next room.

"Damn it," she mutters, shaking her head and turning into my chest.

Her legs fall from around my waist when Rowdy's barking reaches an all-time high, and he begins his obsessive jumping as though he's going to come through the door at any minute or destroy the bathroom. Both of which he's done before. Many times. It's a good thing I can fix drywall and doors.

Have I mentioned I don't like dogs? All I can say is at least it's not a cat.

Madison sighs, her arms flopping against the mattress. "Ridley, he's going to destroy the bathroom again. We should stop."

I pin her hands above her head against the headboard. "Don't you dare stop, Madison." I groan against her lips, my breath catching in my throat as I continue to move in and out of her. "We *need* this."

I'm mostly referring to myself here, but judging by the wetness coating my dick, she feels the same way.

"I know we do…." She sighs. "But he's destroying the bathroom."

I'm not having this end on account of that fucking dog, so I rise up on my hands to change the angle. "I don't care. I'll fix it."

I nearly come when we switch positions because when you've been denied sex for so long, even the slightest movement can make you come because it's literally been so fucking long since you've had any stimulation down there.

All that aside, I can hear Callan outside the door with the baby. Thank goodness I locked the bedroom door.

"The kids are up."

"I don't care," I mumble, shaking my head. And I don't.

As in most situations, when I have something in my head, I need to finish. A mission like this, there's no stopping me. You probably know this by now.

It's then that damn dog starts in with his howling.

"Come on, baby. Stay in the moment," I grunt, my hips moving at a steady pace, focused on getting both of us off in the next five minutes.

Just as she's beginning to relax and finally be in the moment, the baby begins crying.

"Mommy!" Callan yells, knocking on the door. "Evie wants you, and Noah is drinking out of the toilet again."

There's no way Evie got out of her crib on her own, so he must have snuck into her room and grabbed her. While it's cute when he does that, it's annoying right now because I still haven't finished.

And what the fuck, Noah? Really, dude?

Despite all this, I don't stop and instead speed up my movements as a growl emerges from deep in my throat. I'm determined to finish.

At that moment, the fucking dog bursts through the wooden door of the bathroom and into our room and starts to hump the bedpost.

Welcome to the life of a couple with three kids and a goddamn dog.

"What's going on in there?" Callan asks when he hears the door breaking. "Are you guys okay?"

"We're fine. Just take the baby downstairs," I yell back, my mouth only parting from Madison for a moment before I go back to work, kissing her.

Only she's just lying there laughing. Look at her. She's fucking laughing like it's funny. It is, a dog humping the bed, me trying to hump her, two of our kids at the door and one drinking from the toilet, but still. Laughing kinda hurts my ego if we're being honest.

It's quiet for about a half a second when Callan, still outside our door, asks, "What's that noise?"

I stop for about a half a second and then continue despite the squeaking bed springs. "Nothing. Go downstairs."

"Ridley, maybe we should—"

"Hold on, I'm *so* close." My arms give way, and I collapse against her chest, my hands moving to her ass driving her into my determined thrust.

Just as I'm right about there, the goddamn dog I never wanted jumps right on my back and barks in my ear. I hate this dog.

"Goddamn it." I sigh, rolling to the side and pushing the dog on the floor. With my arms resting on my stomach, I move them to my face, exhaling heavily, scrubbing them over my tired eyes. "At some point, I'm going to have sex with you again without all these distractions."

Madison laughs, her hand resting on my stomach. God, I wish she'd put her hand lower and rid me of this need I know is going to drive me crazy all day long.

I peek one eye open at her. "I'd settle for a hand job at this point."

She laughs and removes her hand. "We can't. It's already almost seven. We're gonna be late."

Fuck.

"You go take a shower," I tell her, sighing. "I'll get the kids ready."

I wait for my hard-on to go away, which is depressing as shit because why waste a hard-on? I then go downstairs to see Callan putting Evie in her high chair and Noah getting cereal off the floor. At least he put it in a bowl this time.

Rowdy's right next to him eating Captain Crunch with him.

Smiling at them, I turn to Callan and Evie. He's now reading a book on nuclear bombs to her.

I scratch the side of my head and reach for the coffee filters in the cupboard. We moved into the new house right before Evie was born in November. We've been here about six months now, and I can honestly say, it's a lot more comfortable than our old house.

"Should you be reading that to her?" I ask Callan when I sit down with a cup of coffee at the table.

He shrugs and continues to read. "This is information she needs to know."

Noah gags on what I think is dog hair in his mouth and then goes back to eating his cereal.

I nudge his butt with my foot and he sits up to look at me. "Don't drink from the toilet anymore." We have to tell him this like twice a week. His doctor says it's not horrible, but he shouldn't be doing it. If you ask me, it's worse than gamma radiation.

"Why?" he asks, staring at me with a look of complete confusion.

I can't believe I'm having to explain why toilet water is disgusting. "Because it's gross."

Rowdy licks the side of Noah's face. "No, it not. Rowdy do it."

"He's a dog though. He licks his own ass and doesn't know the difference."

Maybe I shouldn't have said the last part?

Undeterred by anything I'm saying, Noah points to his chest. "I Wolverine."

And we're back to that. He's four now but still hasn't outgrown the Wolverine stage. He might be going to college someday and asking girls out by growling and telling them he's Wolverine. And you know what, they'll probably buy it and be all over him.

Madison comes downstairs, her hands on my shoulders. "Do you want to take a shower before work?"

I nod, standing up to drag my body against hers. She sighs, her lashes lowering as her lips part carefully. It's a shame we didn't get to finish because all I can think about is those lips wrapping around my dick. "You could join me."

She kisses me, once, and then pulls back. "I can't. I have to get these kids fed and the boys to school."

Noah started pre-school and if we thought Callan's tactics to display his annoyance for school were creative, Noah's pretty simple. He bites everyone. We're thinking of home schooling him until we can, you know, get him to stop. But let's look on the bright side here, at least he never draws blood.

Did you notice Madison didn't mention needing to get to work herself?

We both agreed, mostly me, she didn't need to be massaging and waxing nut sacs anymore. And the new house was an hour drive from the salon, so that solved that problem. And you know, three kids are a handful, especially when one's a baby.

Don't believe me, you can watch all three of mine for a night and I'll take my wife out.

And I know what you're thinking, I had her quit her job because I didn't want her cradling dicks all day.

Well there's that, but no, I didn't have her quit her job. She did that one on her own.

Judging by the look on your face, you're also thinking, what did her quitting solve? She was upset you were never around.

Well guess what? I work less these days.

You don't believe me, do you?

Well, I do.

We took on a few more employees and it helped me not have to be there as often and spend more time with Madison and the kids.

Am I happy?

Yes. I can honestly say I am. I miss having my hands on everything with the business, but I take pride in the fact that I still own the company and my hard work over the years built it.

Wanna know what else I built?

This family. It was literally made with my smooth balls.

Take a look at all of them. Callan reading to his baby sister as she chews on the pages he's turning. Noah and his pet dog. Yes, we got Rowdy for him. Or it was more along the lines of it showed up on our doorstep like Beethoven. We later found out it was Brantley's doing, but how are you going to tell your kids you're not keeping the dog?

And after he peed on Noah once and he didn't kill it, I figured we could keep the adorable drywall eating black lab.

And then there's Madison, my beautiful wife and mother of my children. She's never looked more beautiful as she does now with pieces of Captain Crunch in her hair.

I forgave her pretty easily after what she did. She gave me a blow job.

I'm kidding. She really did give me a blow job that day but that wasn't why I forgave her. Only a fraction of why.

I forgave her because of all this around me right now. The house, the kids, her, I wouldn't have this today if I hadn't forgiven her, and it's far better than the alternative.

Sure, I was pissed about what happened but because of Madison filing for divorce, it woke me up to what was happening around us. I not only saw I was a bad husband for not doing my job and treating her the way she deserved to be treated, but I realized I was a bad dad. The relationship I have with Callan now is what I should have had all along.

By the way, in case you're wondering, we planned our trip to Ukraine. It's not until he's twelve, but still, we're totally going with hopes of at least having the ability to turn green when we return home.

And Noah, he hasn't killed anymore animals since I've been around more. That's gotta count for something, right?

While everyone's getting ready for the day, I sneak upstairs, take a quick shower and then I'm back in the kitchen kissing the kid's good-bye.

I may not have mentioned her much yet but do you see my daughter there in her high chair? The one who's a spitting image of Madison in every way but has my green eyes?

That's Evie, a little six-month-old princess who has all the boys in her family wrapped around her finger. Cutest thing ever, isn't she? Hell, even Wolverine, who's handing her a banana as a peace offering for stealing her teddy.

She also never stops crying at night. We love her anyways, her and her impressive fucking lungs.

"How's my princess?" I pick her up after she's had a couple of slices of her banana and I should have paid more attention to the fact that she had a banana. Mostly because after smiling at me and then she pukes all over the front of my shirt.

She hates me. I'm sure of it.

"Well shit," I say, staring at the puke.

"Yuck!" Noah gags again when he sees the puke. He has a weak stomach. And yet he drinks from the toilet. Just the smell of toilet water would make me gag.

Did I mention Evie doesn't like bananas? Why would she? They're disgusting.

I gag just thinking about the slimy dick-shaped fruit. No men actually eat bananas. At least I don't. I don't eat any dick-shaped food. Bananas, hot dogs… all no goes for me.

How did we even get on this topic?

Oh, right. Baby puke. All down the front of me. It's disgusting. Banana baby puke?

Even worse.

But you know what, the smiling little girl in my arms whose tummy feels better is worth the baby puke. And I wouldn't change it for the world. Just my shirt.

Madison sets her head on my shoulder and then kisses my cheek. "Poor daddy. He's having a rough morning."

Shifting Evie to my hip, I reach around to put my arm around Madison and pull her hair. "And mommy's going to have a *rough* night."

She slaps my hand away, laughing. "You're going to be late."

Right. I am. And my feelings on being late haven't changed.

Setting down Evie in her high chair, I run upstairs to change my shirt. Just as I'm pulling it over my shoulders, Madison comes in the bedroom, shuts the door and locks it. "Callan's playing with Evie and Noah. We have five minutes."

I can totally be late for this.

"Fuck yeah," I say, unzipping my pants as she drops to her knees before me.

You can look away now. We need our privacy. After the dog incident, I don't want anyone else watching us.

So that's it. My story. Interesting, huh?

Final thoughts?

I'm not sure I have any, I mean, I'm kinda busy at the moment but I've got some advice for you.

Saving a marriage doesn't happen overnight. It takes a lot of hard work, a lot of talking and mostly fighting.

Fighting for what you want.

I wasn't sure if Madison and I would ever be what some would call a perfect couple, but we were perfectly happy annoying the shit out of each other and attempting to parent these three crazy kids and the dog I didn't want.

The End

ACKNOWLEDGMENTS

I don't think I've ever had this much fun writing a book since *Happy Hour*. Ridley was so easy to write. Everything flowed, and I loved every minute of writing him.

Marriage is hard. And I don't say that to make mine sound difficult, because it's really not. I married my best friend and not a day goes by where we don't laugh at something one of us has said or done. Most of the time it's because of something funny our daughter has done, but still, we laugh and I think that's important. As you probably noticed with Ridley and Madison, through it all, they still laughed with one another.

I met my husband when I was fourteen and started dating him when I was fifteen. We were high school sweethearts. You know, the kind of love they tell you doesn't happen anymore. It does happen, it's not easy, takes a lot of work, but it still happens.

We got married at eighteen, just out of high school, though everyone told us it was a dumb decision, but we didn't care. All we cared about was being together. And though we certainly had our ups and downs, it's been the best eighteen years of my life. I wouldn't change anything we went through because of what it taught us. It's why I wrote, *"Real love is taking two hearts, two bodies, two souls and creating one that can laugh and have fun together despite what's going on around us.*"

I'm sure a lot of you can relate to this book in some way, and that was my intention here. With the help of some very special girls, I wanted to create something fun yet completely relatable if you've ever been in a committed relationship or married.

This book also opened my eyes to a lot about what I'm sacrificing by working so much and in turn, I'm learning to take a day off every once in a while.

So to my husband, thank you for showing me what love is and why it's worth fighting for.

And my little girl, thank you, baby, for allowing Mommy to work during the day.

Thanks to Lauren, Ashley and Janet for working on this novel with me and the girls in the BETA group for all your suggestions and love for Ridley.

To the Sheynanigans, thank you for being so excited for this one when you read the first chapter.

Becky, thank you for letting me break every single rule you've taught me to write *Bad Husband* the way I wanted to. I enjoyed it so much!

To my readers, thank you for allowing me to live my passion! Love you.

Thank you!
Shey Stahl

MEET THE AUTHOR

Shey Stahl is a *USA Today* best-selling author, a wife, mother, daughter and friend to many. When she's not writing, she's spending time with her family in the Pacific Northwest where she was born, and raised around a dirt track. Visit her website for additional information and keep up to date on new releases: www.sheystahl.com.

YOU CAN ALSO FIND HER ON FACEBOOK:

https://www.facebook.com/SheyStahlAuthor

ADDITIONAL WORKS BY SHEY STAHL

Racing on the Edge

Happy Hour
Black Flag
Trading Paint
The Champion
The Legend
Hot Laps
The Rookie
Fast Time
Open Wheel
Pace Laps
Dirt Driven (TBA)
Behind the Wheel (TBA)

The Redemption Series

The Trainer
The Fighter

Stand Alones

Waiting for You
Everything Changes
Deal
Awakened
Everlasting Light

Bad Blood
Heavy Soul
Bad Husband
Hostage (TBA)
Pause (TBA)

Crossing the Line

Delayed Penalty
Delayed Offsides
Delayed Roughing (TBA)

Unforgettable Series

All I Have Left
All We Need (TBA)

The Torqued Trilogy

AVAILABLE ON AUDIBLE AS WELL

Unsteady ~ Reddington
Unbearable ~ Raven
Unbound ~ Rawley (January 2017)

ENJOY A SNEAK PEEK AT UNSTEADY
BOOK ONE IN THE TORQUED TRILOGY ONLY
AVAILABLE IN THE PAPERBACK VERSION ON BAD
HUSBAND.

the TORQUED trilogy

SHEY STAHL

"There's parts of her that were completely untouched until my dirty hands pulled her in, marking her in all the ways she needed."

Desperate to find a new mechanic, the last thing Reddington expects is a woman to show up, let alone one with a sinful body, sharp tongue, and the inability to just do her job and not give him lip.

He can't deny he's hoping to catch a view of her bent over a hood, but there's not a chance in hell that's going to happen. As much as Red wants to take her for a test drive, he knows he needs to keep his priorities straight.

"Have you heard of Newton's third law of motion? Every action has an equal and opposite reaction? It all goes back to one saying. You're able to choose but you're never free from

the consequences of your actions. There's no reset, there's no takeback, there's an action, and an outcome."

After fleeing from an abusive ex, Lennon hopes the garage bays of Walker Automotive will keep her dark secrets hidden from her past. What she doesn't expect is a sexy, brooding, tattooed boss with an attitude.
Neither of them can ignore their attraction as they struggle to make sense of their connection. And what happens next will no doubt be unsteady.

"I'm not going to let him hurt you anymore, Lenny. I won't let him anywhere near you."

Red

chapter 1

WISH YOU WERE HERE

A HYSTERICAL CRY greets me as I unlock my front door. It's nothing new. Our little girl is headstrong and has no problem letting you know when she's not pleased.

My keys fall out of my hand when I open the door. As I lean down to retrieve them, I yell for my wife.

"Nevaeh?" I call out, closing the door with my foot as I set my lunchbox on the floor. "Where are you?" For a second, I listen for her to yell back, but I can't hear anything over Nova's hysterical crying from her bed. She does this at night sometimes, cries until one of us comes and gets her.

Jogging down the hall, I open her bedroom door and find her standing on her bed holding her pink teddy bear by its foot. Tears stream down her red face as she shakes. Immediately I know this is not her normal fit. The look on her face is pure fear. My heart pounds in my rapidly beating chest, and my hands tremble as I hold her close. "Shhhh, darlin'. Calm down."

She doesn't. Instead, she picks up with more hysteria and points toward her door. "Mommy! Mommy!" And she screams that, over and over again, so loud I can't help but think again, this is more than just her nightly thing.

"Okay, okay," I say, kissing her temple, attempting to comfort her by rubbing her back. "Let's go find Mommy." I keep her in my arms as we walk down the dark hallway, a lump rising in my throat with every step.

The moment I notice the light from the kitchen on, my chest tightens. It claws at me knowing something's very wrong. The walls are closing in, suffocating me, and demanding I see what's wrong.

As I come around the corner, her bare feet are the first thing I see, and then her legs. She's lying on her back, eyes closed, looking like she's sleeping. Only she's not. The sight punches my chest.

Nova's screaming hasn't stopped ringing in my ears as she struggles to get free. Nevaeh doesn't move amidst the devastating cries from our daughter. She's so still, undeterred by the noise.

I notice the blood next, a small amount pooled under her head. Everything seems to move in slow motion once I see that. Me setting Nova down, her screaming for Mommy, me scrambling for the phone. It's just like the movies, caught in the middle of a nightmare as I try to shake her awake.

She's not waking up. Her lips have a bluish tint to them, and her face seems to have faded to gray. "Nevaeh, honey… wake up." I shake her again. Nothing. No movement at all.

Oh God. No. This can't be happening. What do I do?

"Hold on baby, please." I'm trying to keep my cool with Nova in the room but I know I'm scaring her. "Hold on!"

I know she's hurt. Badly. Gently, I cup my hand under her head as blood wets my hand and I hold the phone with my other hand. "911, what's your emergency?"

"It's my wife." My voice shakes around those three words. "She's bleeding. She won't wake up."

"What's your address, sir?"

"Uh, 877 Kees St." Beside me, Nova lets out a hysterical cry as she runs down the hall, and I can't help but think I've subjected her to something she shouldn't have seen.

Fuck!

"Is she breathing?" the dispatcher asks.

I check, my fingers pressed to her neck as I hold the phone against my shoulder and ear. Nothing. No pulse. "No, she's not."

"Okay, sir, I've dispatched paramedics to the scene. They're about a minute away."

A minute? I don't have a minute. I don't have seconds.

Twisting my head to bury my face into my shoulder, I let my hand fall away from her neck. I know in my heart she's gone already, and there's no bringing her back. It's clear looking at her.

This can't fucking be happening. *No.* I want to vomit. It's rising up as the dispatcher rattles off things for me to check, but I don't. I stare at my wife, the mother of my child, wondering what the fuck could have happened. "Breathe, baby. Please just fucking breathe for me. Take a breath," I sob, clutching her hand to my chest. "Open your eyes!"

"Daddy!"

Nova's screams are like a knife in my body, over and over again. "Daddy, wake up!"

I blink at the screams, trying to focus on Nevaeh and how I can save her. Only I know there's no hope. She's gone.

...

"Daddy! Open your eyes!"

...

"Daddy!"

I startle awake with a jolt and gasp, sitting up in the bed. My chest heaves with memories racing through my head. Swallowing back tears stinging my eyes, I look at the side of my bed that's now empty. The place where Nevaeh used to sleep.

"Daddy?" I jump at the sound of Nova's voice as she touches my forearm. "Did you have a nightmare again?"

Blinking rapidly, I make out my daughter's face beside me, dressed in her princess pajamas with her hair a wild mess. Her eyes hurt me, so badly, because they're Nevaeh's eyes.

I nod, still trying to control my breathing as she pushes her teddy bear in my face next. "Hold Teddy. He might help you." He's always a peace offering for her, so she must think I need him too.

I take the bear and then wrap my arms around Nova, bringing her up on the bed with me. "I'd rather hold you," I tell her, pulling the blankets back and yanking them over our heads.

It's not the first nightmare I've had about the night Nevaeh died, and certainly not the last.

Nevaeh had an ex-boyfriend, Viktor, who I never cared for. He was one of those guys you just didn't trust, and I *never* did. I wouldn't say he gave me a reason not to. I mean, I didn't get the vibe from him he was mentally unstable. I wish I would have, at least then I would have seen it coming.

Nevaeh and I were together about a month when I met him for the first time at a party. He got in my face and immediately regretted it. About three years later, he got his payback when I was working late one night, and he came into my home and killed her. I'm not sure he intended on killing her, but she hit her head on the counter in the process and ended up dying from that.

Two days later, they found him in his car, dead. He'd blown his own head off. Then I understood he was mentally unstable and later learned it was something he had been struggling with his whole life. Did it make it any better?

Nope. He took my wife from me and now I'm raising our daughter by myself. Nothing makes that okay.

Nova giggles as my breathing tickles the side of her neck, snuggling up against my chest with the bear in between us. "What are we doing today?"

I know she thinks it's weird I haven't gotten up to go to work yet today. I guess she's more perceptive to change than I realize. "We have to go to the church today."

Nova considers that and pushes her hair from her face as she stares up at me. I love how wild it is in the morning. She doesn't say anything for a minute, and then she wiggles. "You're squishing me, Daddy." And then she rips the covers off us and moves to sit up, watching me. "Why do we have to go to the church?"

"We just do."

My Uncle Hendrix shakes his head, drawing in a deep breath. "Damn, Red. I don't even know what to say right now. Whatever I can do to help with the shop, let me know."

Since my father passed away, his shop, our family business, is now mine and today, the shop is the last thing on my mind.

Even though I know my uncle cares, there isn't anything he can do that's going to make this any easier on me or the little girl at my feet wondering why life is changing once again. She's only five, and I can't bring myself to look at her knowing the look I'll see. The one of loss.

Her tiny hand slips into mine, her cheek pressing against the back of my hand as she grips it. Looking toward the sky, I draw in a heavy breath and struggle to calm my racing heart. Though this loss is different, the pain is equally crippling.

Before me, my father's being laid to rest and about fifty feet away, fresh flowers surround my wife's grave, the bright yellow and pink lilies almost blinding against the cloudy sky above us.

Once again, I am holding our little girl's hand as she wonders why someone she loves was taken from her so suddenly.

It breaks my heart that she looks to me—her daddy—the one person who is supposed to have all the answers, because honestly, I certainly can't explain this. I don't even understand it myself. One minute he's standing in front of me, drinking a beer on Monday night and winding down after another long day at the garage and the next, I'm on the ground performing CPR on him. It didn't matter what I did. Not the CPR, not my begging him to hold on and not to leave us. Nothing changed. He still died that night of a heart attack. Healthy man, worked hard, maybe drank a few too many beers but dropped dead at fifty.

"Daddy, why is Papa gone?"

Dropping to a knee next to her, I take her precious face in the palms of my hands to brush locks of brown curls from her cheek. Innocent blue eyes, a beautiful reminder of her mother, blink away tears. “Papa’s heart was sick, and he had to go too,” I say, choking back tears. “It was his time to go.”

“Go where?”

“To heaven.”

What else would I say? She doesn’t have a concept of time let alone what happens when you die, or where we go.

Nova considers my words, her eyes dropping to the ground and then raising back up. “With Mommy?”

It’s like a knife is plunged into my chest when she says that. Though it’s been two years since Nevaeh was laid to rest, it never gets any easier. I doubt it ever will. She was my true love, the one, and she was taken from me, brutally.

“Yes, in heaven,” I finally answer, blinking back tears. “Like Mommy.”

I’m hoping that’s where her questions will end because I’m not sure I believe in heaven anymore. The more questions my daughter asks me about why her mommy and grandpa were taken from her too soon, the more I doubt that I believe in religion for that matter, but I won’t push my beliefs on my daughter.

“But they’re going to put dirt on him.” Nova stares at the grave, her brow furrowed. “He can’t breathe with it on him.”

“I know.”

She lets go of my hand. “Tell them to stop.”

Pushing her curls from her face, I draw in a deep breath. “They’re only doing their job. Papa doesn’t need to breathe anymore.”

Oh God, did I really just say that?

I probably shouldn't have said that but what else was I going to say? There's certainly no manual on explaining death to a child.

Thankfully, I hear footsteps. Turning my head, I see my mother. She places her hand on my shoulder. "Red, honey, can you go find Rawley for me? I haven't seen him today, and I'm getting really worried."

If I know my younger brother at all, he's fucking out his sorrows in the bathroom with some chick. No way am I telling my mother that.

He didn't come to the gravesite, and I don't blame him. It's a tough day for a lot of us.

You wouldn't think it looking at her today, but my mother is the strongest and most selfless woman I've ever met. On a day like today where she's saying good-bye to her husband of the last thirty years, she is putting aside her own grief and is focused on finding my troublesome younger brother and making sure he is okay.

I nod, standing and reach for Nova's hand again. "Wanna help me find Uncle Rawley?"

Nova nods, but doesn't say anything as she squeezes my hand.

"Where do you think we should look for him?" I ask, looking down as she walks beside me. I love the way she walks, so confident even at her young age with her head up and sassy demeanor. You'll never tell my little girl she's wrong or what to do. Even as a parent, I can't tell her what to do. I have to give her options and let her decide. I don't care what anyone says about that either. I parent her the way she wants to be parented, the way that works for her. In turn, it works for me.

"I think he in there." Nova points at the church.

Walking up the stone path, I take the first step and then look back when I notice Nova's let go of my hand. "What's the matter?"

"You go." She doesn't look at me. "I gonna stay here." And then she sits on the steps; her arms crossed over her chest.

See? No convincing her otherwise.

The corners of my lips lift. "Okay, darlin'."

Turning, I hesitate to step foot inside the church, one I haven't been in since Nevaeh's funeral. I actually told myself I'd never step foot in this place again. Looking back at Nova, I bet that's why she won't come in here. Yeah, she was barely three years old when her mother died, but part of me still thinks she remembers being inside the church. I pray that's the only thing she remembers about her mother's death.

As I enter, I glance to my left and can't help a small smile that comes to my lips realizing that once again, Nova was right. Rawley's in here, seated in the last pew with his feet up and arms behind his head staring at the ceiling. I can tell he's been crying, but I'd never say anything. Not my place. We are all dealing with this loss in our own way, and I've shed quite a few tears today myself. If you knew my father, you'd understand why.

Silently I take a seat next to him, slouching. There's an eight year age difference between Rawley and me, so sometimes it's hard to know how to talk to him.

Rawley lets out a heavy breath but doesn't move. "What are you doing in here? You hate churches."

I shrug. "Ma sent me lookin' for ya. She was worried when she didn't see you at the funeral."

"Yeah, well, I stayed in the back." Leaning forward to rest his elbows on his knees, he clears his throat. "She needs to stop worrying about me so much. She acts like I'm a baby."

"You'll always be my baby brother." I reach forward, ruffling his hair with a soft smile, though it feels forced.

He snorts. “And nobody in this family will let me forget it.” I know what he’s referring to. The last time Rawley spoke to our dad was an argument where dad told him it was time to grow up and get his shit together. Start acting like an adult.

Rawley’s nineteen. I remember being nineteen and what it was like starting out, thinking you’re untouchable, and then quickly realizing you’re not. Only with Rawley, he hasn’t quite reached the “you’re not” stage.

Mine didn’t come until Nova was born and I knew then I had to grow up for her. Even more so now that Nevaeh wasn’t around.

“Don’t be so hard on yourself,” I tell him before standing, giving a nod outside. “Come on, man. Ma’s waiting for us.”

Drawing in another deep breath, he gives the church one last look and stands beside me.

Rawley doesn’t talk much, unless he’s been drinking and then you can’t get him to shut up. He’s more of a recluse compared to the other men in our family. Maybe that’s why he’s such a great musician. He’s got that brooding personality that’s perfect for it.

“Hey, princess,” Rawley says, messing with Nova’s curls on top of her head.

She doesn’t look up at him. Instead, she glares in the distance. She’s upset today, and I know it’s gonna take a while for her to come out of this, just like it will everyone.

My father, Lyric Walker, was someone special. Even the name was badass and he, well, I’ve never met anyone like him. He was the hardest working man I knew.

Owning his own garage and working his ass off so he could provide us with a good life. He built his business from nothing and earned a trusted reputation through hard work.

When it came down to it, there was no better mechanic than my dad. He could fix anything with a set of tools. But the truth is that as great a mechanic as Lyric Walker was, he was an even better father.

Not a day has gone by as long as I can remember that I didn't know my dad had my back. When I told him I wanted to be a mechanic just like him, he never hesitated to teach me. Probably because I kept taking the engine in his truck apart, desperate to learn, and he wanted me to know how to put it back together.

Whatever my siblings and I wanted in life, my dad was right beside us encouraging us. The only thing he ever asked in return was for us to take responsibility for our lives. No excuses, just hard work. Rawley and Raven are still kinda working on that last one.

"I want cake." Nova stands, her hands on her hips. "Grammy said we having cake."

I smile, picking her up off the steps. "Grammy said that, huh?"

Rawley reaches up and tugs on her hair, just to annoy her. She swats his hand away and stares at me, intently. "I *need* it."

I give Rawley a sideways glance. "She's workin' me, isn't she?"

He nods, smiling but doesn't say anything.

Just as we're beginning to walk toward the cars parked near the grave, Raven, my younger sister finds us. Nova immediately reaches for her. I'm so grateful Nova has my mom and sister in her life. With losing her mom so young, I constantly worry that I'm not enough. But knowing my mom and sister will always be there for her, guiding her through the things I can't, brings me some relief.

As much as I'm grateful for Raven being in Nova's life, I have to keep a close eye because while I love my sister, she can find trouble like no one else. Like Rawley, Raven hasn't reached her "you're not" stage in life. She's a bit of a troublemaker, and if Nova turns out like her, I'm gonna need a gun strapped to me at all times. Don't think I haven't thought about it.

"Jesus, Red, did you brush her damn hair today?" Raven asks, trying to tame Nova's hair down by running her fingers through it.

All that did was annoy Nova, who whipped her head around. She hates people touching her curls.

I glare toward Raven. "I did brush it." I'm actually not sure if I did, or not. I might have just ran my fingers through it to get the knots out. Apparently, I didn't do a very good job because I see a knot in it now.

Raven rolls her eyes and reaches to take Nova from my arms. "Sure you did."

As we're gathered by the cars now, arguing about whether or not I brushed my daughter's hair, Mom approaches us. "Are we all ready?"

Raven smacks my shoulder as she pushes past me. "Yeah, Ma. We're coming."

The five of us pile inside my other baby, an old Chevy Nova that's definitely a work in progress and head up the street to my parents' house. Though our family isn't all that large, my father was well respected and widely loved, so the small house seems crowded when we get there. On any other day, this wouldn't bother me, but because today's a day where I want to be alone, even the smallest gathering seems like so much.

NOVA AND I keep to ourselves, seated on the couch with a small plate of food. She stays on my lap, her head resting on my shoulder while she plays with the collar of my shirt and nibbles on a carrot. She has this habit of taking a piece of material between her thumb and index finger when she's tired and rubbing it back and forth. I find it incredibly adorable and hope she never grows out of it.

"Do you want to take a nap?" I ask, kissing her forehead.

She shakes her head, adamantly refusing. I don't think Nova's willingly taken a nap in her life. Even as a baby, I would have to trick her into sleep, or take her for a drive.

Raven's watching us from the kitchen. I can see her from my place on the couch with a slice of cake in hand, her legs dangling off the counter. "You want some cake, darlin'?"

Nova perks up, her head bumping my jaw when she sits up straight. "Yes."

Laughing and rubbing my jaw, I stand with her on my hip and make my way into the kitchen. Sliding off the counter, Raven immediately holds her hands out for Nova, who willingly goes to her. She sways to the music softly playing in the background, holding her close.

I take that moment to get her a piece of cake. Just as I'm cutting into it, someone bumps my shoulder.

Turning, I nearly roll my eyes. It's my young neighbor. And I say young because she's seventeen. "Hey, Red," she says, sticking a fork in her mouth to lick frosting off it. I know she thinks this is a seductive way to get me to look at her mouth but honestly, all it does is make me cringe.

I keep my eyes on her eyes as always. Sam's a nice girl, but shit she's young. She watches Nova for me sometimes but even then, I try to keep those instances to a last-resort situation only. "I'm sorry about Lyric."

"Thanks, Sam."

When I have the cake on the paper plate, I begin to walk away when she says, "If there's anything you need, let me know."

Is she serious?

She bats her eyes.

Yep. Serious.

I know what she means. She's never been shy about letting it out there she's interested in me. I don't understand it. Honestly, there's a ten-year difference between us, and I know there are plenty of guys her own age who would be happy to take her up on her offer. I find it uninteresting. And illegal. There's one thing I've noticed since my wife died. Women, especially the younger ones, they have a soft spot for a single dad. And when I say soft spot, I mean they spread their fucking legs easily.

I'm sure some would wonder why I don't sleep with any of them, but I just can't. Hell, it took me a fucking year to remove my wedding ring and even now, I carry it around on my key chain. If that doesn't scream widower with issues, I don't know what would.

Tyler gives Sam a smile as he approaches, and then bumps my shoulder. "A few of us are gonna head down to the shop to you know, honor Lyric the right way."

Sam walks away, watching me as she passes by.

I kind of chuckle because I know what Tyler means by that. This is nice, all of this my mom and aunt set up, but it's not my dad.

He'd want us to be at the shop. The same place we had his fiftieth birthday party a few months back where he and Hendrix did shots of Jägermeister off the table when the bottle spilled.

That memory of them laughing and holding each other up.... Fuck, it hurts he's gone now.

"Hang on, let me see if my mom can keep an eye on Nova for a bit." I leave Tyler in the dining room and find mom in the kitchen with Raven.

"Hey, Ma?" She turns and looks over her shoulder at me. "Can you watch Nova for just a bit? I'm gonna run to the shop with Tyler for a while."

She gives me a tender smile, the one she always gives me. It's the same smile that tells me she'd do anything to make my life easier.

She just lost her husband, yet she's worried about her kids.

I remember when Nevaeh died, I locked myself in our room for a week. I didn't eat, or shower or God forbid take care of my kid. I couldn't even function. I'd never experienced true devastation until that moment. I could barely breathe. The thought of continuing my life without Nevaeh seemed impossible.

But here Ma is, making food for everyone and forcing a smile six days later. Raven props herself up on the counter next to the plate of cheese, which Nova has taken a bite out of every piece and put it back. "Try not to get shitfaced."

Nova comes running through the kitchen, her brown curls all over the place. She stops in front of me and pushes them out of her face, eyeing the keys in my hand. "Where you going? Can I come?"

I kneel to her level. "I'll be back before bed. I just need to check on the guys at the shop. I won't be long." I want to promise her I'll be back later, but I don't promise anything anymore. The last one I made was never granted.

"I promise I'll be home in an hour and make it up to you."

Well, that hour turned into three hours, and when I came home, Nevaeh was dead. Had I been home when I was supposed to, maybe it wouldn't have happened. At least that's what I've been telling myself.

Nova does that thing where her brow scrunches together, and her hands go to her hips. "You promised to read *Pete the Cat*!"

I hate seeing this face. She does it a lot because she always wants to keep me in her eyesight. Nova won't talk about that night, and I don't ask what she remembers from the night her mom died, but she remembers being alone for hours before I came home to find her. They tried to get me to take her to counseling afterward; hell, they tried to get me to go, but it wasn't for me and I couldn't see forcing her to go either. We needed to heal on our own.

"I will, darlin'. I just have to do a few things, and I'll be back."

My mom rescues me, wrapping her arms around Nova and picking her up. "Come on, now, little lady. Let's let Daddy get going so he can get back quicker and read you that book. You can hang out with me and your auntie."

Naturally that distracts Nova enough I'm able to sneak away.

TYLER AND I pull up to the shop, the gravel crunching under the tires as we bring the car to a stop. It's weird being back in here again without my dad and even more so hearing his favorite song without him playing it.

As Bruce Springsteen's "Devils & Dust" moves through the steel building, my eyes immediately go to the spot on the floor where he collapsed, and my chest hurts. My mouth is unusually dry and a knot that hasn't gone away for days lodges in my throat as though it's a permanent reminder that no day from here on out will ever be the same.

All the guys are there, Colt, Uncle Hendrix, my cousins Jude and Eldon… everyone who keeps this shop together. We closed the shop down for a week on Tuesday, the morning after his heart attack, but Monday we'll be opening back up with me as the new owner of Walker Automotive.

Colt Davis, one of the mechanics in the shop, hands me a beer. "Hey, Red."

I take it, running my free hand through my dark hair. The moment we're standing in a circle, tossing back beers, I want to laugh at the irony of this. We did this very same thing the night my Grandpa Carson passed away.

"Hell," Colt breathes in deeply. "I still remember the day he hired me. We were just two kids who didn't know a goddamn thing about making a business work, but somehow did it."

Clearing my throat, I shift my stance slightly, my hand shaking as I bring the beer in my hand to my lips, but don't take a drink. "I know this isn't going to be easy on any of us, but I'll do my best to make it work."

As I finally do take a drink, silence spreads over us, and I should say something more to these guys as they share stories about ways my father made them feel like their presence here was needed. Each and every one of them understood they were family to him. And they were. His theory on running a business was you take care of your employees and they'll in turn take care of your business. He was right on that.

"Fuck I don't even know what to say. I can't make this any different," I tell them, my gaze on the concrete floor where I tried to revive him. "If I could, I would." My voice cracks, shaking with each breath I take. Squeezing my eyes shut, I nod a few times and swallow back the emotion building. I'm at a loss for words as I struggle to say more.

"We're gonna be all right here, man." Tyler bumps his beer to mine, the sound making a ping through the air. "We're gonna make this place work for him."

I'm not sure we can, but I'm damn sure going to try.

When someone dies, there's nothing you can do about it. You can't change it no matter how much you try. And once the angers gone, you accept it because you have no choice. Eventually you'll be forced to.

Reality's a bitch like that.

Made in the USA
Monee, IL
17 October 2020

45433040R00193